E.R. PUNSHON
TEN STAR CLUES

Ernest Robertson Punshon was born in London in 1872.

At the age of fourteen he started life in an office. His employers soon informed him that he would never make a really satisfactory clerk, and he, agreeing, spent the next few years wandering about Canada and the United States, endeavouring without great success to earn a living in any occupation that offered. Returning home by way of working a passage on a cattle boat, he began to write. He contributed to many magazines and periodicals, wrote plays, and published nearly fifty novels, among which his detective stories proved the most popular and enduring.

He died in 1956.

Also by E.R. Punshon

Information Received
Death among the Sunbathers
Crossword Mystery
Mystery Villa
Death of a Beauty Queen
Death Comes to Cambers
The Bath Mysteries
Mystery of Mr. Jessop
The Dusky Hour
Dictator's Way
Comes a Stranger
Suspects – Nine
Murder Abroad
Four Strange Women

E.R. PUNSHON

TEN STAR CLUES

With an introduction
by Curtis Evans

DEAN STREET PRESS

To

THE SIREN

Whose irresistible song so often lured
away the writer from his work.

LONDON. *September—October 1940.*

INTRODUCTION

The tale of the alleged lost heir who has returned home to claim his patrimony in the face of strenuous denials of his identity has proven a perennially popular one in English crime fiction. Probably the most well-known example of the plot today is found in Josephine Tey's much-admired suspense novel *Brat Farrar* (1949), although with *The Traveller Returns* (1945) (in the US, *She Came Back*), the popular Golden Age crime writer Patricia Wentworth preceded Tey into print by four years with a feminine variation on the theme. However, E.R. Punshon anticipated both women on the subject with his fifteenth Bobby Owen detective novel, *Ten Star Clues* (1941), a classic British stately home mystery wherein Bobby, in his first investigation carried out entirely in the Midlands county of Wychshire in his capacity as detective-inspector and private secretary to Chief Constable Glynne, tries his best to solve the baffling problem of just which Wych is Wych. Confused? Read on!

Somewhat unusually for an E.R. Punshon detective novel, *Ten Star Clues* starts with an extended section devoted to detailing the rising tensions among the novel's cast of characters, with Inspector Owen not making his first appearance until a quarter of the story has elapsed, after murder has finally struck. In this opening section of the novel, Punshon introduces the individuals connected to Castle Wych, located near the village of Brimsbury Wych. ("One of England's show places and not without its niche in history," Punshon observes of the castle, "open to the public on Saturdays and holidays on payment of one shilling, for the benefit of the funds of the Midwych General Hospital.") These individuals are the elderly Earl and Countess Wych; Anne Hoyle, their masterful granddaughter, debarred by her sex, much to her irritation, from inheriting the Wych title and estates; Ralph Hoyle, their plainspoken great-nephew, estate manager and heir presumptive; Arthur Hoyle, another great-nephew, next in the line of succession after Ralph and a wealthy, smooth-talking company director who resides, Punshon wryly notes, "in some style in an imposing mansion known as The Thatched Cottage, presumably because it was neither thatched nor a cottage"; the absentminded Reverend Louis Longden, vicar of Brimsbury Wych, and his demure daughter, Sophy, companion to the ailing Countess Wych; Clinton Wells, "youngest partner in the old established firm of Wells, Clinton, Wells and Blacklock that for many years had been in charge of all the legal side of the Hoyle estates"; and Martin, the odious new butler at Castle Wych, "[p]lump, soft-footed, complacent—too complacent."

Into this mix of vintage English mystery characters comes a highly disturbing element: a bumptious individual from the United States claiming to be Bertram Hoyle, grandson of Earl and Countess Wych. The family had presumed that Bertram met his demise a decade ago in the United States, yet Earl and Countess Wych quickly embrace the young man as Bertram, displacing Ralph Hoyle as heir presumptive to the Wych title and estates. Deeply disgruntled by this development, Ralph proclaims loudly to all and sundry that his "cousin" Bertram is a scoundrel and fake, and that he, Ralph, will prove him such. Not long afterward someone is shot dead in the library at Castle Wych, leaving Inspector Bobby Owen and Chief Constable Glynne tasked with unmasking a wily murderer. Late in the novel Bobby lists ten clues, dubbed by him "star" clues, which he believes are the keys to solving the crime—can you, in contrast with the flummoxed Colonel Glynne, beat Bobby to the solution?

At several points in *Ten Star Clues* characters reference the famous Victorian case of the Tichborne Claimant, in which an Australian butcher named Thomas Castro appeared in England in 1866 to claim that he was Roger Tichborne, the missing heir to the Tichborne baronetcy, who was widely believed to have expired in a shipwreck off the coast of Brazil a dozen years earlier. The case--of which it has been stated that "[n]o detective novel has a more complex and absorbing plot"--became one of the great causes célèbres in Victorian England, and has since stimulated the imaginations of English writers of both crime fiction and criminal history. In 1936, Frederic Herbert Maugham, elder brother of author Somerset Maugham and a prominent lawyer who had been recently ennobled as Baron Maugham, published *The Tichborne Case*, a classic account of the affair, while two years later the great locked room mystery writer John Dickson Carr drew on the Tichborne imbroglio for his acclaimed detective novel *The Crooked Hinge* (1938).

While not as singular a production as Carr's fantastically eerie and unnerving mystery, Punshon's *Ten Star Clues* is composed in the author's very best vein. Simultaneously intriguing and charming and peopled by a splendid gallery of keenly observed characters, the novel is a model of Golden Age English mystery. In his review of *Ten Star Clues* in the *Spectator*, Punshon's Detection Club colleague Nicholas Blake (the poet Cecil Day Lewis) allowed that *Ten Star Clues* has a "traditional atmosphere of Earls, libraries and sinister butlers," but he nevertheless declared that the novel rose above convention "by soundness of characterization and the personality of Mr. Punshon's detective." He also deemed Bobby's solutions to the dual puzzles concerning the identities of the claimant and the killer "not only exciting but plausible."

Another interesting facet of *Ten Star Clues* is its setting in England during the so-called "Phoney War," the early phase of relative inactivity in the Second World War that fell between the German-Soviet invasion of Poland in September 1939 and the German attack on the Low Countries that commenced in May 1940. Bobby's newly-wedded wife, Olive--formerly Olive Farrar, owner of the chic shop "Olive, Hats"— dutifully attends ARP (Air Raid Precautions) lectures, where she incidentally meets Sophie Longden. ("I liked Miss Owen," Sophy girlishly gushes to Countess Wych. "She seemed very nice, only rather awfully stylish. Oh, and her hats....Each time she had a different one, and each time it was nothing really and yet perfectly wonderful. She used to have a hat shop before she married, someone said.") After England's declaration of war on Germany, Bobby for his part handed in his resignation from the police force in order to enlist in the armed forces, but his resignation, we learn, was "instantly rejected." County martial preparations ultimately play a key role in Bobby's solution of one of the novel's central mysteries.

War was much on E.R. Punshon's mind when he wrote *Ten Star Clues*, in a two-month period over September-October 1940. With his gently wry humor the author tellingly dedicated the novel to "THE SIREN", "Whose irresistible song so often lured away the writer from his work." He of course refers ironically to the air raid siren, which after the Germans commenced the Blitz sounded many times throughout those months on Nimrod Road, Streatham, where Punshon resided in London with Sarah Punshon, his wife of thirty-five years. Presciently the author had evacuated Bobby Owen and his wife Olive from London to comparative safety in Wychshire, a rural Midlands county of his splendidly fertile imagination, but both Punshon and his wife themselves steadfastly remained in London to face the horrors of German air bombardment. In my introductions to the next set of Dean Street Press reissues of Bobby Owen detective novels, I will discuss more about the matter of E.R. Punshon and the Second World War, while continuing the chronicle of Inspector Owen's battles with crime in Wychshire.

Curtis Evans

CHAPTER I
AFTERNOON TEA

Tea was ready on the great south terrace of Castle Wych, one of England's show places and not without its niche in history, open to the public on Saturdays and holidays on payment of one shilling, for the benefit of the funds of the Midwych General Hospital. Plump, soft-footed, complacent—too complacent—Martin, the new butler, was putting the finishing touches to the tea things. Somehow, correctly conventional as he was in movement and appearance, he yet managed to give an impression of a secret, gloating satisfaction. Ralph Hoyle, leaning against the parapet, found himself reminded of a vulture, a filthy, obscene vulture, hovering over a dying man. Ralph knew this was absurd. It was his own imagination, he was well aware, a result of the tension of the moment. Nevertheless the impression remained. He glanced at his cousin and fiancée, Anne Hoyle, wondering if she felt the same. Apparently not, for she was absorbed in twisting his engagement ring round and round upon her finger. But then Anne seldom noticed servants, not, that is, so long as they carried out their duties satisfactorily. She said abruptly:—

"I can't think why grand-dad doesn't just send for the police."

"Well, I don't like the chap myself," Ralph agreed, "but why the police? Sack him. I don't know why you ever let Uncle Ralph take him on. Of course, it's no end of a job, getting decent butlers these days."

"Don't be a fool," snapped Anne. "You know I didn't mean Martin."

"No, I suppose not," agreed Ralph. "I expect I was trying to be funny. I always do when I'm a bit nervy."

"Nothing to be nervy about, is there?" Anne asked.

Ralph did not answer. She knew as well as he did how much or how little there was to be nervy about. It was the length of the interview in the study from which they had been excluded that was troubling them, that was giving to Martin his air of a secret and malicious satisfaction. They had both thought it would have ended long ago, and it still went on. Neither of them could imagine why. But it meant that both were becoming conscious of a vague and increasing unease.

Anne was still absorbed in apparent contemplation of the engagement ring on her finger. It was a nice ring. It had cost a hundred pounds. She knew the exact figure, because her grandfather, old Earl Wych, had told her as a great secret. But it hadn't been Ralph's hundred pounds. For one thing Ralph hadn't a hundred pounds, hardly a hundred pence for that matter. Her grandfather—who was also Ralph's great-uncle—had provided the money for this ring. That was a proof of how greatly the formal engagement had pleased him. Because he was not an old man who parted very easily with his money. Not a miser, of course, but his dislike of drawing cheques had always been marked, and had increased with age. All the same it was a nice ring. Turning it round and round upon her finger, Anne thought:—

"Suppose it's true. If it is... but it can't be... it can't."

She looked up at Ralph. He was tall, well built, with the fair hair, blue eyes, dominant nose of the Hoyles, who for some hundreds of years had lived and flourished at Castle Wych and owned most—but less now than formerly—of the surrounding country. In accordance with the present fashion, he was clean shaven, so that one could see the big mouth with the thin, straight lips that were also a characteristic of the Hoyles. His big, square chin stuck out, too, in a way reminiscent rather of the earlier than of the later Hoyles, who had generally owed their continued success to a certain nimble suppleness of mind rather than to that thrusting energy of which such a chin is supposed to be a sign. It was certainly a sign very apparent in the effigy of the founder of the family, the first Baron Hoyle, who had undoubtedly been a bit in the traditional robber-baron line.

Since those far-off days, however, the Hoyles had generally preferred to be lawyers, politicians, high ecclesiastics— place holders, in brief—rather than soldiers or adventurers. So they had flourished exceedingly, adding acre to acre, sedately progressing from baron to earl, sending out many off-shoots, destined, they, too, to reap where they had not sown and gather where they had not strewn. Then when place holding became a depressed industry the family took to finance, since holding directorships and drawing fat fees therefor, seemed almost the same thing as holding a sinecure or two. Unhappily, it hadn't worked out quite like that. More than once unscrupulous persons had taken advantage of the Hoyle aristocratic indifference to detail that they expected subordinates to attend to. Also, the trade, profession, or occupation of landlord had in its turn become something of a depressed industry. True, as in the days of Carlyle, if a tenant plucked two nettles to make soup, then of those nettles the landlord could still claim one for himself. But to-day there wasn't always a tenant to do the required plucking. Alternatively, as the lawyers say, the market for plucked vegetation of all kinds was sometimes so bad that even transport costs could not be covered.

This is known as agricultural depression, and Ralph, as heir to his great-uncle, the present aged but still vigorous earl, had long ago decided that when he inherited title and estates Castle Wych would have to go. Possibly it might be presented to the nation or to the Wychshire County Council, if either nation or county council could be cajoled or persuaded or otherwise induced to accept the sprawling white elephant of a place. Some of the outlying property would have to be disposed of, too, and the rest managed on very different lines from those followed at present. There was still money to be made in agriculture, Ralph was persuaded, if one had capital and adopted modern and scientific methods. Unfortunately in his present position as agent to his great-uncle he had command of no capital, nor was he permitted to employ or introduce those new methods for which he yearned. Indeed these suggestions that he had more than once urged upon the old earl had led to somewhat strained relations between them, and to one really gorgeous row when Ralph had let slip his intention of somehow or another getting rid of the castle, the ancient seat of the family.

"But for the entail," Ralph had remarked afterwards to Anne, "poor old Uncle Ralph would have booted me out then and there. He told me I was a degenerate Hoyle and a disgrace to the family name. I suppose it is hard luck on him he has no direct heir now."

Anne had made no comment. Her common sense told her some such step as Ralph proposed might very well be necessary. But she meant to make very sure that it was necessary. Countess Wych, presiding over ancient and historic Castle Wych, would be a much more imposing person than a Countess Wych in a London flat or occupying the dower house which was as old and inconvenient as the castle itself, and very much less magnificent; in fact, not magnificent at all. Besides, she had a genuine sense of the historic significance of the old place, where news had come of Agincourt, from whose towers beacons had blazed to tell of the coming of the Armada, where Charles the First had first raised his standard even before flying it at Nottingham, where galloping messengers had brought so often news of peace and war, of triumph and disaster, where three times over in the war of 1914-18, telegraph boys had come cycling up the long avenue with the tidings that once again the heir had died in battle; Mesopotamia, Gallipoli, France, all taking their toll in grim succession.

Turning now her ring round and round upon her finger, she was telling herself that things would have to be very bad indeed before she would consent to parting with the old historic dwelling, for so long the seat of the family. Certainly not merely to raise money for agricultural experiments. Always she had been accustomed to getting her own way, and she meant to have it about the old house, too. Only, somehow, glancing up at Ralph, as he leaned moodily against the stone parapet, she was aware of an uncomfortable feeling that that square, stuck-out chin, those clear and steady eyes, suggested a will as decided as her own.

Then, too, there was this new development, though that, it appeared, need not be taken too seriously. Ralph himself, at any rate, who had seen and talked to the fellow, had waved him aside as an obvious, almost bare-faced impostor. And Mr. Clinton Wells, the family lawyer, was very much of the same opinion.

Only why were they all three, earl, lawyer, claimant, closeted so long in the library? Or perhaps the police had been sent for and the delay was merely till they arrived?

Bitterly she reflected, with the sense of grievance that never left her, that the claim now made would not have mattered but for the absurd and unfair sex disability under which her natural rights were disallowed. She felt herself as competent as any man to look after the estate or to take part in those activities that in England are part and parcel of an ancient title. Indeed, her clear-cut features; her chin, smaller and rounder no doubt than Ralph's, but sticking out in much the same manner; the firm lines of her mouth, too big, like that of all the Hoyles; the direct and haughty gaze of her clear eyes so ready to show disdain or anger; all spoke of much the same reversion to the original bold-baron type whereof Ralph also seemed an example. She was a handsome rather than a pretty girl, largely made, fond of all outdoor sports, a good rider to hounds, an excellent shot, inclined to despise tennis to which she sometimes referred as 'pat ball,' but almost in the championship class at golf. Not that she ever really enjoyed any game so much as she enjoyed a day's shooting—deer stalking in the Highlands for example—or a good run to hounds ending with a kill in the open. The very first thrill in her life had been the old ceremony of blooding she had gone through at the age of five, after one of the best runs the Wychshire hounds had ever known. Nor probably had Castle Wych, in all its long history, ever been so well run as since Countess Wych's increasing age and infirmities had confined her to her room and caused the reins of management to fall into Anne's hands. The domestic staff held her in wholesome awe, though, like the schoolboy in the story, they would probably have admitted that if she was a beast, at any rate she was a just beast.

A girl came out from the house, small and hurrying and a little breathless. She was Sophy Longden, daughter of the Reverend Louis Longden, vicar of Brimsbury Wych, the village and parish dominated by the castle. Mr. Longden had not been vicar long. It is not always easy to-day to find incumbents for small, badly endowed country livings, and the bishop had been glad to hear of an East End curate who, threatened with a breakdown after twenty years' hard work in a poor district, was willing to exchange the smoke and noise and squalor of the East End for the fresh air and quiet of Brimsbury Wych.

The change had been very successful in filling in Sophy's small, thin face, with the broad low forehead and the pointed chin. She was even beginning to show roses in her cheeks, and her eyes had become less strained, and quieter. Fruit and vegetables from their own garden were still a treat, bewilderingly different from the stuff of the same name, bought from London greengrocers. Nor had Sophy as yet quite recovered from her awe of the castle and those who dwelled therein, especially of the tall old man, so very upright and dignified, who treated her when they met with a lofty courtesy that not only deeply gratified her, but somehow left her more than ever conscious of the enormous difference between Earl Wych and the younger daughter of a country parson.

It had been an added wonder, a kind of Cinderella tale come true in real life, when quite unexpectedly she had found herself actually living in a real castle, rising each morning, going to bed each night, in one of England's stately homes—Sophy knew her Mrs. Hemans—and able in her leisure time to sit with her book or sewing in one or other of those magnificent rooms; even in the west drawing-room, for instance, where, according to legend, Queen Elizabeth had once held council. It was as a kind of part secretary, part companion, part nurse to the bed-ridden Countess Wych that she was there, and though the salary was small enough, it paid for her clothes, there was one mouth less to feed at home, there was even often a little over to help her mother with the housekeeping, and she was still able to help her father in such small ways as taking a class in the Sunday school, arranging flowers in the church, and so on.

Indeed Sophy thought herself an extraordinarily lucky young person, even if she did not fully realize that she was doing twice the work any maid would have done for less than a half of the wage. Not that any one else realized it, either.

She was genuinely fond of the aged Countess Wych, and really liked to listen to those interminable tales of her young days Anne would have cut very short indeed. Of Earl Wych she stood in deep awe, tempered by a lively gratitude that he permitted her to breathe the same air as himself. Anne she worshipped from a great distance, absolutely convinced that Anne was the most perfect and altogether wonderful creature the world had ever seen. She was more than a little doubtful of Ralph, though, holding him quite unworthy of her paragon, but loyally accepting him, since Anne had deigned to do the same. Still she liked him the least of the family. She found a trifle alarming his silences, his abstractions, there was something about him she felt vaguely disturbing. Not for the world would she ever have been alone with him, and once when he had offered to drive her into Midwych on some errand or another, she had looked so startled and scared that he had burst out laughing and gone off without her.

That had been hard to forgive; for her dignity, of which she was seldom aware, had really been ruffled on that occasion. On his side he had put her down as a colourless little thing and had never since taken much notice of her. She said now, a little breathlessly:—

"Oh, I'm so sorry. I didn't know tea was ready. Would you like me to pour out, Anne?"

(Yes, she was allowed to call Anne by her Christian name, and Anne quite often called her 'Sophy'. Countess Wych, too, who had begun with 'Miss Longden', had progressed to 'Sophy', and now seldom called her anything but 'dear' or 'dear child'. It was all very wonderful, and if only Earl Wych had been a trifle less alarming and Ralph a trifle more friendly, she would have felt herself entirely at home.)

Without replying directly to her question, Anne said:— "Are they still in the library?"

Sophy nodded and looked grave.

"I think," she said, "they must be giving him a—talking to." She looked graver still as she thought of how awful it must be to be 'talked to' by Earl Wych. She said severely:— "I don't know how any one can be so wicked as to pretend to be some one they aren't. I could kill them." Then she saw Ralph smiling, and that really annoyed her. It was nothing to laugh at. She said quite loudly:— "Well, I could," and indeed at the moment she felt there was nothing, however desperate, she was not capable of to defend this great House of Wych against disaster.

"Another Joan of Arc come to Castle Wych," Ralph said, amused, and yet a little impressed, too, by the sudden note of will and energy in the generally quiet, clear little voice.

"Sophy's not saying she's a Joan of Arc," interposed Anne, who felt that if any Joan of Arcs were required, she herself was quite ready to supply the need. Sophy looked at her gratefully, thankful for this defence. Anne added:— "What's the good of talking like that? The man's an evident impostor."

All the same there was a touch of renewed unease in her voice. Why were they so long in the library? why hadn't the fellow been thrown out long ago? Sophy began to pour out the tea. Anne had not answered her question directly, but Anne had a habit of not answering questions. She expected her wishes to be understood. She expected people to know what they ought to do and to do it. A regal attitude, but Anne had a regal turn of mind. The fact that Sophy was rather quick at understanding what Anne wished was one of the reasons why she had found favour in Anne's sight— Sophy having anything but a regal turn of mind. From the parapet Ralph said:—

"Here's Arthur coming. The gathering of the clans—or is it a case of the eagles and the carcase?" and Sophy thought the remark in dreadfully bad taste.

A stout, comfortable-looking, middle-aged man was walking towards them across the lawn. He was Arthur Hoyle, next in succession in the direct male line—or so till now it had been assumed—though it was four generations through which he traced descent. His grandfather was the only member of the Hoyle family who, venturing into the city, had there been not shorn but shearer—an expert shearer, too. Arthur's father had been less successful, but Arthur himself was supposed to have more than retrieved their fortunes. He was an accountant by profession, a director of many companies, engaged in various complicated financial operations, and he lived in some style in an imposing mansion known as The Thatched Cottage, presumably because it was neither thatched nor a cottage, and situated between the town of Midwych and Wych forest. He was a widower, having lost his wife some years ago, and there were no children. Rumour said there were many willing to do their best to bring him consolation for his loss, and rumour was busy, too, with the passing consolations he was supposed to be finding for himself.

Fortunately rumour can generally be disbelieved, and these were no more than rumours. He was still a good-looking and in his way an imposing person, with the Hoyle blue eyes—a colder blue in his case perhaps—the fair hair, the wide mouth and the thin lips, these last more tightly pressed together than with most of the Hoyles. On the whole, belonging to the more recent Hoyle type, the supple, smiling, ready-witted type rather than to the direct and dominant type to which both Ralph and Anne belonged.

He ascended the terrace by one of the short flights of steps that led up to it from the lawn, and waved them a cheery greeting.

"Hullo!" he called. "Thought I would drop in and hear the news. I heard Clinton Wells was bringing him along. I suppose he's here."

Ralph nodded an assent.

"They're in the library," he said.

"Well, you ought to be there, too," Arthur remarked.

Ralph made no comment but looked as though he were of the same opinion.

"You're an interested party," Arthur said. "So am I, I suppose, for that matter—or would be, if you weren't so disgustingly healthy."

He collected a chair and sat down. Sophy, whose existence he had acknowledged with a brief nod, poured out another cup of tea for him. Silently Anne pushed over a plate of cakes. She was still turning round and round the ring on her engagement finger. Ever since her earliest childhood, it had always been understood that she and Ralph were to marry. It was, in a way, her right. That absurd sex disability whereby she was barred from her natural right of succession might have had some sense in it in days when occasionally rights had to be defended by the use of lance and battle axe. Not that Anne didn't feel perfectly capable of wielding axe and lance herself, if necessary. But in settled days of law and order, this sex disability business was a ridiculous and disgusting anachronism. Had she been the grand-daughter of an American millionaire instead of an English peer of ancient lineage, sex would not have mattered in the least. Her rights would not have been affected in any way by the totally irrelevant detail that she generally wore skirts and not trousers. True, the American millionaire could leave his money as he liked and the English peer had no say in the matter, all that being regulated by the entail. But Anne felt as fully competent to deal with supposititious American millionaires as with equally supposititious battle axes. She would have liked to see any old millionaire grandfather disinheriting her, just as she would have liked a chance to wave a battle axe in the thickest of the fray. So the engagement to Ralph, heir to title and estates by the mere accident of having been born to trousers and not skirts, had always been regarded as no more than her right, the simple compensation due to her. Turning the ring round and round, she thought:—

"Arthur's awfully rich. Money matters to-day. If you've money you've everything. Ralph wouldn't have a farthing, if he wasn't heir, and he has no profession except managing the estates. I wonder if Arthur would give him a job—five or ten pounds a week perhaps. What's the good of that?"

"You both look a bit down," Arthur said. He helped himself to another cake. "I can remember Bertram," he said. "I was here when we heard of his death. Cheek for this bloke to turn up now and claim to be him. Clinton Wells has seen him, hasn't he?"

"Yes. He told me there was nothing in it," Ralph answered.

"Well, he's a lawyer and he ought to know," Arthur remarked.

"Oh, the fellow's an impostor all right," declared Ralph. "He's managed to get hold of poor old Bertram's papers— stole them after Bertram died most likely. Now he has his tale pat, but there are all kinds of things he ought to know that he hasn't any idea of. You could see it. When he got here he was gaping all round, like one of the Saturday shillingers. He wasn't remembering familiar things, he was noticing and trying to remember new ones. Bertram wasn't bad at cricket. The first century he made in anything like a good match was for Wych and District against an M.C.C. team. No chap ever forgets his first century in a good match. Couldn't if he tried," pronounced Ralph, who himself bowled a good fast ball and was a fair, if somewhat impetuous, batsman, generally good for runs if he didn't get out in the first over. "But this fellow hadn't a notion what I was talking about when I tried him with it."

"Wonder why he has waited so long?" Arthur mused, half to himself. "If he managed to get hold of Bertram's papers after his death, that's all of ten years ago, isn't it?"

"To explain why he has forgotten such a lot," Ralph suggested.

"Yes, there's that," agreed Arthur. "Handy excuse. Or he may have been screwing up his courage."

"Grand-dad ought to send for the police," Anne interposed sharply. "I can't think why he doesn't. Perhaps he has," she added hopefully, "and they're just waiting for the police to get here."

"Well, about that," Arthur pointed out, helping himself to more cake, "I don't know what he could be charged with. I don't quite know what just saying you are someone you aren't would come under for a police charge."

"The Roger Tichborne man was sent to prison," Anne reminded him.

"Wasn't that for perjury committed at the first trial?" Arthur asked. "Do you know, Ralph?"

Ralph didn't answer. He didn't like Arthur's tone very much, and he liked still less the touch of mockery, of malice indeed, he felt beneath the smoothness of Arthur's voice. It has the voice Arthur used, he felt, when Arthur was explaining to someone that he, Arthur, had got the best of the bargain, and there was nothing the someone could do about it. Of course, it all made very little difference to Arthur since his prospect of inheriting had always been negligible. Ralph's expectation of life was perfectly good, he and Anne had every intention of producing a large family. Besides, when a chap was as rich and prosperous and successful as Arthur Hoyle, he had no need to worry about losing so small a chance of inheriting. There were, no doubt, those vague rumours about Arthur having dropped a packet recently on the Stock Exchange, but rumours don't amount to much, and certainly there was no sign of any change in the luxurious style of living at The Thatched Cottage, any more than there was any sign of worry to be seen overshadowing Arthur's accustomed air of plump prosperity. He was well into his fifth cake now, by the way.

Through the french windows that opened on the terrace from the small drawing-room, three men came in succession. First was old Earl Wych, aged, white-haired, erect, looking stern and intent, with so set and grim an expression indeed that Sophy found herself thinking of a soldier advancing to the attack. Not that she had ever seen a soldier advancing to the attack, but that was the thought that came into her mind. Behind the old earl was a much younger man, evidently very nervous, a nervousness that showed itself in restless eyes, an occasional twitching at the corners of the mouth, a perpetual fidgeting with handkerchief and cigarette case, and so on. Sophy remembered, too, later on, how when he stood still she could see his toes working inside his long, narrow, shiny, patent leather shoes. A natural nervousness perhaps in a man claiming to be the long-lost heir and uncertain of his reception. At the moment the thought in Sophy's mind was that if you said 'Boo' to him very loudly and very suddenly, he would probably run away. Unfortunately, it occurred to no one to try the experiment. Besides, it may be Sophy did not quite understand the kind of timid desperation, of frightened obstinacy, some people can display.

Behind these two came a tall, very good-looking young man, athletic in build, with strong, eager features, a bronzed complexion, a general air of brisk and confident authority. He had not at all the appearance of the traditional family lawyer. But it might come to that in time, for he was still much the youngest partner in the old established firm of Wells, Clinton, Wells and Blacklock that for many years had been in charge of all the legal side of the Hoyle estates, and he would certainly not have been here to-day but for the accident that the senior partner, Mr. Blacklock, was ill, and the second partner, another Blacklock, was away on holiday. So this young man, Clinton Wells, combining in himself the original Clinton and Wells strains, found himself in full charge. Gossip whispered that he was an ambitious young man, showing no signs of settling down as a country solicitor, and even entertaining political aspirations. It was reported he had

been heard to say that what a little Welsh lawyer could do, a
solicitor from the Midlands could do, too. More ill-natured gossip
remarked that he had the pale-blue eyes of the Hoyle family, and
hinted that a certain unavowed mixing, outside legal bonds, of
Hoyle and Clinton blood a generation or two back, accounted for
the favour with which old Earl Wych always seemed to regard the
young man. But these were only whispers none dared repeat
aloud, whispers without a shred of proved foundation. True, there
were always those clear, rather pale-blue eyes characteristic in the
Hoyle family, showing, for example, both in Anne and in Ralph,
though in Ralph's case the blue often seemed to be a grey, so that
Sophy, at least, was never quite sure whether they were really blue
or really grey.

There advanced slowly the little group—the tall, commanding
looking old man; the nervous young man; the handsome, youthful
lawyer, looking as distinguished in his way as did the old earl
himself. The group by the tea table were all on their feet now.
Arthur had an air of complete bewilderment. Ralph waited, utterly
expressionless. Anne gave the impression of holding herself in
check, of being ready to spring at any moment, of a coiled-up
spring indeed that the smallest touch might release. To Sophy's
mind the comparison between this advance of the three men with
the advance of soldiers upon a firmly held position, grew still
stronger. She became suddenly afraid. In a clear, loud voice, with
little in it of the frequent shrillness of old age, Earl Wych said:—

"This is my grandson, Bertram, we all believed dead so long. I
am sure you will welcome him. At first I failed to recognize him,
but now I am convinced of his identity."

CHAPTER II
CHIVALROUS OFFER

There followed a bleak silence, broken only by a quick, deep-
drawn breath from the claimant, the soi-disant Bertram Hoyle. It
was almost as if he experienced a sudden relief, as if until then he
had not been quite sure of what the old earl would say. No longer
had he the appearance of being ready to run if any one said 'Boo'

to him. Instead, and instantly, he took on an air of swaggering confidence, and, looking at the others, seemed to be asking them what they thought of that.

What Ralph thought, it was not easy to tell. His features were utterly expressionless. The only change was that he no longer lolled against the parapet but straightened himself and stood upright. The earl was looking straight at him; and Sophy, watching, had an odd sensation that silently the old man was pleading with him, asking for sympathy and understanding, almost for help. But Ralph's own gaze was averted, directed towards that wide expanse of countryside, of field and wood and pasture, of hedge and grove and spinney, all lying there in the quiet afternoon sunshine, all of it land over which for centuries the Hoyles had borne sway and rule.

Arthur was still gaping, open-mouthed, open-eyed. The impression he gave was of a complete and indeed incredulous astonishment. One expected every moment to hear him burst out laughing and remark that it had been a good joke and now let's be serious. Anne was leaning forward, her hands on the tea table, her eyes intent upon the claimant. There was questioning and doubt and anger in her gaze, and something else as well that Sophy, at least, did not understand, something of poise and calculation as at secret, unknown thoughts. Yet what Sophy remembered best in after days, when thinking over that strange scene, in the first moments at least so strangely silent, was neither the dark impassivity with which Ralph listened to his great-uncle's declaration, nor the change in the claimant's attitude from nervousness to swaggering assurance, nor the suggestion in Anne's eyes of hidden, secret thoughts, nor Arthur Hoyle's almost ludicrous surprise, nor yet that impression as of a pleading for sympathy, even for help, Earl Wych seemed to her somehow to convey, but rather the sharp intake just behind her of the lawyer's breath, and of how when she turned for a moment to look she saw his strong white even teeth so firmly clamped upon his under lip that spots of blood showed here and there.

No one had spoken. The only person who had even moved was the claimant, who had dropped into a chair, where he lolled with a kind of insolent self-assurance, as if now perfectly at home. Angrily Sophy thought to herself:—

"Yes, but it wouldn't take much to send you running again."

In a perfectly level, expressionless voice, as if he were merely remarking that it was a fine day, or that he would like another cup of tea, without letting his eyes wander from their contemplation of the fair countryside before him, Ralph said over his shoulder and almost casually:—

"That's a lie."

There followed another silence. Earl Wych went very red and then very pale. He struck his hand heavily on the back of a chair near. Then he said:—

"That's the first time in my life I've been called a liar."

Ralph turned and faced him.

"It may be the first time that you have lied," he said.

Earl Wych still had his hand on the back of a chair. But now it seemed less in anger than for support. Sophy had the idea that he might fall, and instinctively took a step or two towards him. He seemed to understand, and, instead of resenting her action, to be glad of it. He said to Anne:—

"Give your cousin Bertram some tea."

Sophy found suddenly that the old man was leaning a little heavily on her shoulder. He began to walk back towards the castle, still availing himself of her support, of which indeed he was evidently glad. She had the impression that his sight had become dim, that he no longer saw surrounding objects very clearly. She heard him muttering to himself, but she could not tell what he said, though twice over she heard the word 'Bertram' pronounced, and once the phrase 'wretched boy', and then again she heard: 'No lie, no lie. Bertram's there.'

But what this meant she could not imagine.

They entered the castle through the great open french windows of the small drawing-room—its length, by the way, was about thirty feet, its breadth in proportion— and then on to the library where the earl was accustomed to sit. At its door he paused and looked at Sophy with a slight air of surprise, as if wondering who she was and why she was there and why he was leaning on her shoulder. He said:—

"Thank you, my dear. I shall be all right now." Then he said:— "Ralph should take it better. Bertram has his rights. Can't the boy trust me?"

He pushed open the library door and went in, leaving Sophy on the threshold as if he had forgotten she was there, as indeed very likely was the case. Evidently he wished to be alone. Sophy hesitated for a moment, not quite knowing what to do. But she was a young woman with a healthy appetite and she had by no means finished her tea, which, indeed, had been a somewhat interrupted meal. She decided to go back to the terrace and see if anything to eat was still there. She found herself wondering if the old earl had been quite fair to Ralph in saying he should have taken it better. To her surprise she discovered that she was feeling a little sorry for Ralph. Odd, to feel sorry for that strong, aloof personality. She was on the terrace now and she was aware of Martin, the butler, hovering at a distance. She had a disagreeable impression that he was watching. By the tea-table no one seemed to have moved or even to have spoken. Except that Anne had poured out for her newly-discovered cousin a cup of tea, which he was sipping with an air of smug triumph that made even Sophy long to box his ears. His earlier nervousness had entirely disappeared and he had an almost bragging air of possession, even though he did still keep a wary eye on the still and silent figure by the parapet. Sipping his tea as he spoke Bertram was saying now:—

"You know, Cousin Anne, I remember you perfectly. I should have known you again anywhere, any time. So would you me perhaps?"

"No," said Anne, though in a queer, detached, unemotional voice.

"Too bad," Bertram smiled without a trace of discomposure. "I expect I've changed more than you, though. Now Cousin Arthur—" He paused and looked at Arthur, who still had not lost his manner of extreme and indeed incredulous bewilderment. "No," Bertram decided. "I should not have known Cousin Arthur again. One forgets a lot in ten years, especially in the sort of rough and tumble life I've had out there, not to mention a whack on the head I had that got me six months in hospital without knowing who I was or how I got there. Of course, they had me remembering again after a time. That was from getting mixed up in a street row, and when the cops came along, well, they just naturally clubbed every one around. They're handy with their night sticks, those lads, and if you get some when they're handing it out, well, it's just too bad, and that's all there's to it."

He paused and looked round with a kind of sly triumph, and there came into Sophy's mind a sudden, sure conviction that the man was a liar and an impostor, and that he had put forward this story to explain a probably soon apparent ignorance of things he ought to have known, that a genuine Bertram would certainly have known. No one made any comment. The story had been too crude, its intention too evident. Even Bertram himself seemed to feel its reception unsatisfactory. He stared around with what Sophy felt was an insolent defiance, challenging them, as it were, to express disbelief. He drank up his tea and handed the cup to the silent and the watchful Anne.

"May I have another, Cousin Anne?" he asked, and, addressing himself for the first time to the impassive, sombre Ralph, he said:—"Cousin Ralph I hardly remember at all, but then we never saw much of each other, did we? Only in the hols., and not always then."

"I never saw you before to-day," Ralph answered slowly; "and please don't call me your cousin. I believe you to be a liar and an impostor."

"Now, now, now," protested Bertram. "I can make allowances for the way you feel about it, but what's the good of taking it bad? You heard what grand-pa said. I ask you, is it likely grand-pa would accept me as his grand-son and heir if he wasn't satisfied?"

"Have you seen the Countess?" asked Arthur abruptly.

"I have so," Bertram answered readily. "Dear old grand-ma." He shook his head. "Made me go all queer like, here," he said, tapping the spot where he—erroneously—supposed his heart to be. "She just simply couldn't believe it at first, but bless the old dame, she came round as soon as we had talked a bit. Knew me at once then. 'Bertram, my dear boy,' she said, 'this is the happiest day of my life. Now I can depart in peace, same as the Bible says.' The very words she used," he added defiantly, aware that all this was being received with some incredulity since his listeners knew very well that old Countess Wych was extremely unlikely to have said anything even remotely resembling such expressions as he reported. He went on a little quickly as if anxious no more should be said about his interview with the Countess:—"You know, I can quite understand the way you feel; just the way I should myself in your place, if you see what I mean. I shan't take offence. A bit thick to call the old boy a liar. But you can trust me. I'll tell him to forget it. I realize Cousin Ralph is a bit upset. Any one would be. What I say is, let's all shake down together and try to make the best of it. I know just how Ralph's feeling. Natural. But there it is. I've come back and here I am, and I'm more than willing to be friends. What say, Ralph?"

"I say," answered Ralph in the same quiet, conversational tones, "that you're a barefaced and impudent fraud, that I intend to prove it, and I don't think it will be difficult either. I saw you when you got here. I saw the way you looked round. You had never been in the place before. Everything was strange."

"Well, of course, so it was," agreed Bertram easily. "Likely to be after ten years. I went away a boy of nineteen. I come back a man of twenty-nine. I don't feel the same person. In a sense I'm not the same person. Same thing here. It's all the same, but it's all different. Things I remember aren't there any longer and things I don't remember are there instead. Strange isn't the word."

"Do you remember whose portrait used to hang in the library over the fireplace?" Ralph asked.

"Oh, well, if we are going to play the memory game," Bertram answered promptly, "I'll agree at once there are probably a whole heap of things I've forgotten—I daresay that's true of you, too. Do you remember what happened that day we tried to cook a hedgehog gipsy fashion?"

"I don't know what you are talking about," Ralph retorted.

"There you are, you see," smiled Bertram. "It just shows. Clear in my mind as if it was yesterday and gone clean out of yours. Funny, isn't it? I daresay we could go on asking each other things like that all day. Only where would it get us? Likely as not, now I've reminded you, you'll remember all about that hedgehog business and what happened afterwards. When we got together those days you were always the leader, and likely the things you did made more impression on me than they did on you because I admired them so. I remember when we were playing Indians—"

"We never played Indians," interrupted Ralph.

The other shook his head doubtfully.

"Well, what did we play at, if it wasn't Indians?" he asked.

But this time Ralph saw the trap.

"Don't talk about 'we'," he snapped. "There's no 'we' in it."

"You mean it was you all alone?" smiled Bertram. "I expect you just thought I didn't count. Well, what did we play at? Indians if you ask me. All boys play Indians."

Ralph made an angry step forward, his fists clenched, his eyes blazing, and Bertram's expression of a smug complacence was crossed by a quick look of apprehension. Sophy noticed that he even edged his chair a little nearer Anne, as though he felt safer closer to her. Sophy was sure, too, that Anne also had noticed that instinctive movement, and that in some odd way Anne was not displeased by it. This puzzled Sophy enormously. Impossible to suppose that Anne wanted her newly-returned cousin to be a coward—if he really were a coward, that is, which Sophy found a surprising idea. Because she had always taken it for granted that all men were always enormously brave just because they were men, and just as she knew herself to be a dreadful coward, because, she supposed, she was only a girl. Cows, for instance—a painful line of thought Sophy did not attempt to follow up. Of course, Ralph had looked very dreadful, almost for the moment as if he could have killed the other. No wonder perhaps, after all, that Bertram, though a man, and therefore strong and brave, had looked quite frightened. Anyhow, that slight movement towards Anne could not have been an instinctive seeking protection from her vicinity, because as Sophy knew, it was against the nature of things for a man to seek protection from a woman.

Such thoughts flashed swiftly and confusedly through her mind, and it was only later that she understood them clearly. At the moment her chief impression was of relief that that terrible look passed from Ralph so quickly, the ancient look of the man who sees before him his enemy and thinks only of instant attack. A momentary throwback to primitive emotions inconsistent with twentieth century tea tables nicely laid with cake and cream, and with civilized, cultured people gathered round.

Anyhow, it was a considerable relief when Ralph's hands dropped to his side and he turned away. He felt he had nearly made a fool of himself. For the moment he had seen red. It passed, but he still had the sensation of having been trapped. That insidious use of 'we', for example. His own remark 'We never played Indians' that might so easily be twisted into an avowal that they had played together at other things. Why hadn't he said instead: 'We never played at anything because you were never there to play with', or something like that. For the first time he was conscious of what was almost fear. Was it like this, he wondered, that the fly felt when the first invisible threads of the spider's web began to entangle it? He found that Clinton Wells, the lawyer, who hitherto had been silent, watchful and eager indeed but silent, was at his side.

"Ralph," he said, "this is serious. You must be careful. It's no good doing anything rash."

"The fellow's an impostor, a rank impostor," Ralph said. "I ought to have kicked him out at once."

"Can't do that," Clinton answered dryly. "Can't kick people out of other people's houses."

"The fellow's a rank impostor," Ralph repeated.

"I know he is," Clinton answered. "I am as certain of that as you are. But both Earl Wych and the Countess have acknowledged him as their grandson and heir."

"Yes, I know," Ralph said, and stood still. "Well, why?" he asked. "Why? what's it mean?" he asked again, bewilderedly, in the utter blank bewilderment only those can feel who see all their familiar accustomed world vanish at a touch. "Why?" he repeated.

"I don't know," Clinton answered. "Only there it is. We must face facts. If you'll let me say so, it doesn't help to call your great-uncle a liar."

"Did I do that?" Ralph asked. They had walked away from the tea table group and now had reached the end of the terrace, where stone steps led down to the grounds.

Ralph came to a halt there. He said:— "So I did, didn't I? Well, he is."

"No," Clinton declared. "Not consciously at least. It's their sub-conscious longing for their grandson to return that's done the trick. Natural enough in a way. Probably in secret, almost without knowing it, they've been longing for a direct heir. Thinking if only Miss Anne were a boy, if only one of the boys had lived. They've had a tough time, you know. Their own three sons killed in the last war, two grandsons killed in a motor accident, the third dying as a child. It's a tragic record. You can't wonder if two old people, their age telling on them, brooding very likely over their losses, should be only too willing to be convinced by the first fellow who comes along with a plausible story. And it is plausible—as plausible as butter. He had it all pat as you please. Most convincing."

"Do you mean?"

"No, I don't," Clinton interrupted quickly. "I'm a trained lawyer remember. The story is full of holes to me. But I can see how a jury might react, and your great-uncle and aunt—well, with them it's just wishful thinking. They wanted a grandson. A grandson appears. They fall on his neck. There you are."

"Well, I'm not going to fall on his neck," Ralph growled. From where they were standing together at the end of the terrace, he looked back towards the tea table. Anne was in the act of handing cakes to the claimant. Not falling on his neck, of course. Indeed, she was showing no more than the bare civility due to a guest introduced by the head of the house. All the same, Ralph scowled. He would rather have seen the plate of cakes smashed on Bertram's head. "Making himself at home already," he said angrily.

"Very wise on Miss Anne's part, too," declared Clinton, who had detected the note of resentment in Ralph's voice. "For the moment, the only thing to do is to go softly. Remember he's been accepted and introduced by Earl Wych himself."

"Look here," Ralph said. "All that sub-conscious stuff and wishful thinking is all very well. Only Uncle Ralph"—Ralph was the traditional name of the first born in the Hoyle family, it was why Ralph himself had been given it—"only Uncle Ralph's not like that. There's precious little wishful thinking about the old man. He knows that fellow's an impostor as well as I do."

But Clinton shook his head again.

"My dear fellow," he protested, "Earl Wych is the very last man to welcome an impostor. Why should he? Why should any one? Inconceivable, doubly inconceivable in your uncle's case. You know his family pride. No one could possibly think Earl Wych would knowingly and deliberately, of malice aforethought so to say, accept as his grandson someone he knows to be an impostor? You can't really think that?"

"Only I do," Ralph answered. "Uncle lied, and he knew it, and knew that I knew it."

Clinton Wells shrugged his shoulders.

"Well, don't say that to any one else," he advised. "Blind credulity in a very old man—that's natural. Wilful deceit is out of the question. Wishful thinking, that's all. Remember Lady Tichborne. She accepted as her own son—not grandson—a blatant, obvious fraud. This fellow at least is plausible. Arthur Orton wasn't. But look what it took to prove the truth. All because Lady Tichborne wanted her son back so badly she was ready to believe anything. Every lawyer knows there's nothing more difficult to prove than the truth. If you've a lie to prove, you back it up with other lies, and that's all right. But the truth has to stand on its own legs, and sometimes they're pretty shaky legs, too. And if you aren't careful you may prejudice your case from the first. What do you mean to do?"

"I suppose I can bring an action—"

"What about?" interposed Clinton. "I suppose in theory you could apply for an injunction to prevent this fellow putting forward his claims or your great-uncle from acknowledging them. But I certainly never heard of such an action, and I don't know quite whether it would stand. You see, the point is this. Courts of Equity will redress any wrong. That's what they're for. If you have suffered any wrong, the courts are open to you and it's for them to find a remedy. But at present you've suffered none."

"What—" Ralph was beginning in something like a roar but Clinton stopped him with a lifted hand.

"In the eyes of the law," he said quietly, "your position is exactly what it was. That is, you had no rights before and therefore they have not been affected. While the holder of the Wych title and estates is alive, the heir has no rights whatever—except that under the entail he could stop any sale of land or other goods covered by the entail. But no such sale is contemplated. On the death of the holder naturally any claimant can petition for his rights to be acknowledged. But at present you are, so to say, an uninterested party. In theory, Countess Wych might die, Earl Wych might marry again and might have a son. Then both you and this impostor fellow would be out of it. I believe it's not a physical impossibility for a man of that age to have a son. Of course, it won't happen, but the courts can't act on the 'it won't happen' idea."

"Do you mean there's nothing I can do about it?" demanded Ralph, looking very much as if he very firmly intended to do a good deal about it.

"I've been giving you my opinion," Clinton answered, "my unconsidered opinion though. I mean, it's a new point. I can't remember anything of the sort before. I didn't bother to look it up, because, when I brought the fellow here, I fully expected your uncle to ask a few questions and then clear him out for the obvious fraud he seemed to me—he still seems to me. But it didn't turn out like that. The fellow rolled out his yarn and your uncle took it all in. You must see that makes his position immensely strong."

"I'll go and ask uncle—" Ralph began and was about to move towards the house, but Clinton stopped him.

"No," he said firmly. "You're in no state to do that. It would be dangerous. Dangerous for him, dangerous for you, too.

Remember, he's an old man. If you take my advice—" He paused abruptly, so abruptly indeed that Ralph looked at him in some surprise. Clinton moved away a step or two and then came back. He had the air of a man who had suddenly seen a new and startling aspect of the problem before them and was a good deal shaken. He seemed to make up his mind with a gesture of striking one hand into the other. "All right, all right," he said aloud, and then he looked directly at Ralph. "I take it you intend to fight for your rights?" he asked.

"I do that," Ralph answered. "Not only for my rights but because I don't mean to let a filthy fraud like that fellow get away with it. I've got some family feeling left. If a real heir turned up, all right, I'd get out and I shouldn't grumble either. But I don't mean to let a stranger boss it here." He turned as he spoke and looked out again over that wide expanse of fair countryside where he knew and loved almost every tree and bush and field, every stream and woodland path. "No," he said again. "Or there," he added, nodding towards the ancient pile in whose shadow they stood. "Oh, I'll fight all right," he said. "Only why has my uncle done this thing?"

"If you fight," Clinton went on slowly, "you'll want legal advice. I want you to understand my position. We —the firm, I mean—we act for the Wych estate. That's been so for a good many years. The Wych estate—I won't say it's the bulk of our practice, but it is the most important part. Your uncle has a perfect right to change his lawyers at any moment. He will certainly do it if he finds we are acting for you in an attempt to prove a common swindler the man he has publicly accepted as his grandson."

"Yes, I suppose so," agreed Ralph. "You know, I'm sorry. This thing has come so suddenly, I hardly know where I am. I quite see what you mean. That's quite all right. Very natural. I must try to get someone."

"What I'm thinking," Clinton Wells went on, "is there's no one could help you the way we could. I know that sounds a bit conceited but I think it's true. We have, so to say, the atmosphere of it all, in a way that's just not possible for any one coming in fresh. What I'm going to suggest is this. I'll dissolve partnership. I daren't, I don't think it would be right, ask the other two to run such a risk. They're married, got responsibilities. Besides, I don't know what view they'll take. I can't suggest dragging them into it. But if I resign from the firm, I can act for you freely. There'll be no reason for Earl Wych to take his business away, once I've taken myself away. And I think I can say without too much egotism that I can be ten times more useful to you than any one could be only brought in now."

"Look here," said Ralph, a good deal moved. "I mean to say—well, it's awfully good of you. Only—well, it's a big risk."

Clinton nodded.

"Very big," he agreed. "It'll be for big stakes—all in. If we lose, we shall both be done for. But I don't think we shall. I'm utterly convinced we can prove this fellow is a fraud. And I feel I can do it. Mind you," he added, with a little nervous laugh, "I know I've a lot to gain as well as lose. If we bring it off, my name will be made. Clinton Wells, the fellow who pulled through the big succession case. That's what people will say. I shall be a made man."

"You're taking a big risk all the same," Ralph repeated. "I shan't forget. No reason why you shouldn't have stood out. I—I—" he stammered a little, something like a lump in his throat. "I'm grateful," he said and impulsively he held out his hand.

Clinton Wells took it. For a moment they stood so, their hands firmly clasped. Clinton Wells said:—

"Do nothing at present. We must lay our plans. I must be free first. You understand until I am free from my present obligations to your uncle and my partners, I can't take any steps whatever. That's no harm. Just as well to wait for their next move. The first thing to do will be to dig up who this fellow really is. For the moment, we must just wait and see. You understand?"

Ralph nodded silently. It was action he wanted, but he realized the force of the other's arguments.

CHAPTER III
SOME DOUBTS

Although Bertram had been drinking tea and eating cakes and
sandwiches with, as Mr. Winston Churchill might have said, a
'certain relish', none the less all this time he had also been
watching closely Ralph and Clinton Wells as they talked together
at the end of the terrace. Obviously he was uneasy at their
prolonged conversation, and would have very much liked to know
what they were saying.

At the tea table itself few remarks were made. Arthur was still
plunged deep in puzzled thought, and every now and then would
stare hard at Bertram and then abruptly look away again. Sophy
thought to herself: 'Mr. Arthur doesn't believe in him, but he is
wondering how he can turn it to his own profit,' and quite
suddenly she realized she had always known that Mr. Arthur
Hoyle, as a good business man, always thought first of how to turn
any unexpected situation to his own profit.

Anne only spoke to make occasional and conventional
observations, such as 'Do you take sugar?' and so on, but in her
case Sophy was sure she was perplexed and doubtful, bewildered
by her grandfather's announcement, unable fully to accept it and
yet also unable to understand why the old man should say such a
thing unless it were true. Sophy thought, too, that Anne was
looking at Bertram with a good deal of personal interest. He was
certainly good looking for those who liked that style, and he had a
kind of appealing, friendly way with him, a little like that of a well-
trained dog. Sophy felt it was a manner likely to appeal to Anne,
who always wished to feel herself dominating others. It was one of
the reasons why she herself always got on so well with Anne,
because, of course, it was natural for an insignificant little thing
like herself to accept the domination of such a brilliant, forceful
personality as Anne. Then Sophy thought:— "No, he isn't a bit like
a well-trained dog, more like a cat that can purr, and scratch, too,
if you don't mind." Aloud she said, very much surprised:—

"Oh, Mr. Ralph's going."

Ralph, in fact, had descended the terrace steps and was striding away across the lawn. It might have been a flight. It had not that air. More like a march to the attack, Sophy thought. The tall, upright figure, the head held high, the whole impression of strong intention and resolve his bearing gave, denied any notion of retreat. They all watched him and they all alike understood that from him energetic action in defence of the position he had held as heir, was to be expected. Bertram said uncomfortably:—

"Got it in for me all right, so he has. Gee, I'm keeping out of his way dark nights."

To Sophy the surprising thing was that in Bertram's voice as he said this there was evident fear—plain, sheer physical fear, as if he expected Ralph would soon be back, armed with some lethal weapon.

"Well, you can't wonder, can you?" Arthur said.

"Glad this isn't God's own country across the herring pond," Bertram remarked with an uneasy laugh. "You don't go in for gun play over here, do you?"

"It all depends," Arthur answered, with such evident malice that Sophy was convinced he, too, had noticed the fear in Bertram's uncertain tones.

"He must be a real coward," Sophy told herself, for the first time recognizing the fact that even a man might prefer running to fighting; and that, if cows seldom scared the masculine race, yet members of it might be all the more afraid of other dangers and perils.

One good thing about that thought was that Anne, who was certainly no coward, who cared nothing at all for cows and who really seemed to like holding a car at sixty or seventy miles an hour on the open road, would have no further sympathy with the intruder. To Sophy's further astonishment, however, Anne was watching Bertram with a small, amused smile that was not at all unfriendly, or even contemptuous, that was, in fact, almost pleased. Sophy's glance turned towards the departing Ralph. He was just vanishing behind some ornamental bushes. Odd that that disappearing back, as it might be in retreat, gave so strong an impression of determination and resolve. As odd indeed as that

Bertram, sitting there in apparently full possession of the field, gave an equally strong impression of nervousness and alarm. Then Sophy had a fresh shock. Anne had watched Ralph vanish from sight, and her eyes were hard and questioning. She looked back at Bertram, and they took on a much softer and yet strangely calculating expression. Sophy found herself thinking:—

"She is telling herself she could never boss Ralph but she could Bertram, and she does always want to boss every one."

But this thought seemed to her so treacherous and unfair that hurriedly she put it out of her mind.

Clinton Wells came back to the tea table. He did not sit down. He said:—

"I think perhaps I ought to tell you that Ralph does not intend to accept this new situation, and that I have promised to act for him."

"You?" almost shouted Bertram. "Why, you can't, you—" He stopped abruptly as Clinton gave him an angry and authoritative look. "Oh, well, I suppose you know what you are doing," he mumbled.

"I am well aware," Clinton said coldly, "that I am a partner in a firm charged with the interests of the Earl Wych, who has accepted you, sir, as his grandson and heir. My firm is in no way implicated in my action. I shall naturally sever my connection with it. Impossible to act for two persons whose interests appear to be opposed, one of whom indeed is contemplating taking proceedings against the other."

"Well, what can Ralph do?" Arthur asked. "If grandpa says, here's my grandson, what can any one else do? Cousin Bertram was just thanking his stars we don't go in for gun play over here and don't carry six-shooters around in our pockets."

"In point of fact," observed Clinton Wells grimly, "Ralph has a pistol—an automatic, I believe. Keeps it in the safe in the office. The old land agent got a licence for it years ago, when a bank was raided outside Midwych. There were often big sums in the office when the rents were paid—in cash, too. Some of the smaller tenants still pay in cash. But he won't use it in this connection. The gentleman introduced to us as Mr. Bertram Hoyle need not be afraid of that."

"Of course not," agreed Anne, "the idea's nonsense."

"Nonsense," confirmed Arthur. "Ralph will take care the case is proved all the way home and back again, but that's all."

But Bertram did not look too convinced.

"I've seen a fellow look the way he did," he said, "and mighty soon the fellow he looked at was dead, pumped full of lead."

"Oh!" Sophy gasped, so loudly that they all looked at her.

Anne laughed abruptly.

"Our Joan of Arc again," she said teasingly. "Sophy could do it herself, I believe."

"Oh!" gasped Sophy again, quite overwhelmed, even more horrified by a sudden conviction that Anne had had a glimpse in her of depths she herself had never dreamed existed.

Was it possible, she wondered, that others knew more of you than you ever knew of yourself? Was it possible Anne was right about her, and that if she were put to it she would be capable of things she had never dreamed of? Or was it possible she was right about Anne, and that for power, the power to dominate and rule, Anne would go to any lengths? Disturbing thoughts, and thoughts that once again Sophy put resolutely from her.

The others had not been paying much attention. Arthur was saying again to Bertram:—

"My dear fellow, this is England, not Chicago."

"Got no killers in England?" Bertram asked, and that was a question no one answered.

"If Ralph shot you, he would be hanged, you know," observed Anne dispassionately.

"Well, that's a thing to say," complained Bertram. "What good would hanging him do me?"

Again a question no one attempted to answer. Bertram took out his handkerchief, not a very clean handkerchief, and wiped his forehead. Perhaps it was the hot tea he had been drinking that had caused those drops of perspiration he was wiping away, but Sophy did not think so. What she did think was that Anne had made her remark for the sole purpose of once more testing Bertram's nerves, and that his response had pleased her, or why had she once again that look of secret satisfaction?

Sophy thought regretfully of a recent day when they had all been having tea, all except Bertram, of course, on the terrace, just like to-day. Only then everything had been simple and straightforward, normal as tea itself in the open air on a fine day. Now she had a feeling of being out of her depth, of being surrounded by much that was beyond her comprehension. Why had old Earl Wych introduced to them as his grandson and heir this young man whom Sophy, in her own mind, firmly believed to be an impostor? Why had Anne become strange and remote, as if all at once she had seen opportunity hitherto denied her? What opportunity could there be for her in the appearance of this stranger claiming to dispossess the man she was engaged to? Why was Clinton Wells, who had never struck Sophy as a knight errant, so ready to throw up position and prospects to fight so forlorn a battle against such odds? Why was even Mr. Arthur so silent and brooding as if he, too, all at once had become aware of hidden implications that both alarmed and attracted him, horrified him and fascinated him, but that at present he did not fully understand? Above all, why did they talk in that horrible way about pistols and shooting? Uncomfortably Sophy realized she could very well think of Ralph as facing danger with a weapon in his hand.

The departure of Ralph had certainly in no way relieved the situation. The reverse indeed. Even the claimant seemed to have lost his appetite for cakes. He was looking moodily in the direction in which Ralph had disappeared. It was almost as if he thought Ralph might be lurking there, ready unexpectedly to spring out again. In fact, he was rapidly taking on again that air he had had before of being likely to turn and run if somebody suddenly said 'Boo' to him. From the house, Martin, the butler, was approaching, picking his way carefully, now and again pausing and then coming slowly on again. The impression he gave was that of a hovering vulture, waiting its opportunity. None of the others seemed to notice his approach. He said softly in Sophy's ear:—

"His lordship's compliments and her ladyship would he glad of your presence, when convenient."

"I'll come at once," Sophy said, not sorry for a summons that removed her from an atmosphere that seemed to her so full of hidden thoughts and currents, of the significance of which she had no idea. It was like, she thought, sitting still in an arena full of flying bullets and poisoned arrows, discharged by hidden adversaries at enemies of whose purpose and whose presence she had no knowledge.

She got up and hurried towards the castle and when she was quite near it, there came to her the thought that this was the tremendous prize for which combat had now been joined—this ancient and historic building, the broad lands that went with it, the peerage that gave so privileged a place in the old habit and establishment of British life. All this and more she realized now stood at stake, and for such a stake the game might well be played with desperation. Partly from a sheer instinctive modesty that made her a trifle shy of using the great reception rooms more than was necessary, partly because on the whole it was as short a way as any, Sophy did not enter by the great open French windows of the first drawing-room through which old Earl Wych had issued with claimant and lawyer in attendance, but by a smaller side door into a dark and narrow passage that led on to the inner hall and the central stairway. By contrast with the warmth and sunshine of the summer day without, this passage was so chill and gloomy that Sophy stood still and found herself shivering, with that odd sensation which in olden times was supposed to be caused by someone walking over your grave. She glanced back over her shoulder, afraid, though she knew not why, and then saw again the tea table on the terrace and the tiny group round it, the whole scene looking so peaceful, so ordinary, so normal, she told herself she must be getting quite hysterical.

She hurried on her way and upstairs soon became too busy with Countess Wych to have time for much further thought.

The old lady was evidently very disturbed and upset. The shock and excitement of her grandson's return, for that she accepted him as grandson was made plain by her so referring to him twice over, had plainly been great. Sophy's suggestion, for she was really a little alarmed by the old lady's condition, that the doctor should be sent for, was however firmly rejected.

"No, no, I want no doctor," she said with energy, and then later on, after she had quietened down a little, she fell into a troubled sleep from which in about half an hour she woke abruptly. Looking at Sophy, who was sitting near with some sewing, she said:—

"Harm will come of it, much harm."

Sophy came to her side and tried to persuade her to sleep again. But she was still restless and evidently in no fit condition to be left alone, so Sophy sent down word that she would not come to dinner if she might have something sent to her on a tray. The tray was duly brought, but by Martin himself instead of by one of the maids. He asked how her ladyship was. Sophy answered that she was dozing, and tried to think Martin's inquiry was of good will, but in this did not quite succeed.

"He's gloating," she thought, astonished by the word that had so suddenly presented itself to her as the only one to describe Martin's attitude. "They're all like that. Why? That's silly. They can't be. Only they are." Natural, she supposed, perfectly natural, inevitable indeed, that this sudden appearance of an heir long believed to be dead, should cause many unexpected complications. It was the nature of those complications that puzzled her, for she felt that all concerned had seen possibilities and chances that were utterly beyond her understanding, and yet that she felt vaguely to be full of strange, dark implications.

From the bed, Countess Wych called her.

"Sophy," she said, "is he still here?"

Sophy hesitated:—

"Do you mean—?" she began and paused, not quite sure how to refer to the claimant.

"Ralph," the countess said. "He was here, wasn't he? Did he stay—when he knew?"

"No, he went away almost at once," Sophy answered, again with a vision of that broad and upright back vanishing behind the ornamental shrubs.

"Did he say anything? Did anything happen?"

"He was very upset," Sophy answered cautiously, thinking it no time to go into details. "I suppose any one would be. It was such a surprise."

"I was afraid," the old woman said. "He is young and fierce. He won't give in easily. I was almost afraid he might—" She seemed to be about to leave the sentence unfinished and then added:—"be unwise."

"Oh, Mr. Ralph would never do anything silly," declared Sophy, though not with entire conviction, for she, too, had been afraid that Ralph's self-control might slip, as indeed whose might not under such a blow that reduced him in one moment from the position of heir to a title and great estates to that of the poor relative dependent entirely on a rich cousin's bounty.

The old countess was lying back in bed and her aged eyes were heavy with trouble and with fear.

"If Ralph—you see, Sophy, Ralph doesn't understand, and he may ruin it all, all."

"Yes," Sophy said, not understanding this. "Dear Countess Wych, won't you try and forget it now and get a little sleep and then to-morrow it will be easier to realize what it all means."

"It means mischief," the old woman answered. "Mischief will come of it. There was nothing else to do but mischief will come of it and worse—much worse."

Some soup Sophy had asked for, now arrived, brought again by Martin. Sophy could not understand why he was so attentive, for he was certainly not as a rule inclined to go outside his ordinary duties. Did he feel there was distress and bewilderment in the room and did he hope to get some hint of its cause? or did he know that cause already and did he merely find pleasure in assuring himself that that distress existed? The soup was good and appetising, but Countess Wych could only be persuaded to take a spoonful or two. Resolutely she pushed it aside, cutting short Sophy's attempted coaxing with the sharp remark:—

"When you went to those A.R.P. lectures, didn't you meet some policeman's wife?"

For this was at the time when the shadow of a war that to many seemed so wanton, and therefore so fantastically incredible, was already beginning to creep across the land. A.R.P. precautions were being taken. Ralph, to his huge disgust, had been informed that he was 'reserved', and that his war service, if a thing so wholly unnecessary and absurd and improbable as war did occur, was to consist in increasing the production of food from the land. Evacuation plans were being made. It had already been arranged that in case of what was then called an 'emergency'—an emergency some of the papers were declaring every day would never come into being—a wing of Castle Wych would be used for the accommodation of a girls' school. The villagers also were being asked to get ready to receive children, and in connection with these plans, and then again at A.R.P. lectures, Sophy had met the Mrs. Owen to whom she supposed Countess Wych was now referring.

"You mean Mrs. Owen?" she asked. "I don't think Mr. Owen's a policeman exactly," she added doubtfully, for she supposed that only those were policemen who wore a uniform and a helmet and were such a comfort when you had to cross busy streets. "I think he has something to do with Colonel Glynne."

"Well, Colonel Glynne is a policeman, isn't he?" asked the countess, a little tartly. "If a county chief constable isn't a policeman, who is? Isn't Mr. Owen the Bobby Owen man they brought from Scotland Yard to show Midwych how to do detective work? Most unnecessary in my opinion."

"Mrs. Owen did say they came from London," Sophy admitted. "I heard someone at the lecture say he was awfully clever. I only saw him once."

"What is he like?"

Sophy searched her memory. Bobby Owen might be a well-known detective and quite an important person now he was acting as Colonel Glynne's private secretary and more or less as director of the not too efficient or up-to-date Midwych C.I.D., but he had made very little impression on Sophy.

"I don't think he said anything," she observed finally. "He just sat about. I remember looking when that was said about his being awfully clever, but he was just like any one else, only more so. I liked Mrs. Owen. She seemed very nice, only rather awfully stylish. Oh, and her hats—"

Sophy paused with a little gasp of admiration. "Each time she had a different one, and each time it was nothing really and yet perfectly wonderful. She used to have a hat shop before she married, someone said."

"I hope it's only hats we shall ever hear of from either her or her husband," the countess muttered, and Sophy wondered very much why she said that.

"If anything does happen and they do want to send children here," Sophy remarked, "she is to help to look after them. If there is an emergency, I mean."

"It is another kind of emergency I was thinking of," Countess Wych answered.

After that she would say no more, and Sophy was only too glad that now she seemed inclined to rest.

But Sophy slept with the door of her own adjoining room wide open; and once, when in the middle of the night she heard the old woman muttering, she got up and went to her side. She was asleep but quite plainly Sophy heard her mutter once again:—

"Harm will come of it—much harm," and then, loudly and distinctly, the name: "Ralph."

Very thoughtfully Sophy went back to her own bed.

CHAPTER IV
GOSSIP

From the strained and difficult situation at Castle Wych, growing ever more darkly ominous as the hours and the days passed, Sophy, when opportunity served, sought escape in the village. There this day she met her father, noticed with disapproval that he had managed to escape from the vicarage in the shabby, worn out old coat he was supposed to wear only when working alone in his study, and so turned back to go home with him, there to remind Mrs. Longden and the maid of the necessity for a more careful watch being kept.

On the way they talked of the extraordinary development at the castle and the unexpected return of an heir so long believed dead. Nothing else indeed was being spoken of anywhere; the Nazi threat, still only a threat no one took very seriously, was quite forgotten; and Mr. Longden had been very worried to find that through all the gossip and chatter was running a note of strange suspicion.

"I can understand," he told Sophy as they walked along, "that they all sympathize with Ralph, but I do hope and trust there will be no show of hostility towards this young man. It's not his fault."

"I don't like him," said Sophy, suddenly and loudly.

"My dear," said Mr. Longden, slightly shocked, for he thought it only right and natural that every one should always like every one else. "Why, you hardly know him. What makes you say such a thing?"

"He makes me think," Sophy answered unexpectedly, "of keeping my door locked."

Mr. Longden looked very puzzled, and then began a frantic search of his pockets.

"There," he said distractedly, "I must have left my keys at Mrs. Potter's."

The clergy have a reputation, not always well deserved, for absent-mindedness, and in one respect Mr. Longden did his best to live up to it. His path through life was littered with forgotten keys, umbrellas, books, even hats, of late gas masks, too, that he was always putting down upon tables or chairs and then never thinking of again, unless indeed he seized someone else's hat or book or keys or umbrella that happened to be near, and so went well satisfied on his way. In other respects he was careful and precise, and never forgot an engagement or was late for an appointment, though both his wife and daughter declared that this was largely because his diary—foolscap size—was too big to be carried about, had to be kept on his study table, and could not therefore get very badly mislaid. It was, in fact, the first rule of the house, that never, never must the engagement book be taken out of the study; and if ever Mr. Longden were seen wandering away with it under his arm, then everything else had to be abandoned until it was back in its place on the study table.

Possibly a truer explanation was that engagements and appointments concerned the convenience of other people, and that therefore his sub-conscious mind saw to it they were remembered; while such things as keys and umbrellas concerned only himself personally and so mattered less.

However, on this occasion, no harm was done, for a small girl came running up with the keys left behind on Mrs. Potter's table, and Sophy, noticing something else now, said:—

"Dad, where's your umbrella?"

Mr. Longden looked vaguely at his hands, surprised to find them empty.

"I can't have brought it with me," he said hopefully.

But Sophy knew better. Mr. Longden had certain fixed habits. One was, before going out, to open the door and regard the weather. If it looked like rain he nodded with the air of a man who expected no less and turned back for his umbrella. If it seemed likely to be fine, he nodded with the air of a man not to be deceived by appearances and turned back for his umbrella.

"If I did bring it out with me," he decided presently, "I must have left it somewhere."

Sophy agreed that this seemed probable.

"Where did you go first?" she asked.

Mr. Longden said he thought it was the post office, so they went there and found the missing article and a small group of people discussing the lost heir's return—a topic that much talk had done little to exhaust. Mr. Longden, aware again of an undercurrent of suspicion and hostility, pointed out that the heir's reappearance should be a matter of general thanksgiving and must be an overwhelming joy to his aged grandparents. To that they all agreed, and said 'of course', and looked as if they meant the opposite, and one man observed that neither the earl nor his old lady seemed very greatly cheered by the return of the prodigal. He added that by all accounts Earl Wych was going about looking as if he had lost a five pound note and found a bad penny, and that his wife was said to be eating nothing, sleeping not at all, and hardly ever speaking a word to any one.

They all watched Sophy when this was said. She tried to look as expressionless as possible and pulled at her father to come away, observing tartly and disrespectfully as they went that for the future his umbrella would have to be chained round his waist.

"Extraordinary," Mr. Longden declared, "what things people will say. No doubt what's happened is rather overwhelming and I expect both the old people are very worried about Ralph. And that's what makes all this gossip."

"It may be gossip," Sophy answered, "but it's true. Both of them look as if they had done something they are awfully ashamed of and they know harm will come of it. The countess keeps muttering that to herself—that harm will come of it."

"All the same," persisted Mr. Longden, "the young man has his rights, and among them is the right to a welcome home. There's a touch of romance in such a return I should have thought would appeal to every one. I am afraid the butler, Martin, is responsible to some degree. He was at the Wych Arms last night and he seems to have talked in a way that has helped to spread this gossip."

Sophy was silent, but she remembered how like a waiting vulture the soft-footed butler had seemed, hovering and silent and patient at a little distance. She wondered if he could know something, but that seemed to her unlikely. Her father was saying anxiously:—

"I do hope, once the first shock is over, Ralph will take it in the right spirit, and that he will try to be friendly to the young man."

"Mr. Ralph says he is an impostor," Sophy found herself saying, though she had not meant to tell her father that.

Only somehow the words came tumbling out before she was aware.

Mr. Longden stood still and shook his head sadly.

"I am very, very sorry to hear it," he said. "It had occurred to me, but I couldn't believe it of Ralph. I had a better opinion of him. I shouldn't have said that," he added remorsefully. "It must have been a terrible shock to any young man. No one has a right to judge him unless they have been in the same position." This was a favourite remark of Mr. Longden's, and as no one is ever in exactly the same position as any one else, it followed that no one ever had the right to judge another, as is probably true.

They were passing the Wych Estate office now. This was a comparatively new building, in two stories. On the ground floor were three rooms, an outer office for a Miss Higson, the typist, who liked to call herself secretary; a waiting-room; and an inner office for Ralph. Above were rooms occupied by Mrs. Gregson, who was the widow of an old estate employee, acted as caretaker and office cleaner, and sometimes as office boy as well, provided tea every day and occasionally other meals when Ralph happened to be busier than usual. Mr. Longden was half inclined to call in the hope of finding Ralph in a mood which would permit of the offering of a little friendly counsel, but then decided that it was too near the luncheon hour.

"Perhaps," he said as they went on, "Miss Anne Hoyle's influence will help him to get over it better. I do hope she isn't being unfriendly to the young man."

"No, she isn't," said Sophy briefly; and only just prevented herself from adding that Anne was flirting with him as hard as she knew how.

It was an entirely new phase of Anne's character, and one that greatly bewildered and disturbed Sophy. Hitherto Anne had seemed quite indifferent to young men, whom she was often inclined to snub. Older men seemed to attract her much more, and even to Ralph she showed a degree of coldness that surprised Sophy, though she had admired it greatly as a proof equally of feminine reserve and of aristocratic self-control that would permit no display of that love you must obviously feel for the man you were engaged to, or else why are you engaged to him? If doubts had at times tried to enter her mind, Sophy was far too loyal to admit them, and had indeed closed the door on them with such a bang that no wonder they vanished, in a probable panic. All the same, for their mere appearance Sophy felt she ought to do penance, as was her custom when she knew she hadn't been behaving very nicely. Get up half an hour earlier than usual, perhaps, to learn by heart one of the less comprehensible chapters of Jeremiah, or not drink her early cup of tea she always enjoyed so much. Only to leave it would seem ungrateful; to pour it away would be wasteful, so she supposed it would have to be Jeremiah. Sophy sighed at the prospect; and such are the bewildering difficulties of the conscientious life found herself as a result of this distasteful prospect thinking more and more uncharitably of Anne, more and more inclined to believe she really was flirting with Bertram, and thus becoming more and more guilty for harbouring thoughts so lacking in charity.

So to avoid a vicious circle of more penance, causing more and more uncharitable thoughts, rendering more penance necessary, Sophy said:—

"Well, why is Mr. Clinton Wells going to help Mr. Ralph if he doesn't think it's all a horrid fraud?"

Mr. Longden had no answer to this problem. But he remembered that Mr. Wells was a partner in the firm acting for Earl Wych who accepted Bertram as his grandson. It seemed a little difficult to believe Mr. Wells would act against the earl. Like being on both sides at once. So Sophy explained that Clinton Wells intended to resign his partnership, and would he do that, she asked triumphantly, unless he was quite, quite sure?

"It might be," Mr. Longden said thoughtfully, "that he feels he must stand by his friend. If it is that, it's rather fine. The act of a very honest man and a very true friend."

"Yes, isn't it?" agreed Sophy enthusiastically. "I think it's awfully wonderful," and she added obstinately:— "I do hope they prove he is a fraud and I expect they will, too."

"My dear child, you must be reasonable," protested Mr. Longden, "when his grandparents—"

"They haven't seen him for years and years," interrupted Sophy, "and what's more he isn't a bit happy or comfortable, and he's as nervous and jumpy as he can be, and he's always drinking, and he keeps looking over his shoulder as if he thought there was a policeman there, and what's more, he's most awfully scared of Anne." Sophy grew reckless. She threw all thoughts of penance to the winds. She said:—"He thinks she means to marry him and he's frightened to death."

"Sophy," said Mr. Longden in what for him was a terrible voice, "you must not say such things. Have you forgotten Miss Anne is engaged to Ralph?"

"No," retorted Sophy, quite bewildered to find herself sticking up for her own opinion in a way that until now she simply wouldn't have believed possible, "I haven't, but I think she has. I don't understand her a bit. I admired her so awfully, and now it's all a muddle. She may be only trying to find out things. Mr. Bertram and she were talking ever so long together last night."

"Very wise of her," declared Mr. Longden. "Very wise indeed. I trust she may be able to bring Ralph to a more reasonable state of mind, and I do hope and trust he won't do anything rash or foolish, anything really to offend his uncle. You can understand how terribly upset he is. You can understand what a terrible shock and surprise it has been. But he must face the facts like the true, honest fellow he is."

Sophy did not answer, but she felt an instant conviction that Ralph did indeed intend to face the facts; though whether in a way her father would approve, seemed to her less certain.

"Has Mr. Arthur Hoyle said anything?" he asked presently.

"No," Sophy answered. "But he is always there now. He comes in every day. He keeps trying to ask me questions. No one else, only me. I just say I don't know, and I don't." She paused and looked uncomfortable, for something else was in her mind, something uncharitable, 'catty', something that ought never to have occurred to her. She didn't know what had come over her since Bertram's arrival. She seemed only to be able to see the worst side of everything. All the same it came out: "He makes you think he's planning something secret. He said such a strange thing yesterday. He said no one knew now where they were, or whether they were standing on their head or their heels, and most likely it would turn out presently he was the heir himself, and then he would propose to me and we should be Earl and Countess Wych. I was so angry. I thought it was such a vulgar joke, and I told him so, and not a bit funny, either."

"It was a display of very bad manners," pronounced Mr. Longden, looking this time really annoyed. "Most regrettable."

"I believe he thinks it's all some sort of fraud," Sophy continued. "I'm sure he doesn't think Mr. Bertram is the real Mr. Bertram. Only why should that make Mr. Arthur the heir?"

"I don't know," Mr. Longden answered, and suddenly he was afraid, and when he looked at Sophy again he saw that she also was afraid.

CHAPTER V
BUNCHES OF KEYS

During this time, while there were gathering in the east the war clouds of the coming storm, there was going on a languid, half amused, half bored preparation, often looked upon as a kind of play acting or pageantry, serving as an agreeable break in the routine of everyday life.

On a day subsequent to that on which Mr. Longden had held with his daughter a conversation he still remembered as disturbing to a degree, there was to be held in the village parish hall a meeting concerning possible evacuation plans.

According to the usual habits of officialdom all the world over, entirely contradictory instructions had been received from headquarters. One set of officials evidently regarded Brimpton Wych as an evacuation area, since it was so near the great industrial centre of Midwych, and the department would therefore be glad to know what arrangements were being made for the dispatch of the children to a safe district, preferably on the south-east coast, where the children would have the benefit of the sea air. Clacton was suggested as highly suitable. Other equally highly placed officials, however, had as evidently got down Brimpton Wych as a reception area, since it was so far from London, and wished to know at once what steps were being taken to billet the children sent there in the event of an 'emergency'—at this time it was still considered that to use the word 'war' was shockingly bad taste.

Mr. Longden was to preside at this meeting, whereat also Midwych representatives would be present. In connection with one or two preliminary details he called at the Wych Estate office to see Ralph, who for his part was working continuously on the various schemes for increased food production the Ministry of Agriculture was showering upon him by almost every post—not to mention those that arrived by 'phone and by telegraph, many of them of course entirely incompatible with all the others. And any one who has ever had to try to persuade a farmer to cultivate his land other than in his own way and time, can guess what kind of a life Ralph was now leading. Especially as not one single farmer believed for a moment that war was coming, or that, even if it did, there would be any necessity to do much more than sit tight behind the Maginot Line and the British Navy until Germany had got tired of allowing that mountebank, Hitler, to prance about in his big boots.

Ralph was as busy as usual when Mr. Longden appeared, but a trifle relieved that at any rate this interview was not going to be an effort to induce some slow thinking farmer to follow the advice of a London official, entirely and ridiculously ignorant of the difference between the lower field and the ten acre patch, not even knowing that such and such pasture would have to be drained before it could possibly be used for wheat. "They don't even know, them up there, in London," one man had protested amazedly, "that there's springs just under the surface," and as Ralph himself, well as he knew the countryside, had not been aware of that fact, he agreed that very likely up in London they had not known it either.

The business the vicar had called upon in connection with the evening's meeting was soon settled, and then Mr. Longden went on to mention another matter. The church plate was of some intrinsic and of high antiquarian value, and he was beginning to be worried about its safety.

If there were air raids—and Brimpton Wych, like every other village in England, was convinced it would be the special target of every German airman—-would that church plate be secure in the somewhat antiquated safe in the vestry? In case of fire caused by an incendiary bomb, Mr. Longden doubted if that safe would give full protection. Ralph was quite sure it would give very little protection. He suggested the bank; but the difficulty was that the plate was often required for early service, and would indeed be as frequently out of the bank's strong room as in it. As for buying an alternative set, well, Ralph knew the difficulty there was going to be in meeting the next instalment due on the new heating system. But, Mr. Longden pointed out hesitatingly, the Wych Estate office had a fairly new, very large, reputedly fire-proof safe, bought by the old land agent before his death and before Ralph took over the work, and occasionally now referred to by Ralph as a 'white elephant'. There had of course been more need for it in former days, but at present when nearly all rents and payments were settled by cheque, there was seldom any large sum of cash in the office over night. Consequently the safe was often half empty, and was chiefly used for keeping books and papers. In office hours, it generally stood open, as in fact it did now. His attention drawn to it, Ralph agreed that the church plate could quite well be stored there, if and when that doubtful 'emergency' did arrive.

Naturally it would be necessary for Mr. Longden to have keys both for the outer door of the office and for the safe itself. For the safe there were only three keys in existence, one on Ralph's bunch and two in the bank. One of these Ralph promised Mr. Longden should have if the need arose, and he got up to show how the lock worked. It was a somewhat early form of the combination lock, and required to be set in one special way before the key would turn. Mr. Longden, guiltily conscious of how often he managed to mislay his own keys, wondered timidly if the verger could have a third key to the safe, as he had a duplicate key to the vestry safe. But that idea did not much appeal to Ralph, who thought it was one thing to trust the vicar and quite another to let the verger have office and safe keys. Mr. Longden took out his own keys and looked at them sorrowfully, and Ralph suggested that instead, when the time came, of putting the office and safe keys with these others so frequently lost, he should wear them on a string round his neck.

"Quite safe then," suggested Ralph, and Mr. Longden put his keys back in his pocket and thought the suggestion an excellent one.

Or he might, he reflected, give them to Mrs. Longden to take care of. She somehow or another avoided mislaying things. Always knew where things were, and what was more astonishing still, things always were where she said they were. Whereas when Mr. Longden himself knew where things were, very often it turned out that they weren't, but in fact in some quite different place.

Ralph thought putting the keys in Mrs. Longden's care was another excellent suggestion, and then another point occurred to the vicar. The church plate in question was kept in a large, old-fashioned box, said itself to date from the seventeenth century, and Mr. Longden began to wonder if it would be too big to go in the safe. So Ralph had to get out his keys again, open the safe once more, and allow the vicar to take careful measurements with his umbrella, which so far that morning he had managed not to lose. Ralph, beginning to wish the vicar would go and let him get on with his work, took the opportunity to open a small polished case lying on a shelf in the safe and startled Mr. Longden by producing from one of the drawers of his writing table an automatic pistol, a Colt .32. He replaced it in the polished case in which it was evidently kept.

"I've just been oiling and cleaning it," he explained.

Mr. Longden eyed it askance. It had for him, the snub-nosed thing, an ominous, unpleasant air, recalling to him his talk with Sophy and the queer impression that conversation had made on him. Noticing how the vicar was looking at the pistol, Ralph smiled.

"It's been here ever since I can remember," he said. "I don't know that it matters now. There's never anything here motor-car bandits would think worth coming for."

"Why not get rid of it?" Mr. Longden asked.

But Ralph looked grim, put back case and pistol on the shelf in the safe where they were kept, banged the sale door, and went back to his seat at the writing table.

"One never knows," he said. "I thought I would clean it. Must have been years since it was touched, but it's all right now."

Mr. Longden still thought it would be better got rid of, and then turned the conversation towards recent happenings at the castle. To his disappointment, for he had hoped to bring Ralph to a better and more friendly frame of mind, the young man made no secret of his conviction that the newcomer was a bare-faced impostor.

"No more Bertram than I am," Ralph declared emphatically.

"But haven't his grandparents recognized him?" Mr. Longden protested.

"They say they have, and it isn't true," Ralph answered. "I suppose it's old age. I don't know. It may be something else. Only people do go a bit queer when they get old. All I know is that uncle and aunt are lying."

Mr. Longden gasped. Ralph had spoken with an intensity of feeling and emotion that almost frightened him. Ralph lifted his bunch of keys lying on the table and it was almost as though he grasped a weapon—pistol or sword. His grasp relaxed, he put the keys down, but his eyes remained hard and intent. Mr. Longden said protestingly:—

"My dear boy, my dear boy, you mustn't say such things. Why should they? Earl Wych is the very last man to be untruthful. The countess, too. Why should he? both of them?"

"I don't know," Ralph answered, and suddenly looked tired, unnaturally tired, for a man so young and strong. It was a grey face and lined that he showed now, though the eyes were still clear and hard and angry. "I can't imagine. I think and think. All the time it's there." He put his hand to his head with a gesture that in its helplessness had a touch of pathos, too. "Why should uncle— and aunt—both of them—why should they want to put a stranger in my place?"

"But—" began Mr. Longden, still protesting.

"Oh, I know it's incredible," Ralph interposed, "only they are; and yet uncle's always been so keen on the family, on direct descent from father to son. This is the first time it's gone even to a nephew. I'm not in the absolutely direct line, but I do go straight back to the fourth earl, the ninth baron, and now uncle wants to put a perfect stranger in my place."

"Surely—" began Mr. Longden, but Ralph was on his feet now, talking excitedly, walking up and down, evidently glad, though perhaps unconsciously so, of an opportunity to pour out feelings suppressed too long.

"The man's an impostor," he repeated with intense energy. "And uncle and aunt know it, they must know it, so why are they telling lies in the face of all the family tradition has ever stood for?

It's incredible, it's impossible, only it is. Arthur thinks so, too—
that the fellow's a fraud, I mean." He stopped abruptly. "I'm
sorry," he said. "I oughtn't to have said that. He does, but he asked
me not to say so at present. It slipped out. I suppose I'm a bit
excited. Arthur says we must lie low for the present and see what
happens. Business man's idea—wait developments. All very well
for him. I intend to make developments, not wait for them. You'll
keep that about Arthur to yourself, won't you?"

"Certainly, of course," Mr. Longden assured him.

"Arthur doesn't really come into it much," Ralph went on.
"Except from the family tradition point of view. Of course, he
would if I pegged out, but then I don't mean to. I think that's
nonsense. I suppose Arthur's a bit bowled over, too." Ralph flung
himself back again into his chair. "I suppose we're all half crazy. I
think and think till I'm nearly off my head. Why is uncle lying?"

"But if both he and your aunt do persist in saying that this
young man—"

"I tell you it's a lie, and they know it," almost shouted Ralph,
banging his hand passionately on the table. "Don't argue about
that, please," and he gave the vicar once again a look so fierce, so
full of menace, as Mr. Longden had seen only once before, in his
London East-End parish, when a man had warned a blackmailer
not to go too far.

Fortunately that blackmailer had seen wisdom and had
decided to retire, so all had been well; but Mr, Longden still
remembered how for that one moment he had seemed to see
before him the grisly form of approaching murder. Perhaps Ralph
noticed how shocked and disturbed Mr. Longden looked, for his
expression changed at once and he smiled so pleasantly he hardly
seemed the same man. Mr. Longden grew quite ashamed of his
recent thoughts, feeling sure now that he had unpardonably
allowed his imagination to run away with him.

"I'm awfully sorry," Ralph said. "You mustn't mind if I let off
steam a bit. You do understand, don't you? Lord knows, if I had as
much as a moment's doubt, I would say 'all right, very likely it is
Bertram after all', and I would fall on his neck and welcome him
back like a good little boy. I don't want to do any one out of his

rights. The more I feel like sticking up for my own rights, the more I would recognize his. But I shan't give in to a fraud, not for all the senile old men and women in the world. It's the only explanation. Age. People do get into a second childhood. Uncle and aunt were awfully cut up when they were left without any children or grandchildren. They've been brooding, and it's worked on them till they were ready to fall for the first impostor that came along. Arthur thinks he is an American gangster, and he's bumped off the real Bertram. He says I had better look after myself or he'll bump me off, too. That's why I was cleaning up that automatic when you came in." He made a gesture over his shoulder towards the closed door of the safe, behind which Mr. Longden was so thankful to think that the weapon in question was so safely reposing. "But Arthur's wrong there. The fellow is English all right, and he has no need to bump me off so long as he has the old people behind him. More likely I'll bump him off. He has been in America, that's plain, but he is English, and what's more I think he comes from this part. Only," he repeated, turning to the thought never long absent from his mind, "why does uncle—?"

He left the sentence unfinished, and an idea came into Mr. Longden's mind, born of that scene he had witnessed in his East End parish so long ago when a blackmailer had driven his victim beyond what had seemed safe.

"You don't think," he said timidly, shamefacedly indeed, "that it might be blackmail?"

Ralph looked very much taken aback.

"Do you know," he said, "I never thought of that. Blackmail? Uncle? Aunt? It doesn't seem possible."

"It isn't," said Mr. Longden, very firmly. "I don't know whatever made me say anything so absurd." Indeed the word seemed as incongruous in connection with the dignified old earl, the stately countess, as any word well could be—as incongruous indeed as to associate together a night club and Canterbury Cathedral.

Ralph plainly felt that, too. He shook his head.

"Out of the question," he said. "Only there's some reason, and even if I can't find it out, I'll show this fellow up and get him booted back where he belongs. Clinton Wells is going to act for me. It's awfully decent of him. He can't go on acting for uncle, too, so he is resigning from his firm. I didn't want him to, I thought it was too much. But he stuck to it he would. I'll never forget it, never. I only hope I'll be able to make it up to him later. He's coming along to have a talk. Only he says there's not much you can do at present, because he says it hardly arises legally till uncle's death, and of course he may live for ten or twenty years. People do get to the hundred. In a sense I'm no worse off. In the eyes of the law, I mean. Hullo, here is Clinton now."

A car had in fact just driven up with Clinton Wells at the wheel. He alighted and entered the office and after a moment's chat Mr. Longden took his leave and with it Clinton's umbrella instead of his own. Fortunately Ralph saw what had happened and ran after the vicar. Much disconcerted, Mr. Longden wondered what he could have done with his own, and then a passing estate tenant with a grievance pounced on Ralph. Mr. Longden, wondering where his own umbrella could be, went across to the post office where it so often turned up. But this time it was not there, and suddenly he remembered he had had it in the estate office. So he went back there, passing Ralph still trying to get rid of the discontented tenant, and in the office found both the missing umbrella and Clinton Wells impatiently fidgeting at the window and demanding to know how much longer Ralph was going to spend out there with Farmer Young, notorious for his grievances and his demands.

"I'll see if I can chase him away," he announced, adding a brief acknowledgment of the returned umbrella.

Mr. Longden, left alone, collected his own umbrella, making sure it really was his this time, replaced Clinton's in the stand, noticed Ralph's keys lying on the table, triumphantly put them in his pocket under the impression that they were his own, congratulated himself on everything being all right now, and went off. Nor was it till late that night, after a call that had kept him out till nearly twelve, that he discovered as he was preparing for bed that he was in possession of two sets of keys. This puzzled him so enormously that he just sat there looking incredulously at the two bunches, which indeed resembled each other as closely as bunches of keys generally do, so that it was easy enough to mistake one for the other. Close questioning by Mrs. Longden cleared up the mystery, and then Mr. Longden was so remorseful that he would have started out then and there to return the keys to their rightful owner had not Mrs. Longden very firmly objected.

The morning would do, she said, and besides, the vicar had to confess that he was really tired, for before that late summons had come there had been the long and tiring meeting about evacuation plans. It had been a confused, muddled, quarrelsome meeting, and his job as chairman had not been easy. Mrs. Owen, who was present as a Midwych representative, gave her husband, Inspector Bobby Owen, an amused and detailed account.

"I was hoping to see the returned prodigal," she added, for the return of the long lost heir was still the one exciting topic of the day, far eclipsing in interest that approaching dance of death down which Hitler was so soon to lead the nations of the world, "but he wasn't there. Mr. Ralph Hoyle was. He looked awfully strained. They say he is working himself to death over the new food production plans, but it looked to me as if there were more than that."

"Well, you can't wonder," answered Bobby, who had spent a happy, peaceful evening pottering about the garden, putting there into practice trial and error, especially error. "Enough to bowl any chap over. He was the big man in the district as the heir to the title and the estates, and now he's only himself and nothing more, just a pair of hands and a head like any one else."

"People generally seem to like him," Olive observed. "I do myself, what I've seen of him."

"It's one thing to be liked when you're the heir and important, and another when you are just one more in the market place," observed Bobby, and added that all the same the new heir didn't seem to be making himself very popular.

There were the rumours, too, that Ralph was calling the new man an impostor and a fraud and that he meant to put up a fight.

"Difficult to see what he can do at present, though," Bobby observed, "unless he can manage an action for libel or something of that sort. And I don't see how he can work that, if the other fellow lies low and says nothing and spends his time consolidating his position as they say in the army. Of course, if he is the genuine goods, he won't need."

"You would think he must be genuine with both his grandparents accepting him," Olive said thoughtfully, "but there's the oddest feeling about that he isn't. Little Sophy Longden was there. She's such a nice child and she's dreadfully worried."

"What about?" Bobby asked. "Doesn't affect her, does it?"

"No, I suppose not," agreed Olive, "but all the same she made me feel there's something wrong at the castle and she knows it and she's afraid."

"Well, anyhow, it's a civil matter," Bobby observed comfortably, as he went off to lock up for the night. "Like the Tichborne case. Nothing to do with us, thank the Lord."

But early the next morning, before they were up, the 'phone rang, and after he had listened, Bobby turned to Olive.

"I've got to get off double quick time," he said. "I'll grab a bit of bread and cheese and there's some milk, isn't there?"

Olive was out of bed in an instant, her mind full of bacon and eggs, tea, toast.

"I'll have breakfast ready before you're dressed," she said.

"Can't stop," he told her. "I've to be at Castle Wych at once."

"Castle Wych," Olive repeated. "What's happened there?"

"Murder," Bobby answered as he made for the door.

CHAPTER VI

DINNER PARTY

At that confused, quarrelsome meeting held to discuss the evacuation question and destined to prove the prelude to what later on became known as the Castle Wych tragedy, Earl Wych himself had not been present.

Almost unprecedented for any public meeting to be held in the village whereat he was not either chairman or speaker. But since the return of the long-lost heir, that one might have expected would be to him so great a source of comfort and content, the old earl had tended to withdraw from all and every kind of activity or intercourse. He spent hours alone in the library he had always used as his own special retreat. He had had installed there a small wireless set and would listen to it for hours at a time, as though all he wanted were something, anything, to distract his thoughts. Frequently, too, he would not join the others at meals, but would ask simply for a sandwich and a glass of sherry to be brought to him.

Noticeable, too, was it how little disposed he seemed to be for any intercourse with Bertram, the long-lost, newly-found heir. Martin, the butler, went indeed so far as to declare that to avoid Mr. Bertram was the chief reason for the earl's seclusion. The countess, too, now seldom left her room, or if she did so, it would only be for an hour or two in the afternoon when, on a fine day, Sophy succeeded in coaxing her to sit for a while on the terrace. Only rarely did she appear at dinner, so that often it happened that Anne, Bertram, and Sophy were alone. Occasionally, if Sophy thought the countess was not fit to be left, the evening meal became a tête-à-tête, with Anne and Bertram sitting by themselves at one end of the big table.

When that happened, the situation seemed to amuse Anne more than it did Bertram. One of the malicious stories that could in the end have been traced to Martin, recounted that on one such occasion Bertram had fairly bolted out of the room and that Anne had finished the meal alone, smiling to herself with a curiously well satisfied air.

"You mark my words," Martin declared on another occasion, "there's something up between those two. One way or another, she knows she's got him."

But when asked to explain, or to say how there could be anything between two people who had never met before, he merely shrugged his shoulders and looked wise, as is the way of those who have no answer to give to the questions put to them.

On the evening of the day of the evacuation meeting that was to become a sort of landmark in the story of the Castle Wych tragedy, there was, however, a larger party than usual assembled round the table in the old dining-room. Earl Wych had for once emerged from the library. The countess had declared herself feeling stronger and in spite of Sophy's fears that she might be overtaxing herself, she had come downstairs. Both Ralph and Arthur had spoken at the meeting and both had come on to dine at the Manor. Ralph was silent and grim. It had somehow become known that he had asked for a private talk with his great-uncle and there was a general impression that that talk was not going to be a very amiable one. He had been heard to say that he wasn't going to stand it any longer, and that there had to be a show-down, one way or another. Arthur, in contrast, was very cheerful and talkative. He had made a good speech at the meeting. It had been much applauded, and it had been popular because it expressed the general feeling that the government had fallen under the influence of 'jitterbugs', that anyhow Brimsbury Wych wasn't going to part with its children; though if weaker-minded localities wanted to get rid of theirs, Brimsbury Wych would, of course, look after the kids. But the government had to understand that Brimsbury Wych would only accept good, carefully brought up, well-behaved children, like their own. Brimsbury Wych was not going to allow its youngsters to be contaminated by the off-scourings of the big towns.

Arthur's speeches had hitherto generally been made at company meetings when the applause—or lack of it—was in direct relation to the dividend—or lack of it. Of late, both dividends and applause had tended to be scant, so that Arthur found it quite exhilarating to sit down amidst a tumult of cheers.

Possibly it was this feeling of exhilaration which accounted for the fact that he was drinking more freely than usual. Fond though he was of all the good things of life that money can procure, he was generally careful in his indulgences. Bertram, too, was drinking freely, though with him that was not uncommon, and when presently Anne whispered to Martin, with the result that thereafter the wine seemed always out of his reach, and his demand for a liqueur with his coffee appeared to get overlooked, he said nothing but stared at Anne as sulkily as he dared.

Evidently, Sophy thought as she watched this byplay, Bertram knew where the prohibition originated, and she told herself that really it was very nice of Anne to watch over the behaviour of the man who had, however innocently and unavoidably, taken the place and ruined the prospects of her betrothed. Old Countess Wych, too, noticed this bit of byplay, as she noticed most things, and indeed Detective-Inspector Bobby Owen, conducting the investigation into the murder that was to happen later on, remarked in one of his reports that the countess's story of the dinner and what passed at it, was much the clearest and most detailed.

Clinton Wells was also to have dined at the castle. He had attended the meeting, apparently to pass the time, since he was neither a resident of Brimsbury Wych, nor yet a Midwych representative. Afterwards he had asked to be excused from coming on to the castle, making the excuse of a sudden business call. There was an impression, however, that the real reason was his annoyance over Ralph's insistence on having a show-down, to use Ralph's own expression, with his great-uncle. Clinton, it was understood, had advised waiting. Ralph had retorted that things had got to be cleared up. Clinton retorted in his turn that Ralph was in no mood to clear anything up, that indeed in his present temper he was more likely to make things worse. Finding all remonstrance useless, Clinton had thereupon been heard to say that he washed his hands of the consequences and he had gone off in his car back to Midwych, where he lived with an old housekeeper and a maid in a house much too big for his needs.

It stood in an enormous garden, it was very expensive to keep up, but he continued in occupation because he had some reason to believe that the Midwych corporation might buy it presently in connection with a new housing scheme. Obviously one can ask a better price—even a much better price—for a well-kept house and garden, from which one is, so to say, forcibly evicted, than for a house and garden left derelict, and for which no purchaser has been found. Most of the members of the corporation understood all this very well indeed, and it much increased their respect for Clinton, since it was a clever dodge and they admired clever dodges. Besides, it all came out of the rates, anyhow.

All the same the purchase was hanging fire, and Clinton was finding the upkeep of the big house and garden an unpleasant strain, and trying, too, the grumbling of his old, slightly deaf housekeeper over the difficulty of keeping a maid. Girls didn't like to work in such an antiquated barracks of a place, and even grumbled at having so many stairs to climb to their bedrooms on the third floor. Both maid and housekeeper might just as well have occupied rooms on the second or even the first floor, since Clinton Wells only occupied rooms—bed, sitting and bath—on the ground floor, and never penetrated elsewhere. But the old housekeeper would never have consented to make such a change. For her the third floor was for the staff, the rest of the house for the 'family', and that was fixed and unalterable.

Since Sophy was always so quiet at meals, no one noticed that to-night she was even quieter than usual. For one thing she was a trifle uneasy over the decision of Countess Wych to come downstairs. It was as though an abrupt access of somewhat feverish strength had come to her in startling manner. Indeed this had been so marked and so surprising after so prolonged a period of inertia and weakness that one of the maids had in Sophy's hearing said something about the last flicker of the candle before it went out. Sophy had been extremely angry, and had told the maid quite plainly and very severely that she mustn't say such things. All the same it had made her feel uneasy. She was worried, too, by a memory of her talk with Mrs. Bobby Owen, who had been certainly very sympathetic and understanding, but to whom Sophy now felt she had possibly said too much. Not that there was a word she could not have repeated aloud at this minute at this table, but she knew well that behind and beneath what she had said there had been an undercurrent of unease that had awakened in Olive a similar sense of brooding apprehension.

It was an apprehension that grew deeper now as she watched a curious flush grow on Countess Wych's cheek; in her tired and aged eyes a light begin to glow that had not been there for many years, and that Sophy did not think was wholly due to the very special port of an ancient and renowned vintage that, to Martin's surprise, the countess had ordered for herself. Nor was that sense of brooding apprehension lessened as Sophy watched how Ralph and his great-uncle hardly even looked at each other, and how, when their eyes did meet, each looked as grim and hard and resolute as the other. Like a silent duel it seemed between the old man and the young, and the others seemed aware of it, though whether as participants or as mere spectators, Sophy could not be sure. Under its influence conversation grew more and more restrained. Even Arthur's cheerful chatter ceased, and by the time the meal was drawing to an end silence was almost complete. Sophy, for her part, scarcely knew which of the two protagonists frightened her more—the aged earl, erect and stately for all the burden of his years, about him all the prestige conferred by a long tradition of authority and high offices of state filled with success and credit; or Ralph with that set jaw and those fierce and angry eyes in which she felt there showed a determination nothing would daunt, that no obstacle would turn.

'Ralph has made up his mind to something," she told herself, and then blushed, because this was the first time that even in her thoughts she had used his first name without any prefix.

She noticed Anne was looking at her, a deep, curious, searching glance. Was it possible Anne had read her thoughts? Sophy became panic-stricken at the mere suspicion, and made up her mind that never again in all her life would she so much as look at Ralph.

Bertram, trying to filch for himself another glass of port, managed, as he hurriedly poured it out, to splash the wine in a dark red stain on the tablecloth. They all looked at it, but no one spoke. It was Bertram who broke the silence. He said:—

"Looks like blood, doesn't it?"

And instantly Sophy felt that this idea had come to them all, and that that was why all of them had been so silent and had stared so intently at that red stain. The thin old voice of Countess Wych said suddenly:—

"Why, so it does. Yes, so it does."

"Nonsense," snapped the earl from the other end of the table; and it was a measure of the disorientation of them all, both that he should speak so roughly in public to his wife and that it seemed to them quite natural he should do so.

The countess rose to her feet.

"I'll go to my room," she said.

She moved towards the door with a slow dignity that was all her own. Sophy hurried after her to give her her arm. They went into the hall together. In it hung a portrait of some value, formerly ascribed to Van Dyck but now put down to some unknown pupil of his. In any case, an excellent piece of work. It represented a woman in the dress of the civil war period. The countess paused before it. Sophy wondered why. Portrait and living woman might have been exchanging secret thoughts, for it was as though their eyes met with understanding and with knowledge. Presently, still leaning on Sophy's arm, the countess moved on towards the foot of the stairs. She said:—

"That was the Lady Jane Elizabeth Hoyle. When she believed a son of hers was going to betray the king's cause to Cromwell, she took a pistol and shot him. For the honour of the family, she said."

Sophy gave a little gasp.

"Oh, how dreadful," she exclaimed.

Countess Wych withdrew her arm from Sophy's and said:—

"Go back to the others. I wish it. I can manage by myself very well." She repeated:— "Go back. Tell me about it afterwards."

She spoke in a tone of authority that Sophy dared not disobey. But she waited for a moment to make sure that the old countess was really equal to climbing the stairs unassisted. She seemed to be; and Sophy, turning to re-enter the dining-room, had a slight shock when she found Martin, the soft-footed butler, standing behind her. He had some cigars on a tray he was apparently intending to take into the dining-room, but somehow Sophy was certain the cigars were only an excuse, an excuse for spying and eavesdropping. It was from that moment that she began to entertain a real fear of Martin, whom before she had not exactly disliked, because she seldom disliked any one without given cause, but of whom she had certainly more than once wished he were more like the faithful old family retainer she had always supposed went of necessity with these ancestral mansions. He said to her in his smooth, deferential voice:—

"Her ladyship seems much better, doesn't she, miss? She might be twenty years younger going upstairs the way she is."

Then he looked at the picture:— "A tragic story, miss, but of course things like that don't happen now. I believe her ladyship has always been interested because she has the same first names—Jane Elizabeth."

Vaguely resenting the man's words and attitude, Sophy did not answer but went on to the dining-room. Martin followed with his tray and cigars. Earl Wych was standing now. He frowned when he saw Martin enter.

"That will do, those aren't wanted," he said, and waved the man away. When the door had closed behind him, he said:— "They're playing Bach somewhere—Vienna, I think. I want to hear it so I'll leave you."

He began to move towards the door, but now Ralph also was on his feet.

"Uncle," he said quickly, "I told you before I wanted to have a talk with you to-night."

The earl turned and the two men faced each other, age and youth, the contrast made the more effective by the strong family likeness between them, so that the earl might have been Ralph with fifty years added, and Ralph the earl half a century younger. Somewhat absurdly, Sophy found herself remembering the old puzzle about the meeting of the irresistible force and the immovable object. Earl Wych said:—

"Talk will do no good."

Ralph answered:—

"All the same, I mean to have it."

The old man looked more fierce, more angry than ever, more than ever like a hooded eagle on its eyrie.

"That is not the way to speak to me," he said.

"I am sorry," Ralph answered, but his tone too hard and resolute for much sorrow to find expression in it. "All the same we've got to have a talk—and to-night."

More and more angry looked Earl Wych. Sophy wished devoutly she was anywhere but here, anywhere in all the whole wide world. The others sat silent and watchful and uncomfortable. The two protagonists seemed to have forgotten that they were not alone.

"Talking's no good," Earl Wych repeated, as if in a last appeal.

"You've got to talk before you act," Ralph said.

Earl Wych turned towards the door. Already he had hold of the door knob when Ralph said:—

"Uncle, you've got to listen."

"I have no wish to," the old man answered. "It would do no good. There is nothing you can say that will make the least difference."

"All the same I mean to say it," Ralph insisted, his face flushed, his tone very angry indeed.

Earl Wych opened the door. He had recovered his self-possession that for the moment he had seemed on the point of losing. Haughty, upright and unperturbed, he stood in the doorway, his tall, thin old form there framed. He said nothing, but the gesture that he made was eloquent of decision and command. He passed through the door and vanished from sight. Ralph stood still for a moment, looking at the closed door. He glanced back at the table and at those still sitting there and he also said nothing.

"It's no good, Ralph," Anne's cool voice said. "You're only making a fuss—and uncle very cross."

"Ralph, old man," Arthur chimed in, helping himself to another glass of wine at the same time, "we all understand the way you feel, but what's the good? Things are what they are."

"So they are," Ralph retorted, "and also they will be what they will be, and truth happens to be important." He looked across at Bertram, who had managed to get hold of that very special bottle of port Countess Wych had told Martin to bring her. He was doing very well with it, too. Challengingly and not too pleasantly, Ralph said to him:— "Well, what's the claimant got to say?"

"It isn't me that's the claimant, it's you," retorted Bertram.

It was a reply both effective and unexpected. Ralph flushed still more angrily, and from where he stood near the door turned sharply towards Bertram, who apparently took the quick movement for a threat of attack and at once jumped to his feet. He swung up the bottle which by now was empty. Possibly it was the heat of the wine in his veins that made him take up so aggressively the challenge he read into Ralph's movement.

"You keep off," he said. "For just nothing at all, I'd lay you cold."

It all happened in an instant, a scene such as that dignified, patrician apartment had not witnessed since the early eighteenth century when a duel had been fought in it by candlelight. Ralph moved like a flash. Bertram struck with the bottle. Ralph caught his wrist. A short, brief struggle. A chair went flying, crashing against the wall. Bertram followed it, crashing, too, against the wall. Ralph very deliberately and carefully replaced upon the table the bottle he had taken from his opponent. Bertram sat up and looked dazed. He got out his handkerchief and put it to his mouth and cheek which were bleeding slightly. He said:—

"All right. All right. All right. If I had had a gun..."

He did not finish the sentence. The door opened and Martin appeared once more, his small, quick eyes more than ever alert and watchful. Sophy's clear impression was that he had been hanging about outside, waiting to see if anything happened.

"I beg pardon," he began, and got no further.

"Get out," Ralph said, and there was that in his tone sent Martin flying.

Bertram began to pick himself up.

"If I had had a gun..." he kept muttering. "If I had had a gun..."

Anne said:—

"Ralph, you are only making things worse for yourself."

"For—myself?" Ralph repeated; and Sophy wondered if she were right in thinking that he laid a slight emphasis on the word, as if he had noticed, as she had done, how Anne had said 'for yourself' and not 'for us'.

"Anne's right," Arthur chimed in. "If you are going to law this sort of thing won't help you. Put any jury against you at once, set any one against you for that matter."

"Including you?" Ralph asked, his tone anything but amiable. "Perhaps you aren't sorry to think I'm out. Well, I'm not out yet."

"Aren't you?" Arthur snarled. "Looks like it," he said viciously.

Anne got up and walked over to Bertram, now somewhat unsteadily upon his legs again.

"I am so sorry this has happened," she said in her rather high, deliberate voice.

Bertram muttered something inaudible. Anne helped him to a chair. She did it in a quiet, abstracted way, as if her mind were occupied with many thoughts. Sophy thought her expression strange. Enigmatical was the word that came into her mind. She found herself thinking:—

"There's something in Anne's mind... I wonder what."

Bertram was looking weakly from Anne to Ralph and back; and one might have thought from his startled eyes and odd expression that he was not sure which of the two to be the more afraid of. Ralph's expression was of mingled hostility and contempt, but he made no further movement, just stood there with his hands in the pockets of his dinner jacket. Anne's air as she stood by Bertram began to be protective, as if she were shielding him; possessive, too. Sophy found herself thinking now:—

"She's going over to his side. She must think he is really the heir. She didn't before. What's made her change?"

In spite of Sophy's recent resolution never to look at Ralph again, she did so now. It seemed awful to her if he were really going to lose Anne as well as everything else. To her utter bewilderment his expression changed as their eyes met. The hard, fierce, fighting look vanished, he looked no longer formidable, but friendly, he gave the idea, somehow, that by his side there was safety, there was even the beginning of a smile apparent in his eyes and at the corners of that stern, set mouth. Incredible, impossible, absurd, of course, but it really was as if he had caught a glimpse of the sympathy and the faith that almost without her knowledge flooded all Sophy's being.

"Well, I'll go on the terrace for a smoke," Ralph said abruptly.

He vanished. He had not looked again at Sophy, but why should he? She heard Arthur saying:—

"He's behaving like a fool. He can't go to law, there's nothing he can take action on. He hasn't a leg to stand on. So long as both the old folk back Bertram up, that is."

"He got me when I wasn't ready," Bertram said. "Tough guy, isn't he? Mighty tough. If I had had my gun..."

"Good thing you hadn't," Anne told him sharply. "Just remember, we don't use guns in this country."

"Oh, yeah," retorted Bertram, looking at her sideways. "Thought I saw you with one last week."

CHAPTER VII
INQUIRY BEGINS—MARTIN

Since Colonel Glynne, chief constable of the Wychshire County Police, chanced to be spending a day or two in London at the time when there occurred the Castle Wych murder, the preliminary investigations had to be conducted on his own responsibility by Inspector Bobby Owen, who acted both as head of the somewhat sketchy Wychshire C.I.D., and also as private secretary to the colonel; a position which it was generally understood meant that some day on the colonel's retirement, Bobby was likely to succeed him.

From London the colonel arrived in haste and now was listening to what Bobby had to tell him, which indeed at present was not much more than already every newspaper reader in the country knew. For though the news had been too late for the morning papers, the evening papers had given it a prominence that for the time had driven into the background all the accounts of the war preparations that were daily occupying more and more space.

Naturally Colonel Glynne was already well acquainted with the tale of the unexpected return of the long missing heir, and of Ralph's open threats to prove the newcomer an impostor. Now, as he listened to Bobby's report, he shook his head gravely.

"Worse than I thought," he said. "What a situation—a powder magazine and people walking about striking matches at random. Countess Wych muttering that ill would come of it. Ralph Hoyle threatening legal action. Anne Hoyle engaged to Ralph and flirting with Bertram, and what's her idea? Arthur Hoyle making one think that he's waiting to see if he can edge in his own claim. The

Sophy Longden girl dropping vague hints. The butler, Martin, almost certainly up to something on his own. Clinton Wells, a hard-headed lawyer I always thought thoroughly ambitious and self-seeking, throwing up his partnership to support a quixotic forlorn hope. The claimant's odd behaviour. The still more odd behaviour of Earl Wych himself, who proceeds more or less to shut himself up on his heir's return instead of wanting to make a fuss of it as you would expect. And now this incomprehensible, this bewildering thing—the poor old man found shot dead on the terrace outside the library windows. And who can have done that and why?"

"One of those you've mentioned I think, sir," Bobby said slowly; "though it might be someone we've never even heard of. But I don't think so. As for the motive, that's difficult. The obvious explanation is a sudden quarrel. But it may go deeper."

"Hard to see that any one benefits by the old man's death," the colonel remarked.

Bobby said nothing. He felt that motives would be best discussed as each possible figure in the tragedy came up for consideration. The colonel said abruptly:—

"It couldn't be suicide? or accident?"

"There are three bullet wounds," Bobby explained. "A man does not shoot himself three times by accident. No weapon was found near the body, so it can hardly have been suicide, unless of course the weapon was removed. There seems nothing to suggest that. Nor for that matter do suicides often shoot three times over."

"No," agreed the colonel. "That establishes murder."

"As I reconstruct the crime," Bobby went on, "Earl Wych was sitting in his armchair, apparently listening to the wireless and presumably smoking a cigar, since a half-smoked cigar and an overturned ash-tray were found near the chair, between it and the fireplace. There are bloodstains on the chair and it has been pushed violently out of position. My suggestion is that the first shot was fired from the terrace outside, the french windows having been pushed open and the curtains drawn aside. Earl Wych was hit in the body, but not fatally. He jumped up and ran towards the window, perhaps with some idea of tackling his assailant."

"Plucky of him," the colonel said. "The Hoyles always showed pluck though—traditional."

"The murderer then fired two more shots. Earl Wych fell just outside the window and must have died almost immediately. The terrace is of stone and the steps lead down to a gravelled path. I have had a search made but there are no footprints. There is nothing to show the murderer either came or went that way. He may have but there's no proof of it. He—or she—" Bobby corrected himself deliberately—"may have left the house earlier, waited for an opportunity, and afterwards re-entered the house by the library, through the open french windows. The medical evidence puts the time at about half-past eleven. Of course, that allows a margin of error each way. No shots were heard, but the wireless was going, and as the earl was a trifle deaf he generally had it on in full volume. That might account for the shots not being heard. Also the library door is heavy and fits closely. Martin is sure he heard the wireless going at eleven when he was locking up as usual. Bertram Hoyle and Miss Anne Hoyle were in the drawing-room till shortly after eleven when they went up to bed. Neither of them heard anything, and neither of them can be sure whether the wireless was going then. If it was, they didn't notice it. It seems highly significant that the wireless was turned off. If I am right in thinking that at the moment of the murder, Earl Wych was listening and that the wireless prevented the shots from being heard, then it must have been turned off either by the murderer or by someone who was in the room after the murder. If the last, why wasn't an alarm given? Of course, there is the possibility that the earl himself turned off the wireless before being attacked, and that it just happened that no one heard the shots. That is possible. No one sleeps apparently on this side of the house. Walls are thick and doors and windows strong and well-fitting. Also shots are common in the country, and if any one did hear anything, the sounds may not have been noticed or remembered."

"Any finger-prints?" Colonel Glynne asked.

"I thought it important enough to call in Wakefield," Bobby said. "I wired asking them to send one of their most experienced men along as quickly as possible. They sent him in a fast car. I haven't his report yet."

"Criminals never leave finger-prints, they know better,' the colonel remarked pessimistically.

Bobby was inclined to agree, but then in detective work you never know your luck. A crime may be committed in the heat of passion and not a hint or a clue left behind. A crime may be committed after the most careful preparation and the scene simply shriek the name of the perpetrator. Bobby turned to the pile of reports and statements through which the colonel had been glancing.

"Up to and including dinner last night," he said, "the statements made are clear and detailed and all agree. There were more at dinner than usual, I understand, because several came on after the evacuation meeting held earlier. During the afternoon the vicar, Mr. Longden, called at the Wych estate office. Ralph Hoyle was there. He acts as his great-uncle's agent though I suppose he may get the sack now Bertram Hoyle has turned up again. Mr. Clinton Wells, who it seems is going to act for Ralph if the succession case comes into court, was there, too."

"Well," commented the colonel, "I don't see what Ralph can do if both grandparents accept Bertram as genuine—pretty conclusive. Not our business, though. Our job is to find out who shot the old earl. A blackguardly crime. Not logical, I suppose, but somehow it seems worse to cut off an old man's few remaining days. However, that's not the point. What matters is the evidence you've got together. A bit confusing so far."

"Yes, sir," agreed Bobby. "There are two or three points I want to draw your attention to. First, there seems no doubt about Ralph Hoyle and his great-uncle having had a violent quarrel last night. But Ralph left about half-past ten, an hour or so before the murder. So if he is responsible he must have come back."

"No difficulty about that, I suppose?" asked the colonel.

"Oh, no, none. Secondly the butler, Martin, says that Lady Wych was using language earlier in the evening which could be taken either as a threat or as knowledge of a threat from another quarter. Thirdly, one of the gardeners found an umbrella in the castle grounds on a path that is often used as a short cut. It's a private path, but there seems to be a sort of tacit permission for people in the neighbourhood to use it. The umbrella has been recognized as Mr. Longden's. I'm told he has a trick of leaving things about. The gardener who found it had another look round and came across cigarette ends and other signs that someone had been sitting under rhododendron bushes near. So both the vicar and some other person were in the castle grounds last night, apparently about the time of the murder. The fourth point seems important. During the vicar's call at the Wych estate office Ralph Hoyle was handling a Colt point three-two automatic. The bullets that killed the earl were fired from a pistol of that make and calibre. It doesn't follow it was Ralph's pistol, but it was one similar. Ralph says he locked his pistol up in the estate office safe, and that it must be there still because the safe has not been opened. But it appears that the vicar absentmindedly went off with Ralph's keys, including the key of the safe. Ralph says he has no other key by him. The spare ones are kept in the bank, and it seems clear the key was in the vicar's possession before, during and after the time of the murder."

"Nothing to prevent Ralph from having provided himself with a duplicate key, I suppose?" remarked the colonel uneasily.

"Not that I know of. It seems a curious detail that the key should be in the vicar's hands just at that time. Curious and interesting. It may be important or it may not. As soon as I heard of the existence of the pistol I sent a man to keep an eye on the safe. If the pistol is still there, and if the bullets fired last night didn't come from it, we needn't bother about it any more. If it's gone from the safe, or if it turns out to be the weapon used..."

He left the sentence unfinished, and the colonel remained silent for a moment or two, evidently thinking hard and looking very puzzled.

"Odd about that key," he muttered. "Odd about Ralph's having a pistol of the same make and calibre. Still, there are plenty of Colt point three-two automatics in existence." Then he added:—"I know Ralph Hoyle. Not a likely murderer."

"No, sir," agreed Bobby, but a little doubtfully, and added:—
"Murder is never likely, and murderers are still less so. Another
thing that may be worth attention is that there appears to have
been rather a violent scene at dinner between Ralph and Bertram,
and there was an exchange of threats and references to pistols and
shooting. Arthur Hoyle thinks Ralph was the first to threaten the
use of a gun, but isn't sure. Miss Anne says she doesn't remember;
she says anyhow it was only talk. No one actually produced a
pistol. Miss Sophy Longden is quite clear that Bertram was the
only one who said anything at all about a gun. I don't think Miss
Longden approves of Bertram. She gave me the idea she could
have said more about him if she had wanted to."

"Ralph and Bertram actually came to blows, did they?" the
colonel asked.

"Bertram picked up a bottle and threatened to brain Ralph,
and Ralph tackled him and threw him—'gave him a toss', is
Ralph's expression," Bobby added, fumbling among his papers.
"Bertram says: 'Tripped me up when I wasn't looking.' Things
seem to have been strained all through the meal. Even before that,
there was an oddly uneasy feeling about, as if they all expected
something to happen. My wife has met Miss Longden in
connection with the evacuation preparations. She told me before
this happened that Miss Longden seemed nervous and afraid,
though it wasn't at all clear what she was afraid of. There was
another curious little incident at dinner last night, too, they all
comment on. Some wine was spilt, port wine, and it made a red
sort of stain that set them all saying how much it looked like
blood. It was almost as if it struck them as a kind of omen. I
thought that rather significant."

"In what way?"

"As suggesting that the idea of bloodshed, death, murder, was
already present in their minds. It's not usual for people in a
normal state of mind to begin thinking about bloodstains because
a little wine gets spilt. It suggests to me that ideas of threats, or a
dread of violence coming, were already in their minds—
subconsciously perhaps and perhaps not."

"The suggestion is that one of those at the table was already planning the murder?"

"I don't mean that quite, I don't think that follows," Bobby answered. "What I mean is that someone, some time, had heard or even uttered a threat of violence of some sort; that in fact there was a general apprehension and fear among them. Not very clear and I'm not expressing myself very clearly. What I mean is, some such idea was present in some way and the spilt wine incident brought it to the surface."

"Getting a bit out of my depth," Colonel Glynne said doubtfully. "May be something in it, but police work wants facts. I daresay there was an uneasy feeling about. Natural enough in such a situation—every one strained and uneasy." He began to finger the reports lying on the table. Presently he said:— "You don't seem to think much of this butler fellow, Martin. Not been here long, has he?"

"No, sir," Bobby answered. "When the last man left, I'm told Lady Wych had a good deal of trouble in getting any one else. Apparently good butlers are scarce. I gather she was too glad to get hold of Martin to check up on his references very carefully. I thought it might be as well to take him over his statement again."

"I see that from your notes," the colonel remarked. "Well, have him in and carry on."

Martin was accordingly sent for, and Bobby explained that there were one or two points on which they would like further information.

"I notice, for instance," he remarked, "you say you thought things were getting very tricky here."

"Yes, sir, they were that," Martin answered. "No one knew what was going to happen next, but we all felt there was bound to be a flare up."

"In what way?"

"Well, there was Mr. Ralph talking very wild like about Mr. Bertram being a fraud and he meant to prove it. Mr. Bertram acted a bit queer, too. Some of us used to say how scared like he acted—almost as if it was him as was likely to be thrown out. The other ladies and gentlemen, too. Like so many cats on hot bricks, if you see what I mean. Something was bound to crack and something did."

"It did," agreed Bobby. "Now about this incident in the hall. When you heard Lady Wych telling Miss Longden about a seventeenth-century Hoyle who shot her son to preserve the honour of the family. Did you attach any importance to it at the time?"

"Oh, no, sir, none at all. I should never have thought of it again if it hadn't been for what happened last night."

"I suppose you are not suggesting that the countess shot the earl to preserve the honour of the Hoyle family, are you?"

"Oh, no, sir, of course not," Martin answered with a kind of pleased smirk which suggested very strongly that that was in fact precisely what he wished to suggest. "Never even thought of that, sir. Only it did seem rather strange, and then you remember we were all told very particularly everything we could think of we were to mention, whether it seemed to have anything to do with the poor gentleman's murder or whether it hadn't. And it did strike me as strange, what her ladyship said, just as if it were a kind of prophecy."

"The honour of no family is helped by murder," Bobby remarked. "There is nothing else you can tell us, either about your own movements or about anything that strikes you as strange in the light of what happened later?"

"No, sir, nothing at all. Of course, I'm very sorry if I did wrong in mentioning about what her ladyship said in the hall."

"You did quite right," Bobby assured him. "Much better for us to know it now from you than for it to come out later. You locked up at eleven, you say?"

"That was the regular rule—eleven o'clock sharp. If any of the family meant to be out later, they told me, or if they didn't, it wasn't my fault."

"You saw to all doors and windows personally?"

"Yes, at eleven sharp, all on the ground floor, that is. All except the library. His lordship saw to the windows there himself. He used to sit up late listening to the wireless, and he didn't like being disturbed."

"Didn't he take anything for a nightcap before going to bed?"

"No, his lordship was a very abstemious gentleman. He never took anything late. It wasn't often he even smoked a cigar after dinner. His rule was two a day, one after breakfast and one after lunch."

"Did he never smoke cigarettes or a pipe?"

"I've never known him to. He had an idea that smoking at night stopped him from sleeping. He did have an extra cigar after dinner sometimes, but generally only if he were feeling upset or worried. He told me once it was a useful counter-irritant and I expect he felt he needed it after the scene with Mr. Ralph. That would be why he had one last night."

"Oh, yes, I wanted to ask you about that," Bobby said. "Yes. Let me see. Oh, yes, here it is. You were passing through the hall about ten or a quarter past. You heard loud voices coming from the library as you were going down the corridor outside. You recognized Mr. Ralph Hoyle's voice, and you are sure he and Earl Wych were quarrelling?"

"Going at it hammer and tongs," answered Martin confidently.

"Did you hear what was being said?"

"I expect I could if I had listened," Martin replied, his tone now very virtuous, not to say unctuous, "but, of course, I didn't."

"Of course not," agreed Bobby. "How is it you are sure it was Mr. Ralph?"

"Well, if you put it like that," said Martin slowly, "I suppose I couldn't swear it was him, if that's what you mean. But every one knew Mr. Ralph was insisting on having it out with his lordship. Mr. Ralph hadn't made any secret of it. Loud and furious they sounded, and I didn't stop. I didn't want the door to open suddenly and them find me there. It might have meant the sack and no character, both of them worked up the way they were."

"You noticed also that Mr. Ralph looked very excited —very strange and excited you say in your statement. That was when you let him out?"

"Yes, sir, that's right, sir," agreed Martin, but now a trifle uneasily, as if somehow he had detected a warning note in Bobby's voice, nor did that touch of uneasiness in his manner diminish when Bobby reminded him that he would be asked to repeat on oath all that he was now saying.

Bobby continued:—

"Mr. Ralph left about half-past ten, you think. He didn't go to the drawing-room to say good-night to the others. You thought that was because of the scene during dinner. You locked up at eleven as usual. You are quite clear that the library wireless was going then. You went to the drawing-room where you found Miss Anne and Mr. Bertram. Miss Longden had gone to bed. You asked if there was anything more. You were told there wasn't and you went to your own room, read a little, and were in bed by about a quarter to twelve. You heard nothing in the night and you were dressing this morning when you heard of the discovery of his lordship's body outside the closed—not fastened—french windows of the library. You had not been near the library or outside the house since Mr. Ralph Hoyle left."

"No, sir, that's right, sir," Martin answered. "I can take my Bible oath on that, sir."

"What is puzzling me," Bobby explained, "is exactly how you come to know that your master smoked a cigar after Mr. Ralph's departure? He did so, because we found a half-smoked cigar on the carpet where it had burned a small hole. So it seems likely that it was actually being smoked at the moment of the attack. Mr. Ralph's evidence is that his great-uncle didn't smoke during their interview or before. How did you know?"

Martin hesitated, plainly at a loss how to reply.

"I heard someone say something about a cigar end in the library," he stammered at last.

"Who was it?" demanded Bobby.

"I... I don't remember."

"No one who knew about it would be likely to mention it in your presence," Bobby said. "Only our men knew, and our men don't chatter. I'm afraid you are telling lies, Martin. Come, out with it. How did you know?"

"Well, I didn't actually know," Martin answered, recovering his self-possession. "It was just a guess. I knew his lordship's ways so well. I said to myself after I had let Mr. Ralph out, I said: 'They've had an almighty dust up. That'll mean his lordship sitting up late smoking most like, to settle his nerves down, then he'll be awake all night, and then he'll be in a rotten bad temper to-morrow and we'll all have to look out for squalls.' You'll remember, sir, I said just now, I said: 'If his lordship smoked a cigar,' I said."

Bobby turned to the shorthand writer, sitting unobtrusively in a corner of the room.

"Have you 'if' down?" he asked.

"No, sir," came the prompt response. "There wasn't any 'if'."

"You mean you didn't hear it," said Martin calmly. "A little word like that, it's easy overlooked or not heard. 'If' is what I said, and I'll take my Bible oath." In spite of his recovered self-possession, his glib replies, the man was plainly shaken. He was moistening his dry lips with the tip of his tongue; he was making little restless movements with his hands and feet. "I won't sign nothing that hasn't 'if' in it, like I said," he declared. "You can't make me, neither. I know my rights," he declared defiantly.

"Just a little too well," commented Bobby. "Suggests previous experience. Ever had any?" Martin did not answer. "Your protest will be noted," Bobby said formally. "But I think you had better consider your position very carefully. If you wish to say anything more, let me know. And remember: Murder has taken place and murder is a serious matter. Murder is a hanging matter. You can go now."

Martin put his hand to his throat with an odd, hurried gesture as though to relieve a pressure he felt there. He gave Bobby a scowl of mingled fear and dislike and then went off, looking a good deal less self-satisfied than before. The colonel said:—

"You don't think he's our man, do you? what motive could he have?"

"It's all too difficult and obscure even to begin forming an opinion yet," Bobby answered slowly. "At least, that's how I feel. The motive may be as hidden and difficult to understand as the whole position seems. Martin was certainly lying part of the time, and the cigar business shows he was back near the library after Ralph Hoyle left. But by itself that doesn't prove much, except of course that Martin is a liar. He may have gone back to the library door and listened out of mere curiosity, and smelt cigar smoke, and yet not want to admit he was doing a bit of more or less harmless snooping. Or there may be more to it. Hard to tell. He could let himself in or out of the house as he liked, for that matter there is nothing but his own word to show he went to bed when he says he did. He is playing his own game, and it may be a more dangerous game than he realizes."

The colonel nodded again.

"Yes," he agreed. "There's a murderer loose about here, and a very cool and desperate murderer, too."

CHAPTER VIII
VICAR—BUSINESS MAN

There was a knock at the door and a constable appeared with the information that the vicar had now arrived in answer to the message sent him requesting his attendance once more at the castle. Bobby, after consulting Colonel Glynne, told the constable they would be glad to see Mr. Longden at once. While they were waiting for his appearance, Bobby remarked to the colonel:—

"He was here earlier, but I didn't ask him for any statement. I understood he came along only as the parish priest to see if he could help in any way, and there seemed nothing then to suggest he knew anything relevant. It was only after he had gone that I heard Ralph Hoyle had been seen handling an automatic in the Wych estate office. A bit suggestive with a murder happening shortly afterwards. And then, after that, the vicar's umbrella was picked up in the castle grounds, so apparently he was somewhere about here last night."

"How do they know whose it was?" the colonel asked. "Initials or something?"

"No, not that. I believe the man who found it recognized it as Mr. Longden's. It seems he has a reputation for leaving odd belongings about; umbrella, gloves, anything."

The door opened and Mr. Longden himself appeared. He was plainly nervous and distressed, and began at once, without waiting for questions, to talk of the horror of such a crime in that quiet and peaceful village.

"Is it certain it was murder?" he asked. "Couldn't it possibly be accident—or even suicide? That would be very dreadful, very dreadful indeed, but not—not murder."

"I fear there's no doubt," the colonel answered gravely. "My assistant, Inspector Owen, is in charge of the inquiry, and he would like to ask you a few questions. I need hardly say that both he and I rely upon you to give us all the help in your power."

"It is a duty, a plain duty," Mr. Longden answered, very much as if he wished it wasn't. "Anything I can tell you, of course."

"I ought to begin," Bobby said, "by explaining that an umbrella was found in the grounds here, leaning against a tree." He produced it, as quaint an exhibit as has ever played a part in the investigation of a murder. "I'm told it is yours. Do you recognize it?"

"Dear me," exclaimed Mr. Longden looking quite excited. "Is that where I left it? I knew I had it with me last night but I thought I must have left it at Mrs. Vigor's. I was meaning to call there to-day to ask."

"At Mrs. Vigor's?" Bobby repeated.

"I was called to her house late last night," Mr. Longden explained. "Her baby, only a few days old, was very ill and she wished me to baptize the poor child. Most happily, immediately after the baptism, there was a most marked change for the better. A wonderful change. I must not attribute it to the baptism, but still—the change was extraordinary. Most impressive. On my way back, I took a path—I have permission—through the castle grounds. It saves going a long way round. When I got near the house I could hear the wireless playing and I noticed the french windows of the library were partly open. It was a warm night."

"Were they wide open?" Bobby asked.

"No, no, just a few inches. But then I saw someone from the terrace open them wider and go through into the library, pulling the windows to afterwards."

He paused, evidently embarrassed. When he did not continue, Bobby said:—

"Did you recognize who it was?"

"I... I couldn't be sure," the vicar answered. His embarrassment was evident. He hesitated, stammered a little as he went on:—"I... I couldn't be sure. No. I certainly couldn't be sure. I suppose it was then I put down my umbrella. I think I prayed for guidance. I... felt so bewildered. I felt I must be mistaken."

"Whom did you think it was?" Bobby asked, very quietly but with a note of insistence in his voice that evidently the vicar recognized, and that as evidently made him still more uncomfortable.

"You see," he explained, "I'm not sure. Really, I don't think it would be right for me to mention a name. It was only a mere passing glimpse. Very likely, I was entirely mistaken. I might," he pointed out pleadingly, "be misleading you in a most unfortunate manner."

"I am afraid," Bobby insisted, "it is necessary for us to know what you thought at the time. We realize it was only an impression and possibly a mistaken one. If it was, we can soon get that cleared up. The point is that even a mistaken impression will be a guide and a help, and it is essential to know who was and who was not near the spot at the time of the murder. That is what we call establishing identity. Identity of time, place, and any possible suspect." The vicar was evidently thinking this over. Bobby did not try to hurry him. The vicar said with unexpected insight:—

"That means me—includes me as a suspect?"

"Well, yes," agreed Bobby, though in point of fact he had not thought of that before. "Still, we can leave that aside for the moment. What we are asking for now is the name of the person you thought at the moment you recognized. We have got to know it," he added with that hard resolve which was at the core of his character though it so seldom appeared, "for we do not intend that the murder of an old, inoffensive man like Lord Wych shall go unpunished."

"It will not," the vicar said with a sudden and a curious severity that matched—outmatched indeed—the hardness in Bobby's tone.

"It cannot, indeed, for the punishment is in the deed itself. No punishment is greater than impunity."

Bobby did not attempt to argue that point. He thought to himself that perhaps it was a punishment, this of impunity, that might well encourage crime and still more crime. But he was not sure, for he thought that at least he could catch a glimpse of what the vicar meant. He waited quietly, and with a sigh Mr. Longden spoke.

"I want to say again," he began, "that very likely I was utterly mistaken. At the time I know I felt I must be. It seemed it was incredible. But certainly at the time it did seem to me that I had seen the Countess Wych."

Neither Bobby nor the colonel could quite conceal their surprise. It was the last name either of them had expected. Colonel Glynne indeed drew his breath in sharply, in a very audible gasp of astonishment.

"Lady Wych," he exclaimed incredulously.

"No doubt I was utterly mistaken," repeated Mr. Longden eagerly, turning quickly towards the colonel as if hoping to escape from Bobby's hard insistence. "Incredible, of course. In her state of health."

"She came downstairs to dinner last night," Bobby remarked thoughtfully, half inclined to belief on the old principle: 'I believe because it is impossible'—or, in this case, so highly improbable. The impression made on the vicar must have been strong, he felt, to have produced such a statement. "Anyhow, you feel sure it was a woman?" he asked abruptly.

"Well, yes, a woman," the vicar agreed, "yes, I think so, but really, it was only a glimpse, as—whoever it was— opened the window, pushed back the curtain, entered the room."

"The wireless was playing?" Bobby asked.

The vicar was quite clear on that point. He distinctly remembered hearing it playing. But he had heard nothing in the nature of pistol shots. Concerning the exact time, he was less certain. Somewhere about half-past eleven, he supposed. Nor could he be certain what exact piece of music was being played, or what portion. Classical music certainly, but he had not recognized it. His knowledge of music was limited and his ear by no means first rate.

There is one thing more where you can help us possibly," Bobby continued, when it became clear that nothing more definite could be extracted from the vicar's somewhat vague recollections. "Not far from where you were standing, judging, that is, from where the umbrella was found, there are traces of footprints. Cigarette ends are lying about. Under some rhododendron bushes. It looks as if someone had been sitting there for some time, and it appears to be about the only convenient spot from which the castle can be seen comfortably. There is an uninterrupted view of the library windows. Apparently whoever it was remained there for some time, just as if he or she were watching. It may have been the murderer waiting a favourable opportunity. There may be some innocent explanation. Did you notice or can you remember anything to help us there? Did you smell tobacco smoke, for example, or see a lighted cigarette?"

Mr. Longden looked a good deal disturbed at this new suggestion.

"Do you mean," he asked, "the murderer may have been hiding there and that I may have passed within a few feet of him?—dear me, a most uncomfortable idea."

Disturbing as he evidently found the suggestion, he was unable to say anything to confirm it, and Bobby did not press the point.

"There's just one thing more," he said. "You were a good deal surprised when you saw Lady Wych, so much so that I think you said something about praying for guidance. I don't quite understand what guidance was necessary."

Mr. Longden flushed and hesitated.

"I was conscious of a certain temptation," he said. "My daughter has undertaken duties towards Lady Wych, whose health is very bad. My first feeling was that Lady Wych oughtn't to be out there at that time of night, and that her being so might imply a certain neglect on Sophy's part. I wasn't sure what to do, I was tempted to do nothing for fear of drawing attention to what might have been a fault on my daughter's part. But there was, after all, no reason why Lady Wych shouldn't be up and about. It was not very late and it was a warm, fine night. Yet I felt uneasy. I don't know why. I wasn't sure what to do, and when I feel like that, it is my habit to seek guidance. Then I saw Lady Wych turn back into the room and pull the curtains to behind her. I felt that was an answer, and showed there was no need for me to do anything. I went on home. That is all."

"Thank you," Bobby said, touched and a little puzzled by the simplicity of the tale and the natural way in which it had been told.

He asked one or two more questions about what had passed in the estate office the previous day, with special reference to the pistol incident. Mr. Longden was quite clear he had seen it locked up securely in the safe. Bobby went over all this so carefully and in such detail that he felt by the time he had finished that he was aware of every tiny incident of the interview that had taken place that afternoon. Then Mr. Longden returned to the disturbing possibility that he might have been within arm's length of the murderer the previous night.

"If that is so," he said, "he may think I saw him and know who he is?"

It was an uncomfortable idea that had already come to Bobby and he had decided to suggest to the colonel that it might be wise, short-handed as they were, to tell off a plain-clothes man to provide some sort of protection for the vicar. It was not necessary to make the suggestion, however, for the possible danger had evidently occurred to the colonel as well.

"It would be as well," he said, "if you had one of our men within call. I don't take it seriously, of course, there's no real danger, but all the same, precautions mean safety. The murderer may think you know him."

"But if he does," protested Mr. Longden, "and if there's a policeman about, that might keep him away."

"Well, yes, that's why," the colonel explained, not quite understanding, or, rather, thinking that the vicar did not quite understand.

"You see," explained Mr. Longden in his turn, "if he thinks I know who he is he may come to me for help and advice and I may be able to bring the unfortunate man to a better frame of mind. He might be brought to realize his terrible sin and to show his repentance by confession."

The colonel blinked. The idea was not one that had occurred either to him or to Bobby. Nor, in spite of the glowing enthusiasm in Mr. Longden's voice, did they think such a result very probable. What struck them both much more forcibly was the danger that the unknown murderer might try to remove a possible witness. But this, when it was hinted at, Mr. Longden waved aside. In his opinion, no man, laden with the guilt of one murder, could conceivably wish to add that of another to the burden of remorse he must of necessity know himself to be condemned to bear.

"There is no risk of that," he declared with emphasis. "Quite out of the question. And if any such danger did exist, it would be quite unimportant against the smallest chance that this most unhappy man may come to me for help."

None the less, when Mr. Longden had departed, Bobby, with the colonel's consent, took such steps as were possible to ensure that an unobtrusive watch was kept on the vicarage. They were both inclined to take the danger seriously, and then Arthur Hoyle, whom it had been decided it would be best to interview next, made his appearance.

"I was hoping," he said ungraciously, as he came in, "that I could get away long before this. I am a business man with a good many things needing my attention; and dreadful and shocking as all this is, and though I don't want to seem callous, still a good many people are going to suffer if my work is held up indefinitely."

"Oh, not indefinitely," Bobby protested. "There are just one or two points on which we thought you might like to supplement your statement. You remember I mentioned we found footprints and cigarette ends in the grounds at a spot from which these library windows can be clearly seen. It seems certain someone was there for some time, presumably watching the house. Naturally that interests us as there was a murder committed. We wonder if that watcher was the murderer. We wonder if he saw or heard anything."

Bobby paused. Arthur muttered angrily and uneasily:— "Well, how should I know?"

"The footprints," Bobby continued, "are too indistinct and confused to be of much value. But they do suggest that the person making them wore a rather unusually large size of shoe. Most likely a number ten. Perhaps a nine and a half. Difficult to be sure. Except that it was an outsize shoe." He paused and carefully did not look at Arthur Hoyle's feet, encased in number ten shoes, for Arthur, though not a big man, had both big hands and big feet, a plebeian inheritance from his mother's side of the family. Involuntarily Arthur made a movement to withdraw his feet under his chair, and then, recognizing the futility of so doing, thrust them ostentatiously forward. He did not speak, and Bobby went on:—"The cigarette ends were a not very common Greek brand— blend of Grecian and Turkish tobacco. 'Le Proche Orient' it's called. We have made a few inquiries, and we understand it is a brand you smoke and that you have some interest in the manufacture, isn't it?"

"Not in the manufacture," Arthur answered. He spoke more quietly now, and seemed to have recovered a self-possession that for the moment had been badly shaken. "I am a director of a small private company, a distributing company, trying to popularize the use of Greek tobacco. The Greeks are our allies, Greek tobacco is first rate, we think it would be good for both countries and for our own pockets as well, if we could create a demand here for Greek tobacco." He smiled faintly. "Patriotism and profit. Unluckily we haven't had much success so far. Now look here." He leaned forward and spoke with emphasis. "It's plain enough what you're driving at. I'm not the only person who takes a big shoe. I'm not the only person who smokes those cigarettes. I give them away freely myself, I've seen they are on sale in every retailer's in the district, and the company has offered a bonus for biggest increase in sales. We're pushing 'em. I do take an outsize in shoes. I do smoke 'Le Proche Orient' cigarettes. I wasn't anywhere near here last night after I left about nine or a quarter past, after dinner. Got that? Now, something else, I understand your insinuations and I resent them. Got that?"

"I am afraid," Bobby said gently, "that I might reply that we resent your suggestion that we have insinuated anything. I have made no insinuations. I have made a plain statement and asked a plain question. But it would be a pity, don't you think? if we just stand about resenting each other. It is our duty, as police, to find who murdered Earl Wych. I am sure you will agree that it is the duty of every citizen to help us, especially your duty, Mr. Hoyle, if I may say so, since his lordship was the head of your family. I suppose you are in the line of inheritance yourself?"

"What the devil do you mean by that?" demanded Arthur, angry again.

"Merely what the question means itself," Bobby answered. "Indeed, it was hardly a question, more a statement of a fact well enough known. Mr. Hoyle, you are helping neither yourself nor us by taking this tone. Now I must ask you another plain question and please don't ask me what it means, because it means exactly what it says, neither more nor less. You left this house about a quarter past nine. There is, of course, proof that Earl Wych was alive then. He and Mr. Ralph Hoyle were in the library together much later than that. Where did you go when you left here?"

"Home. But if you want to know I didn't go straight home. I drove around for a while. I like night driving. I daresay it was midnight when I got home. Make what you like of that."

"Could you tell us exactly where you went? Did you stop anywhere, speak to any one?"

"No, I didn't," Arthur said. "Why should I? The pubs shut pretty early, you know. I just had an enjoyable drive in the fresh air, round by Wychwood Forest. I couldn't say exactly what roads I followed. I didn't notice. I wasn't afraid of getting lost. It's pretty lonely round there. I don't remember that I saw more than one or two other cars. I didn't notice them and I don't suppose they noticed me. I drove pretty fast. I'm not a speed merchant, but I don't believe in mooching around either. I daresay I had done more than a hundred miles—well, not more, but not far short— when I got home. I'm not the only person taking an outsize in shoes, I'm not the only person smoking those cigarettes, I'm not the only person who was out last night, and I'm going straight from here to have a talk with my lawyers."

"Always more satisfactory to have legal advice," agreed Bobby. "I can assure you we are very well aware of all you've been saying. Certainly you are not the only person out late last night. Very odd if you had been. Mr. Longden for instance, was close by somewhere about the time of the murder, as far as we can judge. In fact, it was through him that we came across the footprints and the cigarette ends I told you about."

"Longden? the vicar?" repeated Arthur with a start of surprise that made Bobby wonder if it would be fair to call it exaggerated. "If Longden says he saw me there, he lies. That's all. It's a dirty lie."

"Really, Mr. Hoyle," Bobby protested, "I said nothing of the kind. Nor did Mr. Longden. I said 'through him'. What happened is simply that he left his umbrella standing against a tree. Apparently he has a trick of leaving odd possessions about. When the umbrella was noticed, naturally further search was made and the cigarette ends and footprints were found. Mr. Longden had nothing to do with it, but if he hadn't left his umbrella there, very likely no special search would have been made in that particular spot. That's all."

Arthur was evidently thinking deeply.

"Look here," he said. "Have you thought of this? If he left his umbrella leaning against a tree—well, doesn't that suggest he wasn't merely on his way home? Looks to me as if he had stopped there for a time. Or why did he put his umbrella down? Thought of that?"

"Well, yes," agreed Bobby, "but no one could possibly suspect him, could they? what possible motive...?"

"He might have been meaning to have it out with the old man, if he had been a bit worried over that girl of his. Anyhow, that's likely enough, and a lot more sensible than talking about outsizes in shoes and cigarette ends."

"You mean Miss Sophy Longden?" Bobby asked. "The young lady who is a kind of nurse-companion- secretary to Lady Wych. Why? do you mean there's been gossip about her?"

Arthur shrugged his shoulders.

"I never paid it any attention," he said. "The old man used to be a bit of a lad in his time—gay Edwardian, that sort of thing. They went the pace before the last war just as much as they did after it, if all tales are true. Anyhow, he still had an eye for a pretty girl, and Sophy Longden is that all right enough. Plenty of opportunity, too. Naturally, the old boy would be in and out of his wife's room at all hours. She has had a sort of separate suite since her illness. Miss Longden has the next room. Not that I ever believed a word of it. My own idea is that that Martin fellow started the talk. Trying to make mischief. Or perhaps just for something to say. A good butler who knows his job may be hard to get and worth keeping when you find him, but I wouldn't have that fellow in my house at any price. Malice and mischief making, if you ask me. But if Longden heard about it— well, he's a clergyman with extra strict ideas, and it might explain why he was mooching around and leaving his umbrella about and saying his prayers and all that. And if there was a row, Earl Wych wasn't the kind of man to stand being talked to. He had a pretty big idea of himself. Natural, I suppose; he was always very much his lordship, the Earl Wych and all the rest of it. Anything might have happened. Mind you, that's only a possibility. I wouldn't mention it to any one but you."

"I shouldn't," said Bobby drily. "But you may be sure it's a possibility we shan't forget. Everything has to be considered, no matter how improbable on the face of it, or how apparently insignificant—even cigarette ends, for instance. By the way, you had already heard about Mr. Longden's umbrella?"

"Every one has," Arthur retorted. "Wasn't it one of the servants who spotted it first?"

"The under-gardener, I think," Bobby agreed, aware that the news of the discovery had been widely spread. "You mentioned that Mr. Longden was saying his prayers. I think that was what you said?"

Arthur's expression changed suddenly. Till now he had looked confident and self-possessed. He had answered every question readily with no sign of hesitation. But now he did hesitate, a wary look came into his eyes, he almost stammered as he said:—

"Oh, well, well now, well, he always does, you know. Hang it,"—the words came more fluently now—"if you ask me, he never sets out to catch the 'bus for Midwych without stopping to pray he may be in time. And that probably makes him lose it, ha! ha!"

But the laugh with which he concluded his sentence sounded forced and unreal, nor did he look at all comfortable under Bobby's steady and questioning gaze.

"Mr. Hoyle," Bobby said slowly, "I must put a direct question. Was it you under the rhododendron bushes last night?"

"It was not," Arthur almost shouted, "and you've no right to ask me such an insolent question."

"I am sorry if you think it insolent," Bobby answered, quite unmoved by this protest, "but we have not only the right, but the duty to ask questions. I must ask you another. Were you anywhere near the castle about half-past eleven last night? If you were, did you see or hear anything unusual?"

"I wasn't and I didn't," Arthur answered sulkily, "I've already told you I like night driving, and I was just having a run round."

"Do you wish," Bobby continued, "to add anything to your remark about Mr. Longden's 'saying his prayers'? I think we must agree that unless there was some special reason, it would be a little unexpected, even for a clergy-man, to be obviously offering a prayer at that time and place. You see, we are wondering what gave you the idea?"

"I've told you," Arthur answered again, and even more sulkily. "It was just a casual remark—a sort of joke it you like. Trying to poke fun at the old boy. That's all."

He turned sharply on Colonel Glynne. "Do you permit this sort of thing?" he demanded. "Trying to catch you out, trying to put meanings into your words?"

"If I had heard anything improper, I should certainly have interfered," the colonel answered stiffly. "In my opinion, you were asked none but reasonable questions. If any suspicion were in our minds—I'm not saying for a moment that there is or was—it is largely, Mr. Hoyle, your own manner and show of temper that would be the cause."

That ended the interview, and when the door had closed behind him the colonel said:—

"What do you make of that, Owen? Think he's our man? Badly scared, I should say, and very anxious to draw our attention to someone else. That prayer business smells a bit fishy to me. Looks very much as if he had been there and been watching."

"I think so sir," agreed Bobby. "That slipped out very much as if he had actually seen Mr. Longden and noticed something in his attitude that suggested the act of prayer. Probably if he did he would think it awfully funny and weak minded and remember it. But even if he were there and did leave those footprints and cigarette ends, it doesn't prove he was the murderer. He is badly frightened certainly, but innocent people are often that, if they think appearances are against them."

"Can there be anything in his nasty little hint about Miss Longden and the earl?"

"I think we must try to follow it up," Bobby said. "There may have been gossip; spiteful, unfounded gossip very likely. The more spiteful and the more unfounded, the better some people like gossip. It's just possible some such talk came to Mr. Longden's ears. It's just possible that he saw a woman entering the library from the terrace. If so, he may have thought at first it was the countess and then been afraid it was Miss Sophy or at any rate felt he must make sure. That doubt might explain his prayer for guidance. If he did try to make sure, a quarrel may have resulted. And it is a fact that Mr. Longden knew there was an automatic in the estate office safe and either by accident or design the key of the safe was in his possession at the time of the murder."

"Put like that, I don't much like it," the colonel said slowly. He shook his head. "Father avenging injured daughter's honour," he said doubtfully. "Take a lot to make that go down with a modern jury. Generally it's not so much murder as an action for damages. And I don't see Longden as a murderer. Still, I suppose you never know."

"No, sir," agreed Bobby. "For that matter, the primitive instincts are pretty strong in some of us still. Scratch the civilized, conventional man, and you find the primaeval underneath."

The door opened. A constable appeared. He had brought the report of the Wakefield finger expert. Among other matters of less interest, it stated that a clear imprint, the last made, on the switch controlling the wireless set, was that of Miss Sophy Longden. Another print, less clearly defined, but still recognizable as hers, seemed also to have been the last made on the handle of the library door.

CHAPTER IX
SOPHY

"And what," said Colonel Glynne, when he had studied this report, "what are we to make of that?" Bobby said nothing, for the good reason that he had nothing to say. In the minds of both men was a memory of Sophy as they had seen her only a little before. Small, gentle, shy, with large, frightened eyes and a tendency to slip away unperceived on the first opportunity. An odd, incongruous figure to crop up in the middle of a murder investigation. One could imagine her clinging trustfully to some strong man's arm. One could imagine her gravely intent on arranging the flowers in the drawingroom or wrinkling that smooth, white forehead of hers over some difficult question of which hat went best with which frock. But to suppose a connection between that dainty little figure and the grim business of murder, seemed more difficult. Yet there were these finger-prints to be accounted for!

"A pretty little thing, too," the colonel said abruptly.

"Yes, sir," agreed Bobby. He had thought so himself when he had seen her with Olive, and Olive had said later on that even though one was apt to overlook her at first, because she was so small and of such quiet, retiring ways, yet her looks took her very nearly into the rare class of beauty. No doubt two or three inches more of height would have been an advantage. "Still, even pretty little things..." he said and paused, not caring to complete the sentence.

"Of course, of course," the colonel said. "We must hear what she has to say. It does seem to fit in rather uncomfortably with Arthur Hoyle's hints and with Mr. Longden's own story. Worrying about those keys, too, and that estate automatic. If Longden saw someone he thought was a woman, went to make sure, found it was his own girl... well, there you are."

"It might be like that," admitted Bobby uncomfortably. "Only if Mr. Longden had the Wych estate automatic with him, then it would appear premeditated."

"We don't know what weapon was used," Glynne pointed out. "Ralph Hoyle seems confident his must be still in the estate office safe. For that matter, the pistol actually used may have belonged to Earl Wych himself. I can't remember if he had a licence for a pistol. If he had, it will be in the Firearms Register. He had licences for several guns, naturally. Owen, are we to attach any importance to what Arthur told us about Longden's having said a prayer?"

"Not the sort of thing it would be any good bringing up in court," Bobby answered. "Defending counsel would make fun of it, and Hoyle had an explanation ready—as pat as the explanation Martin gave over his knowledge of the cigar. But all that does suggest very strongly to my mind that Martin was hanging about outside the library, though he says he wasn't, and that it was Arthur Hoyle who was watching by the rhododendron bushes. And it seems to me that takes away some of the significance of Miss Longden's finger-prints. It does leave it open whether she was the last person in the room. Either Arthur Hoyle or Martin may have been hanging about, and may have been in here later than Miss Longden."

"Well, why was she here at all at that time of night?" demanded the colonel irritably. "Martin is the snooping type. He may have been merely eavesdropping out of curiosity. But if it was Arthur Hoyle under the rhododendrons, what was he up to? No good, I'll be bound."

"I'm afraid it will be difficult to get the truth out of him if he chooses to stick to his motoring story," Bobby observed.

"A tough customer, one of our hard-faced business men," pronounced the colonel. He spoke gloomily, and then brightened up. "Luckily," he said, "it won't be much trouble to get the truth out of the little Longden girl. Girls often lie like blazes, but they soon get scared and all tangled up."

Bobby made no comment on this pronouncement in feminine psychology. Nor was he altogether in agreement with it. In his experience, some girls could not only 'lie like blazes', but could also prove themselves very cool and skilful liars. It all depended on the girl. Probably, he thought, it would be nearer the truth to say that when a girl was a good liar, she was very, very good, and when she was bad at it, then she was perfectly hopeless. As in other things, women tended to the extremes. The colonel cleared his throat and said half apologetically:—

"I think, Owen, you had better let me do the questioning this time. It may come a bit better from an older man, get her confidence and that sort of thing. I can tell her I've a daughter myself just about her age. The chief thing will be to avoid frightening her. Once a girl starts crying," said the colonel profoundly, "you just simply jolly well can't do a thing."

This time Bobby was in full agreement, and now Sophy appeared in answer to their summons.

A forlorn, scared little figure she did in fact present as she stood there facing the two men, her hands clasped before her, a tremulous quiver at the corners of her mouth, her breathing uneven and hurried.

A very pretty, dainty picture she made, too, with her complexion of cream and roses—roses the country air had recently made to blossom in her cheeks—her large, scared eyes that looked up at them so appealingly from under long, curling lashes any film star would have envied, the perfectly-shaped little nose, the two rows of tiny, even teeth like two rows of well-matched pearls, showing, too, to such advantage now as they parted to let that quick, uneven breath come through.

The shorthand writer, unimpressed, for here he was not so much man as stenographer, opened his notebook and hoped she would speak clearly and not too quickly. He did not know whether he hated most the gabblers or the mumblers, but he did know that the world was almost entirely composed of the one or the other. The stenographer's daily cross. But the colonel was impressed, and indeed began to look so extremely paternal that Bobby half-expected him to get up and welcome Sophy with a kiss—an entirely, completely paternal kiss, of course. Bobby wasn't sorry his superior officer was going to do the questioning. He thoroughly agreed that when a girl, especially an unusually pretty girl, starts crying, it's like being up against a royal flush at poker.

Nothing to be done.

"Please sit down, Miss Longden," the colonel was saying—cooing would be perhaps a better word to use. "We just want to ask you a few questions about this dreadful business. We won't bother you any more than we can help, because, of course, we all quite understand what a dreadful shock it has been."

He paused. Sophy did not speak, but Bobby saw how her small hands clasped together before her tightened till the knuckles were white. Her eyes were hidden now, fixed on the floor, concealed behind those long curling lashes. Only a slight movement of the small head showed that she had heard. The colonel continued, still in his most paternal manner:—

"I am sure, my dear young lady, you understand how necessary it is we should know everything that happened last night, even though it may seem quite irrelevant. It's the only way in which we can hope to discover the truth, to bring to justice whoever is guilty of this shocking crime. I know how painful, how distressing it must be to you, but I'm sure you'll be brave and courageous."

He paused, as inviting a reply. When none came, he said coaxingly:—

"We quite understand how dreadful it is for a young girl like you—a young, sensitive girl—to find herself concerned in any way in such a dreadful business. I'll do my best to help you and you will be brave, won't you?"

"I'll try," said Sophy in the smallest voice imaginable. The colonel gave what it is hardly an exaggeration to call a triumphant glance at Bobby. It seemed to say:—'You young fellows may think you score with the girls, but it's us older men they really trust.'

He went on, his voice fairly oozing kindliness and protectiveness and fatherliness:—

"First of all, I've got to explain that everything you are going to tell us will be taken down in writing, and afterwards you'll be asked to sign it to show it's correct. Now, I know that sounds very alarming, but it isn't really, it's only so that we may be able to refer to it if we want to be sure exactly what you did say without having to bother you again with more questions. You do understand, don't you? that anything you can tell us may be used in evidence. That means, you see, my dear," explained the colonel carefully to the small, demure, listening figure, "you might be asked to go into the witness-box and repeat there on oath what you tell us to-day. And after all I don't suppose you would find it such a dreadful ordeal as I expect it seems now. You do quite understand, don't you?"

This time Sophy nodded, and the colonel thought that little forlorn nod so pathetic he had to clear his throat before he could proceed. He almost wished he had let Bobby do the questioning. It seemed such a shame to have to examine officially this timid unprotected child, so utterly helpless. But it was a duty, and it had to be done. And then really it was better for the questioning to be done by a—well, by a man of so to say mature age, one, too, who was himself a father—rather than by a comparative boy like young Bobby Owen. Besides, he wasn't getting on so badly. That 'my dear' he had slipped in so naturally, so paternally, had had, he was sure, a most reassuring effect.

"There is one thing more I must explain," he continued kindly, "you need not answer any question if for any reason you feel you would prefer not to. We can't force you to speak, you know."

He smiled at the mere idea of applying force to the timid little figure shrinking down in the chair opposite, and the stenographer thought suddenly:—

"Old boy fancies himself with the girls. Why the blazes doesn't he get down to it? I could have squeezed the truth out of her in half a brace of shakes while he's been talking all round the show."

"Just one thing more," the colonel went on, "if you wish you can have a lawyer present to help you. Would you like one?"

"Oh, no," breathed Sophy very earnestly.

This talkative old gentleman was bad enough, and Bobby Owen was looking very grim, and the presence of the short-hand writer was awfully alarming, but to have a lawyer there, Sophy felt, would simply be altogether too much. So her "oh, no" was heartfelt, and the colonel beamed approval.

"Very well, just as you like," he said. "I'll repeat. You understand that what you are going to tell us may be used in evidence, that you are under no obligation to answer questions if you prefer not to, and that you can have a lawyer present if you wish it. Now we'll begin, shall we? I want you to start, if you will, with the dinner last night. You were present, I think?"

"If you please," said Sophy timidly, "if you don't mind, I would rather not say."

"Eh?" said the colonel, thinking he had not heard correctly.

"Please," repeated Sophy as timidly as before, "if you really don't mind very much, I would rather not say."

"But... but..." the colonel said, still paternal, though now slightly less so, "I didn't mean you mustn't answer questions. I meant you needn't, and of course we know already you dined with the others last night."

"Yes, I know, of course I did really," Sophy agreed, "only, please, I thought it would be so much easier if I didn't say anything at all about anything."

"Yes... but... my dear young lady... my dear Miss Longden... you must realize... began the colonel, and paused, not quite knowing what to say next.

"You said I needn't answer if I didn't want, and I don't want," explained Sophy, "and so I thought it would be simplest if I didn't."

The colonel blinked. He supposed he hadn't understood, and he was sure she didn't understand. She was looking straight at him now, through those long curling lashes of hers, looking at him very timidly and also very determinedly. Impossible to convey in words the impression of sheer panic, of distress, of absolute resolution, that she gave. It came rather absurdly into Bobby's mind that against that gentle resolution of hers even the old method of thumbscrew and rack would be equally ineffective. She would have shrunk, she would have wept, but not a word would have been wrenched from her. The colonel was struggling to persuade himself that he had heard aright. The stenographer thought:—

"I'd soon get her talking with the help of a good ash plant." Then he looked at her and changed his mind, and thought instead:—"She'd die first. The old man's up against it."

"Miss Longden," the colonel was saying, not a bit paternal now, wholly official indeed, even military, "I don't think you realize how serious what you are saying is. Let me remind you that a murder has taken place."

"Yes, I know," said Sophy, and somehow her tone suggested that it was really rather a waste of time to repeat what was the central fact of the present situation, but that on the whole you couldn't expect men to have enough sense to realize that.

"Miss Longden," said the colonel, "do I seriously understand that you intend to refuse to answer the questions put to you?"

"Well, you said I needn't if I didn't want, didn't you?" Sophy pointed out. "And I don't want," she added as gently as ever.

"If you don't," the colonel told her in tones full of warning and menace, "we shall draw our own conclusions."

"I expect," observed Sophy thoughtfully, "they will be all wrong."

"I think," said the colonel, making another effort, "you had better consult a lawyer."

"Oh, no. What for?" asked Sophy.

"He might give you some good advice."

"But I don't want any," Sophy remarked.

"You need it," almost thundered the colonel.

Sophy said nothing. The colonel glared. Sophy continued to contrive to look at the same time timid, appealing, and scared; and also utterly resolute. The colonel transferred his glare to the stenographer, who luckily was not smiling at the moment; and then to Bobby, who was looking considerably and consolingly puzzled. The colonel said:— "Suppose I told you that your finger-prints had been found on the wireless set in the library and on the handle of the library door. What would you say?"

Sophy made no answer. She unclasped her hands, looked at the tips of her slender fingers as if wondering how they had contrived to leave traces behind them, and continued to be silent.

"It is a fact," said the colonel impressively, "we are obliged to consider highly suspicious. I was inclined to suppose at first that you would have some explanation to offer." He paused, optimistically hoping that even now some explanation might come. None did. He went on:— "Apparently you prefer to say nothing." Again he paused, and again Sophy wondered a little at the masculine passion for stating the obvious. "Very good," said the colonel, plainly meaning the opposite. "The facts are so serious that I am not sure I should not be justified in detaining you."

"You mean you are going to send me to prison?" Sophy asked. "That's what's making me so dreadfully frightened. It must be so awful to be in prison," she sighed, but a sigh with no weakness in it, a sigh of full acceptance of the inevitable.

"Prison," said the colonel regretfully, "is not in question at present. But it soon will be if you show contempt of court."

"Oh, I never should," declared Sophy, quite shocked at the idea.

"Do you know," demanded the colonel, "what is meant by being an accessory before or after the fact?"

"No," said Sophy.

The colonel tried to explain. Sophy tried to understand. Neither was very successful. Sophy said:—

"But you did tell me I needn't answer questions if I didn't want to and I don't. You did, didn't you?"

The colonel scowled. He wished he hadn't now. It would have been quite easy and justifiable to have questioned the girl in an easy, a casual, an informal manner, and only to have administered the customary warning a little later, if there seemed any chance of her really incriminating herself. But he had so wanted to be absolutely fair. And then who could have guessed a child like this would turn so suddenly and so abruptly obstinate. Also it had seemed quite safe. Innocent people never held their tongues. They had no reason to. The guilty never held theirs. They were too anxious to offer their convincing explanations that they had so carefully compiled. But this absolute silence—well, what could one do? Worse even than tears. Tears come and go and talk often follows. But silence is—well, just silence. For about the first time in his life Colonel Glynne took an extreme dislike to a pretty girl. He only wished he could do some of the many things his angry mind was suggesting to him. But he knew he couldn't. So he scowled again and even more deeply, and Sophy said:— "I'm so sorry to have made you so angry. I am really. But I do think, please, I would rather not say anything." The colonel rose to his feet, dignified and severe.

"I consider it my duty," he said, "to warn you that your attitude involves you in the gravest suspicion. I consider it most unwise. There is still time for you to think over your position."

He paused again, and again impressively. Sophy continued to look small and demure and to remain silent.

"Very well" said the colonel. "That will do for the present. Kindly understand, however, that you are not to attempt to leave, and that you are to hold yourself at our disposal."

Probably even Colonel Glynne himself would have had some difficulty in explaining exactly what this last expression meant. But it sounded well, and Sophy looked more frightened than ever.

"Please, what am I to do?" she asked.

The colonel grunted and waved a hand towards the door.

"That's enough," he said. "You can go. For the present."

The last words were snapped out like a threat, but Sophy hardly heard them as she scuttled away, so quickly did she avail herself of the permission to depart. The colonel gave a final glare at the door as it closed behind her and then turned to Bobby.

"Obstinate, pig-headed little fool," he growled. "What do you make of her, Owen?"

"She's shielding someone," Bobby answered promptly.

The colonel considered this. Then he said:—

"Or herself."

"It might be," agreed Bobby gravely.

"She'll have to explain those finger-prints," declared the colonel. "They're there and she's got to say sooner or later how they got there."

"If she won't, she won't, and nothing can make her," Bobby pointed out. "All she has to do is to sit tight. Not many people can—not one in a million. I have an idea Miss Longden may be that one in a million."

"A slip of a girl like that," grumbled the colonel.

Bobby said nothing, but he thought to himself that sometimes even girls can conceal in their slim and tender bodies a will unbreakable. For the strength of the spirit is one thing, the strength of the body another.

"Suppose," the colonel said presently, "suppose there's some foundation for Arthur Hoyle's story. Suppose Ear Wych had been trying to make advances to the girl, as old men do sometimes. He got her to go to the library late last night on some pretext or another. Perhaps she resented it. Perhaps she didn't. I'm prepared," said the colonel sourly, "to believe anything of that girl. And if Longden interrupted them—well, anything might have happened. Or perhaps she did resent it, and there was some sort of scuffle—and again the shooting was the result. I'm prepared," repeated the colonel with still more emphasis, "to believe anything at all about that girl after what we've seen of her this afternoon."

The door opened, opened widely. There entered the Countess Wych. She looked ill, with drawn features and a deathly-white complexion, thin and fragile to a degree. Almost she might have been the dead risen again to walk the familiar earth. When she lifted a hand it was so nearly transparent, the light seemed to shine through it. Nevertheless she held herself upright, and though her voice was the thin, high-pitched voice of age, it was clear and steady.

"What is this nonsense about Sophy Longden?" she demanded, "what right do you think you have to try to bully and frighten a young girl? Is that part of the duty of the police? to bully children?"

The attack was so unexpected that the three men could only gape at her.

"Well," she asked. "Well, have you nothing to say?"

"An investigation is being conducted into the murder of Lord Wych," Colonel Glynne answered then. "Your ladyship must understand that the method of conducting that investigation is our responsibility. Miss Longden, I am sorry to say, has declined to answer the questions I felt it my duty to put to her."

"Quite right, too," retorted the countess. "I have sent for our lawyers. Young Clinton Wells is here, but I prefer Mr. Blacklock. I've known him longer. What made you suppose a child like Sophy Longden could know anything?"

"There is what seems conclusive proof that she was in this room late last night, that she was probably indeed the last to be in here," Colonel Glynne answered. "She refuses to give any explanation. In consequence she renders herself open to very grave suspicion."

Lady Wych looked at him doubtfully, evidently a good deal surprised. She said after a moment or two:—

"Nonsense. She couldn't have been. Why should you think she was?"

"We have evidence which seems conclusive, especially in view of the refusal to answer questions," the colonel repeated.

Lady Wych, however, was hardly listening.

"If that's true, if she really was here, too, she must know—"

"Know what?" Colonel Glynne asked.

The countess looked at him long and steadily before she answered and her dim and sunken eyes were bright again when she said at last:—

"I can't imagine."

CHAPTER X
LADY WYCH

For a moment there was silence. They all felt that Lady Wych had remembered or understood something; but what that something was, they had no idea. Colonel Glynne and the old woman were looking full at each other, as it were in challenge and defiance. But it was the colonel who looked away first, as though he could no longer match the energy and will that blazed in those old eyes, no longer dim and sunken but alight with an inner fire. She turned her glance next upon the stenographer, but he was not interested, for his business was with the spoken word, and in this silent conflict of wills no word was being uttered.

"Well, have you got all that down?" she asked him abruptly.

"Certainly, my lady," he replied, slightly offended, for that was his job and what he was there to do.

She turned to Bobby, who was looking not at her but at the ceiling above his head. He seemed to find it interesting. She frowned slightly, as if she did not much approve of this absorption, and said to him:—

"Well, young man?"

With a slight start, as if recalled to present surroundings, he said:—

"Oh, I'm sorry. I was thinking."

"What about?" she demanded. "What were you thinking?"

"Oh, I'm sorry," Bobby answered again, "but as chief constable of the county, Colonel Glynne is conducting the inquiry."

At that she stared and frowned again, and then laughed harshly.

"I can tell a snub when I get one," she said, and turned back to the colonel. "Is there anything more you want to ask me?" she demanded.

"Now your ladyship is here," he said formally, "there are some questions I feel it is my duty to put to you on one or two points that have cropped up since you made your first statement. Won't you please sit down?"

Bobby got up to find her a chair. She acknowledged the attention with a curt bow. She sat down, upright, waiting, slightly formidable. Fumbling in the pile of papers before him, the colonel said, without looking up:—

"Oh, by the way, you were saying just now that Miss Longden must know something. Could you give us some idea of what it is she might know?"

"You must ask her that," came the quick response.

"Your ladyship," said Colonel Glynne, formal again, "must realize that I am forced to conclude that you are unwilling to reply. In other words, that there is something you know but wish to conceal."

"I am in no way responsible for your conclusions, which do not interest me," she retorted haughtily, indeed more as if she were talking to her butler than to the chief constable of the county. In a more conciliatory tone, she said:— "I know nothing, and I do not choose to talk about things I am not sure of. If you want to know anything about Miss Longden, ask Miss Longden."

"She declines to answer any question," the colonel pointed out.

"Well, then," said Lady Wych as if that ended the matter. "We will leave that for the time," the colonel said. "I think in the statement you made earlier on, you say that the last time you saw Earl Wych alive was at dinner last night?"

"That is so," she answered steadily, and in a voice as steady, she added:— "I have since seen his body."

"After dinner," Colonel Glynne continued, "a trifling incident appears to have taken place, at the foot of the stairs, in the hall. Our information is that you stopped to look at one of the family portraits hanging there and that you remarked to Miss Longden, who was with you, that it was the portrait of an ancestress who shot a son of hers in order to preserve the family honour."

"I suppose Martin told you all that," she remarked. "I remember he was hanging about. You called it a trifling incident. If you really think it trifling, why do you ask about it? If you do not, I should be obliged if in future you would say more exactly what you do mean. Martin's story is accurate. Do you wish to suggest that I said that as a preliminary to shooting my husband to save the family honour?"

"There is no wish to make any such suggestion," the colonel answered stiffly and also going very red. "I must remind you it is my duty to question you on every detail. I hope you will agree it is equally your duty to answer both freely and frankly."

He paused, evidently hoping for and expecting some response. He got none. But the grim old face looked grimmer still, the gaze of the old tired eyes remained as direct and firm and challenging as before. No wavering there. Colonel Glynne continued:—

"I must put this to you: Was there anything in your mind, any fear or apprehension, that any danger threatened Earl Wych?"

"No," she answered. "You know there has been feeling shown, very naturally, over the appearance of—of our grandson."

Bobby noticed that she hesitated over the last three words, as if she had some difficulty in getting them out. She saw he was looking at her and she repeated them loudly:—

"—of our grandson."

"Was that," Colonel Glynne persisted, "why you seem to have said several times that ill would come of it? Or had you some other reason?"

"Ill has come of it," she answered sombrely, and would say no more.

The colonel tried another approach.

"After you had made that remark, I believe you went straight upstairs to your room?"

"I did. I went straight to bed. I had overtired myself by coming down to dinner. When I got to my room I had a slight heart attack. It was not serious. Miss Longden wanted to send for the doctor, but I would not let her. He had left me some pills he told me to use if my heart seemed troublesome. I took one. It did me good and I went to bed. Sophy wished to read to me. She often does. She is a very good reader, with a very quiet, soothing voice. Last night I felt I would prefer to rest quietly, not even listening. Sophy sat by me till about ten. She was sewing. At ten o'clock or about then I told her to go to bed as I felt able to sleep. She went to her own room, next to mine, and got ready. Before actually going to bed she came back to see that I was comfortable and if I needed anything. She came in again during the night. I think it was a little before three. I heard a clock strike. I was restless and she heard me moving and came in to see if I was all right. She often does. I don't believe myself she heard anything. If she wakes in the night she often comes and peeps in. If she thinks I am asleep, she goes away again. If she thinks I am restless, she comes in. She is a conscientious little thing and considers herself entirely responsible for me. I suppose I am old enough to like being cosseted."

She paused, as if inviting comment, and Bobby thought that any one less likely than this grim, upright, resolute old woman either to require or to accept 'cosseting' he could hardly imagine. But then, perhaps, so contradictory is human nature, those were the very qualities that made the 'cosseting' welcome. Lady Wych continued:—

"Early this morning I heard the commotion in the house. I asked Sophy to find out what was happening. She came back and told me. I trust that is a sufficiently complete history of the night to satisfy you." The irony in her tone was evident. As evidently Colonel Glynne didn't like it. She added in conclusion:— "Is there anything further you think I can tell you?"

"There are just one or two other points I would like to mention," Colonel Glynne said. "It seems to have been generally understood that Mr. Ralph Hoyle was insisting on having a talk with his great-uncle last night. I take it you knew that too?" Lady Wych made a slight movement of assent. The colonel went on:— "Did you expect a quarrel?"

"Hardly a quarrel. I knew Ralph meant to protest against our recognition of our grandson. I think Ralph meant to say that he intended to take legal action against us."

"Did Earl Wych resent that?"

"Yes."

"Did he intend to try to stop Ralph?"

"I think he meant to try. I don't expect he would have succeeded. Both of them as pig-headed as most men, more so."

"There seems no doubt," the colonel went on, "that a quarrel did take place. There is clear evidence. The expression of one witness is 'they were shouting at each other something awful'. Indeed Ralph admits as much. He admits saying, in fact he was overheard, he appears to have shouted it at the top of his voice, that he would stop his uncle 'somehow, anyhow'. Lord Wych seems to have retorted by telling him to get out and stay out. In fact a good deal of violent language appears to have been used on both sides."

"Very likely," agreed Lady Wych. "Both of them had the usual vile Hoyle temper. It doesn't last, but it flares up in a minute. I daresay Ralph felt ill used. My husband was not used to opposition. He always reminded me of the man in the Bible—the man who said 'go' or 'come' and it was so. I expect he felt Ralph ought to be prepared to believe that the honour of the family was safe in the hands of the head of the family. I can quite believe they were both so busy shouting at each other that neither heard a word the other said."

"You are still not willing to suggest any reason why Miss Longden should have visited the library last night so late in the evening?"

"I know of none," the countess answered slowly. "I do not intend to guess. It wouldn't be fair. All I can say is that I had, and have, no reason, except what you tell me, to suppose she ever left her room—except to visit mine—or that she was ever anywhere near the library. I don't know anything about this finger-print business of yours," she added, "but even if it's as infallible as they say, even infallibility can be misunderstood and misinterpreted."

"There is another point I must ask about," the colonel said. "Do you know if Miss Longden, who is a very attractive girl, had any reason to complain of the conduct of any one here?"

Lady Wych looked for once a little disconcerted.

"I suppose you have been listening to gossip," she said presently.

"Well, we call it information received," Colonel Glynne answered. "Had it any foundation?"

"I don't know. Perhaps," the countess admitted though still hesitatingly. "She never said anything to me, and I didn't ask her. She is a very steady, sensible, trustworthy child. I have complete confidence in her. There are girls who, without meaning anything much, do invite men to take liberties with them. Flirting and fooling. Sophy is one of the other sort, the self-respecting kind. I remember I told her once that if she wasn't quite happy or comfortable here, or if anything was annoying her, she was to tell me. I think she would have done so. I think she trusts me. I am fond of the child and I hope she is of me, too."

"There is nothing more you can tell us?"

"No. I don't know that I should if I could. I can't, but it's her business. If you want to know more you must ask her. I doubt if she will be much inclined to say anything." The colonel was of much the same opinion, but he made no comment. Changing the subject, he said:—

"I haven't had time to consult the firearms register yet, but I think I remember one of the licences Earl Wych held was for an automatic pistol. We've found in one of the drawers here an empty case that seems to have held a point three-two Colt self-loader, but there's no trace of the pistol itself. Can you tell us anything about it?"

The countess shook her head.

"I believe he had a pistol of some sort. We are insured, but some of the heirlooms would be quite irreplaceable. There's the old silver salt, for instance, said to be a gift from Queen Elizabeth, and things like that. Burglars would probably melt them down. My husband got the pistol some years ago when there was an epidemic of burglaries in the neighbourhood. After that died down, I expect he forgot all about it. I never remember seeing it recently or hearing him speak of it for that matter."

Bobby moved over and murmured something in his chief's ear. The two men talked together in undertones. Lady Wych was beginning to look very tired. The fierce vigour, the dominating air she had shown when she first entered the room had gradually left her. Now she was looking old and feeble. Bobby indeed was growing afraid she might collapse under the strain of so much questioning, bravely as she was bearing up. She had rallied to her aid all the powers, or more, that age had left her, but now they were nearly exhausted. The colonel nodded in agreement to the suggestion Bobby had been making and said to her:—

"Just one more question. You are convinced that the man calling himself Bertram Hoyle is in fact Bertram Hoyle, and your grandson, and therefore now succeeds to the title and estates?"

Lady Wych rose to her feet as if with a sudden flash of energy and resolve.

"My husband publicly acknowledged him," she said loudly and clearly.

When she had spoken she swayed and would have fallen had not Bobby jumped forward in time to support her. She leaned heavily on his arm and then seemed to recover to some degree.

"I am sorry, I am afraid I must go back upstairs," she said.

The colonel, alarmed by her looks, rang the bell and then hurried to open the door for her. She went through leaning on Bobby's arm. One of the maids appeared in answer to the colonel's ring. She was sent to find Sophy. Lady Wych was still leaning on Bobby's arm. She was looking better now, the heart attack that had threatened having apparently passed off. She said to him:—

"Are you still thinking? I wonder what you are thinking?"

"I am thinking," he answered, "that when people do not tell us the whole truth, then it becomes very difficult for us to discover any of the truth."

"That remark approaches the insolent," she said haughtily.

"A police investigation is not bounded by the laws of etiquette," he told her quietly, "and police are not respecters of persons. Or at least, if they are, they fail in their duty. May I ask you another question? A personal one. I suggested it to Colonel Glynne. He did not wish to put it to you officially, but he said I might ask it if I liked."

"What is it?"

"Why you do not wish to tell us whom you suspect of murdering Earl Wych?"

"I suspect no one," she said harshly.

"I will put it another way," he told her. "Whom do you suspect we may suspect?"

"That is another question," she said looking at him doubtfully. "I do not like your questions, young man."

"So you do not answer it. No answer is in itself sometimes an answer. I wonder if you are willing that your husband's murderer should remain unpunished?"

"Young man," she answered again, "when you come to my age you will understand how little punishment matters."

"Yet," Bobby said, "if breaches of the law go unpunished the law will break down, and chaos will result."

She was looking at him now with a certain grim amusement.

"You are an odd policeman," she said. "Do you want to discuss the ethics of punishment? I have heard two Oxford professors arguing about that. They came to no agreement, but they both got very cross, and I am sure would have liked to punish each other with a week's bread and water. A severe punishment, too," she added thoughtfully, "for Oxford professors—especially the water."

"I have always thought of punishment as society's act of self-defence—-justifiable homicide, so to say," Bobby answered. "No doubt a better society would find a better means of defending itself. Will you tell me now whom you suspect?"

"No," she answered.

They had reached the hall. Sophy was running down the stairs towards them. She had only just received the housemaid's message. Bobby and Lady Wych waited at the foot of the stairs, by the portrait of that ancestress of earlier days of whom the tale was told that she had sacrificed her son to the honour of the family. Lady Wych saw that Bobby was looking at it. She said:—

"Well? what are you thinking now?"

"That the honour of the Hoyle family," he answered slowly, "would seem to demand many sacrifices."

"You think too much," she told him frowningly, and then Sophy came up.

To her Bobby relinquished the care of the countess and went back to join Colonel Glynne, whom he found looking very worried and disturbed.

"Well," he asked as Bobby re-entered the room, "what do you make of all that?"

"For one thing," Bobby answered, "that she knows a good deal more than she told us."

"I thought that, too," agreed the colonel. "But what can we do? An old woman like that—one moment all fire and energy. The next on the point of collapse. Impossible to press her too far. Owen."

"Sir?"

"You don't think she can be guilty herself? Jealousy or something like that, if she knew the old man had been trying to fool about with this Longden girl."

"It might be," Bobby said thoughtfully. "To save her honour, the honour of the family, his honour perhaps."

"She's a remarkable old woman," muttered the colonel discontentedly, as if he felt it unfair he should have to do with remarkable old women. "She had me quite scared at times. She would go through with anything. What can she be holding back?"

"I am sure of one thing," Bobby answered. "There is certainly something odd about Bertram Hoyle. Yet she still wants to acknowledge him. So she must be willing to see him take the title and estates."

"Difficult to understand," the colonel agreed. "If he is an impostor, what possible reason can there be for acknowledging him? or for the countess being still willing to accept him? One might suspect blackmail, only with Earl Wych—well, you can't take that idea seriously." Bobby was less sure. The life of any man may hold strange secrets. His imagination played with various ideas. An early bigamous marriage perhaps somewhere in the family that made all acknowledged issue illegitimate. But what was the use of guessing? The colonel interrupted his thoughts by saying abruptly:—

"We'll have him in next. Thank goodness we needn't handle him so tenderly. He isn't a girl and can't start crying, and he isn't an old woman and can't collapse on our hands."

"No, sir," Bobby agreed, "but he can lie. He may prove good at the job."

They had to wait for a few minutes while the message reached Bertram. The barking of dogs outside attracted Bobby's attention. He moved to the window to see what was exciting them. Anne was walking across the lawn below the terrace. She was accompanied by two or three dogs. She was hurrying, almost running. The dogs were leaping and barking at her side, evidently demanding that she should stop and play with them. Bobby had only a passing glimpse, but he noticed that the coats of the dogs were wet. She had apparently been giving them a swim in the ornamental pond that was one of the features of the castle grounds, Bobby watched thoughtfully as they disappeared from view. The colonel said impatiently:— "What are you staring at?"

"Miss Anne Hoyle has been giving her dogs a swim," Bobby explained, "and stopped too soon for their liking."

"Well, never mind that," the colonel snapped. "We can't waste our time on trifles. What's worrying me is this automatic that belonged to Earl Wych. We've got to find it. We've got to."

"Yes, sir," agreed Bobby obediently.

"There's one thing it seems to show. You see it?"

"I can't think of anything special at the moment," Bobby confessed.

"Well, to my mind, if the earl's own pistol was used, then that means the murder was the result of a quarrel. It wasn't premeditated."

"Yes, sir," agreed Bobby. "I see that. Only until we find the pistol we've nothing to show it was the weapon actually used."

"No, I know, that's why we've got to find it somehow," declared the colonel. "It can't be far away."

Before Bobby could answer the door opened and Bertram came into the room and stood there in the doorway, looking at them sulkily.

CHAPTER XI
BERTRAM

Sulkily the man who, by the recent tragedy, succeeded to the ancient title of Wych, the castle with all its treasures accumulated through the centuries, lands that still stretched far around, came slowly forward. With his hands thrust deep into his pockets, his shoulders hunched, he stood there looking at them scowlingly, and Bobby thought:—

"He's angry. He's frightened. He's very frightened. Why?"

The stenographer was thinking:—

"Gabbler or mumbler?"

He soon knew, for Bertram burst into a torrent of angry complaint. They had asked him plenty of questions already. Why did they want to start again? He knew nothing about it. Nothing he could tell them. He had never left his room all the night. Slept all the time. He had heard nothing. Slept like a child. He wasn't going to answer any more questions without having a lawyer present. Clinton Wells was hanging about somewhere. He wouldn't say another word unless Clinton Wells were present.

"My lord," began Colonel Glynne formally, "if your lordship will permit me—"

But the young man interrupted him even more angrily.

"Don't lose any time, do you?" he snarled. "They all started 'my lording' me right away. Can't they wait till the old man's in his grave?"

"You succeed to the title immediately," the colonel told him, looking somewhat puzzled. "There is no interregnum."

"No—what's that?"

"I mean there is no interval," the colonel explained. "The moment the holder of a title dies, the next in succession takes it. You become Earl Wych automatically."

"Not," interrupted Bertram roughly, "not if that guy Ralph can stop me."

"He can, of course, challenge your claim," agreed the colonel, "but I suppose, as you satisfied the late earl of your identity, you will have no trouble in proving it. In any case, that has nothing to do with us. Not a police matter. We are only here to conduct an investigation into a murder. I take it for granted, since you were accepted by the late earl, that you are his grandson, and therefore the present earl. And I do hope you will just answer a few questions. There are one or two things we are not clear about, minor points. You see it's important we should know exactly every one's point of view and what every one thinks."

"Oh, all right, go ahead," the young man answered, and flung himself into a chair, looking now a little less sulky but still wary and uneasy.

Bobby was reflecting that he made no display of grief or even ordinary concern at his grandfather's shocking death. Perhaps not so very surprising after so long an absence. More surprising that he showed no excitement and even little interest in his inheritance. Yet surely it was no small thing to succeed to so ancient a title, such large possessions and responsibilities. Even if, in spite of the recognition accorded him by his grandparents, he were an impostor, one would have expected him to betray some exultation or satisfaction at the prospect of securing so glittering a prize. Yet he seemed merely sulky and worried.

"I believe," the colonel was saying now, "there was some sort of scuffle after dinner last night. Between you and Ralph Hoyle?"

"He got me when I wasn't ready," complained Bertram. "He's sore with me. He was sore with the old man. What about asking him a few questions? Clinton Wells says now he can go into court. Put in a petition or something. He couldn't before, because there wasn't anything to petition about. That's why."

The colonel blinked. He didn't quite follow. Bobby said:—

"You mean you think Ralph Hoyle murdered his uncle in order to bring matters to a head and allow your claim to be tested in court?"

"That's right," Bertram said. "That's why he did it. Or perhaps it was just they started scrapping, and that's the way it ended. Anyhow, he's got it fixed now so the old man can't testify. Only when he's hanged for it, that won't do him much good, will it?"

"There is no proof at present of the guilt of any one," the colonel said, a little stiffly. "I would like to mention another matter. I understand you said in the course of the scuffle with Ralph Hoyle that Miss Anne Hoyle possessed an automatic pistol?"

"That's right," Bertram agreed. "She showed it me. A colt automatic three-two. Knew how to use it, too. You could see that. Bossy that girl is. Bossy. Thinks she ought to run the show here, only she can't, because she's a girl, so she thinks she'll run it all the same, and every one else as well. Bossy," he repeated moodily.

"Did you ask her why she had it, or where she got it from?" the colonel asked.

"No. I don't ask her things," Bertram answered, sulky again. "She does all the asking necessary. And more. But she had that three-two automatic all right, handling it like she knew how." He stopped and stared. A new idea had evidently occurred to him.

"You mean you think it's her?" he said. "I wouldn't put it past her. She's tough."

"Good heavens," exclaimed the colonel, extremely startled by this unexpected suggestion. "Why on earth —well, why should she? I mean murder, her grandfather?"

"Well, that makes me earl right away, don't it?" Bertram replied slowly, "and then if she picks me up, then she's countess and runs the show and me too, she reckons. Bossy, she is, that girl. Bossy. I know it."

"My lord," began the colonel, profoundly shocked, for in his scheme of things, one did not suspect young ladies of the aristocracy of that sort of thing. Girls might to-day be a bit inclined to kick over the traces, but they did draw the line at shooting their grandfathers. At least he hoped so. "Really, really," he protested, while Bobby resumed his abstracted contemplation of the ceiling above his head.

"Well, why not?" asked Bertram, looking quite eager. "Old man was bumped off about half-past eleven. Well, she wasn't in her room at half-past eleven or thereabouts."

"Are you sure of that?" the colonel asked doubtfully.

"Dead sure. The door of her room was open. I wondered why. I had a peep. Just peeped in. She wasn't there. Where was she?"

"That will be inquired into," the colonel said stiffly. "She will be asked."

Bertram looked alarmed again.

"You won't let on it was me told you?" he asked earnestly.

"Nothing will be said that is not necessary," the colonel answered. "Your lordship may be asked to give evidence, of course. Apart from that, nothing will be said that is not essential to the inquiry."

"She'll have it in for me if she gets to know it was me told you," Bertram muttered, and did not look as if he found much comfort in the colonel's assurances.

Bobby and the colonel engaged in a whispered conversation. Bobby received permission to ask a few questions on his own account. To the surprise of Colonel Glynne, these began with a long speech of congratulation to Bertram on his succession to so splendid a position.

"A position the Earls Wych have always so worthily upheld," Bobby went on smoothly. "To-day, with war upon us, there will be so many opportunities. It was when Napoleon threatened invasion that the Earl Wych of that day raised the Wychwood Yeomanry. He was the first colonel. They are mechanised now, and they will be very proud to have once more in their ranks an Earl Wych. The late earl was honorary colonel, you know."

"Yes, but, steady on," interrupted Bertram, "what are you getting at? I'm no colonel. I don't know a thing about soldiering."

"It will have all the more effect," Bobby explained, "when you join up as a private."

"Me?"

"You'll just be in time," Bobby told him. "The Wychwood Yeomanry will be among the first to go to France. Light mechanized troops will be badly wanted for scouting and to head the advance."

"Kidding, aren't you?" Bertram asked doubtfully. "Earls and lords and such like aren't privates. Stands to reason."

"Every one is liable under the new Conscription Act," Bobby explained smoothly. "Dukes and dustmen, earls, lords, and tramps, all of us." He added slowly:— "An Earl Wych who wasn't the first to come forward—why, people would hardly believe he was an Earl Wych at all."

"Oh, that's it, is it?" Bertram growled.

Then he was silent. Bobby continued to watch him closely. Colonel Glynne was looking more and more puzzled. The stenographer seized the opportunity to sharpen his pencil. Bertram said presently:—

"If you're an earl and such like, you don't have to. There's ways. What's the good of being a lord if there isn't? I'm not yellow," he asserted, "but I don't believe in war. What's the sense of sitting about in a trench being shot at and nothing to eat either?" He added darkly:— "If you're so mighty keen, why don't you go yourself?"

"Reserved occupation," explained Bobby carelessly; "police, I mean. But not the peerage."

"Think you're O.K. then, don't you?" Bertram snarled, and Bobby smiled, as if he thought so, too, though indeed his resignation from the police had already been handed in and instantly rejected. Nor were his efforts at using influence to get permission to enlist meeting with much better success. For indeed this was at a time when the gate admitting to the army was as though guarded by a flaming sword turning all ways at once. Bobby went on:—

"By the way, I've just been wondering, it just struck me, talking of the peerage, I suppose. Can you tell me why it is always Earl Wych? I thought you were always Earl of Something—of Derby or Oxford or wherever it is."

"Saying it short, I suppose," Bertram answered. "I don't know. I never thought. Why?" he asked suspiciously.

"Oh, I just wondered," Bobby answered, and Bertram looked still more suspicious, as if scenting a trap but yet unable to imagine what it could be. "Of course, there isn't any place called Wych, is there? There's Midwych and Wychwood and so on, but not plain Wych. Not that it matters. One thing more. You are clear that Miss Anne Hoyle was not in her room about half-past eleven last night?"

"That's right."

"You are certain of that because you saw the door open and you looked into the room and you saw it was empty?"

"That's right."

"You say, too, in your statement that you and Miss Hoyle went up to bed about eleven. You went to your respective rooms. You went to bed at once. You slept all night. You heard no sound."

"That's right."

"You see," explained Bobby, "I don't quite understand how in that case you could be near Miss Hoyle's room at half-past eleven, see her door was open, look inside, and so on. I think her room is some distance from yours, in a different corridor in fact. It looks as if you did leave your room, doesn't it?"

Bertram looked very taken aback.

"I... I..." he stammered, then recovered himself. "Oh, I was just going to the bathroom," he said jauntily. "That's all. I forgot that, didn't think it worth mentioning, anyhow."

"I see," mused Bobby. "But that means you went rather a long way out of your way, doesn't it? There are three bathrooms on the first floor apparently. One near your room. One farther away. Only the third, which is the farthest away of all three, would take you near Miss Hoyle's room."

"Well, that's the one I went to, that's all."

"Can you tell us what reason you had for going to the bathroom farthest away?"

"There was someone in the other—door locked," Bertram explained.

"We must find out who that was," Bobby mused.

"Well, perhaps there wasn't any one, perhaps the door stuck," Bertram suggested. "It often does. See here. Are you trying to fix anything on me? or make out there was anything between Anne and me?"

"Why, no," Bobby answered. "How could there be if she wasn't there? Now, about that automatic. Miss Hoyle showed it you. Why was that? Any special reason?"

"No, of course not, why should there be, just showing it, that's all," Bertram declared, but not too confidently. "She can go to blazes any time she likes and take her automatic with her. Not my style. You won't go and tell her I said so?" he added, again with that touch of uneasiness in his manner.

He was once more assured that everything he said would be regarded as strictly confidential unless and until required for use as evidence. Nor, once again, did he seem too satisfied with the assurance. He explained once or twice that he thought Anne Hoyle a mighty fine girl.

"Though bossy," he added. "Knows she would be just It if she wasn't a girl, and means to be all the same."

"But that is impossible," Bobby pointed out. "There is no provision for female inheritance. The title would become extinct, I understand, and the estates go to very distant cousins in America."

"There's ways," Bertram answered, and looked sulky again. "There's ways. She's got her own idea."

Bobby tried to persuade him to be a little more explicit, but he only shook his head and grumbled again something about 'bossiness' and 'wanting to be It'. He complained, too, of having been led on to talk without Clinton Wells being present, and that it hadn't been fair, and therewith took himself off. Colonel Glynne hardly waited for the door to close behind him before exploding wrathfully.

"The fellow's a coward; a rank, shivering, shaking coward," he thundered. "Got cold feet at the mere idea of active service. You brought that out very well, Owen, but I ought to have stopped you, because, of course, it has nothing to do with the case."

"It might have, sir," Bobby suggested.

"You mean he can't be the murderer because he hasn't the guts?" asked the colonel. "Well, I don't know. Doesn't take much courage to shoot an unsuspecting old man, and murder is a cowardly game." He paused and looked puzzled. "Do you think he can be our man?" he asked. "What could be his motive? His grandfather accepted him, recognized him. So did the countess."

"It might be to make sure recognition wasn't withdrawn," Bobby suggested thoughtfully.

The colonel gave a little gasp, stared, rubbed his head. It was a new idea to him, for he had supposed the recognition given to Bertram to be necessarily final.

"Oh, well," he said, and repeated, "Oh, well." Then he said:—
"That would be a first-class motive, of course, but there is nothing to show it was likely, is there?"

"No, sir," Bobby agreed. "Except that all this has happened since Bertram's return, and it seems to me certain that there is something very queer about the whole business. Recognition by the old people seems conclusive, but Ralph Hoyle doesn't accept it."

"Oh, well," interrupted the colonel, "that's natural. Natural form his disappointment would take. Ralph's a fighter. He won't give up easily."

"I don't understand," Bobby went on, "the man's own attitude. He is very uneasy and disturbed. Is that because he is guilty? But a man who could carry out such a crime as the murder of Earl Wych you would expect to have better control of his nerves."

"He is scared of Miss Anne, for one thing," observed Colonel Glynne with a faint smile. "She's certainly a young woman who knows her own mind. I'm not surprised he thinks her bossy. But then she is engaged to Ralph. I suppose if this fellow is really an impostor he may be afraid she'll dig out the truth!"

"I didn't think it was that was worrying him," Bobby answered. "He gave me the idea of not being too sure of himself, and not very happy at the idea of facing the responsibilities of being the new Earl Wych. It involves a good deal. One would almost think he doesn't like the idea of being so much in the limelight."

"That would mean an impostor who is afraid of his own success," the colonel pointed out.

"Yes, sir. I know it sounds rather absurd put like that," agreed Bobby. "Why start a swindle if you are afraid of going through with it? It might be he didn't realise before what a prominent position an Earl Wych is expected to take in affairs. Possibly he thought it was just a question of getting hold of a big bank balance and drawing cheques. And now he finds there is more to being Earl Wych than that."

"Good God, so I should think," the colonel exploded. "But that's all speculation. We haven't got to decide anything of that sort. Our job is to see that the murderer is brought to justice. Don't you think our questioning was rather straying from the point?"

"Well, sir, I was trying to get the background," Bobby answered meekly. "Backgrounds are important. Like the screen at cricket. You can't judge the ball unless you can see the bowler's arm."

"Don't admit that," grunted the colonel. "It's not the bowler's arm, it's the last lap home of the ball you want to watch. You brought out one thing of importance. Apparently both Miss Hoyle and this fellow—Earl Wych now, if he is Earl Wych—were out of their rooms at the relevant times. Where was Miss Hoyle? Why?

Now you come to think of it, he came pretty near to accusing her, didn't he?"

"He could hardly have made it much plainer," agreed Bobby drily.

"It seemed so absurd, I hardly took it in," the colonel admitted. "A mass of contradictions," he complained impatiently. "No one behaving sensibly or consistently. Why was he hanging round her room? There can't be anything between them, can there? I can't believe that possible. She's engaged to Ralph, has been since they were kiddies. It all seems such a muddle. What is Anne doing with a pistol? If it's true she had one. If she had, can it be the one that seems to be missing from the case in the table drawer here?"

"There are two pistols we've heard of, we must trace," Bobby said. "Earl Wych's pistol, which is missing. And the Wych estate pistol, which, according to Ralph Hoyle, is locked up in the estate office safe. Even if it is there now, that doesn't prove it wasn't used last night. When we do know which weapon was used, we shall be a good deal further forward."

"We had better have in Anne Hoyle next," the colonel said, but not as if he looked forward to the interview with any very great pleasure. "A formidable young woman," he said. "I'm a bit scared of her myself, but not like this Bertram fellow. I can't quite see why he should go all shivery when he mentions her."

"He thinks," said Bobby with a grim smile, "that she means to marry him."

CHAPTER XII
ANNE

Before Colonel Glynne could make any comment on this remark, which had surprised him greatly and of which he strongly disapproved, the door opened and Anne came in. She gave them a quick glance, sat down, and said briskly:—

"I may as well tell you at once that if you think you are going to treat me like poor little Sophy, you're very much mistaken."

"I am not aware—" began the colonel stiffly, but Anne cut him short.

"It won't be the very least bit of good trying to bully me," she announced.

"We have not the least intention—" the colonel tried again, and still more stiffly, and again Anne cut him short.

"The poor kid's so scared," she said, "she can't get a word out. Just sits and soaks into her handkerchief."

"If you are suggesting—"

"I'm not like that," Anne told him. "You won't reduce me to a state of speechless tears."

"Madam—" began the colonel, and his voice was certainly both loud and stern.

"It's no good shouting at me," declared Anne even more sternly if less loudly. "If you can't behave with ordinary decency, you can't. But you won't frighten me by shouting."

"Miss Hoyle—"

"One thing," Anne explained carefully, "to bully a poor little bit of a thing like Sophy who wouldn't dare say 'Boo' to a goose. I think you'll find I'm different."

"Will you be so good as to allow me to say one word?" asked the colonel pronouncing each separate syllable with an almost awful restraint.

"You may say as many as you like," answered Anne. "That's what I'm here for, isn't it? just to listen to what you want to say."

"I'm glad to hear it," said the colonel with an emphasis Anne failed to notice.

"I'm only telling you it's no good trying to bully me," she explained once more. "I'm not Sophy, poor little wretch. Grandmother's very annoyed. She may snap Sophy's head off herself, but she doesn't like other people doing it. Her privilege. She's talking about going to see the Home Secretary."

Colonel Glynne snorted. Home Secretaries may be Home Secretaries but Chief Constables are Chief Constables, and fully prepared to talk with Home Secretaries in the gate or elsewhere at any moment required. Anne, who knew little of the powers and the status and the dignity of the chief constable, who indeed has no superior save God and the king, went on in a milder tone:—

"I only wanted to let you know I'm not Sophy. I expect she was easy. I'm not. I'm waiting," she added, adopting a listening attitude with her hands clasped before her and her head inclined to one side, as though tendering an attentive ear. "And, oh, would you mind being as quick as you can, please. I've no doubt you have lots of time, but there are a great many things to be seen to. Grandmother is hardly fit to attend to them, and I have to do my best by myself. There's no one else. Even Sophy's too upset to be much good."

"Please try to understand," said the colonel, now very red in the face, for that hint of an appeal to the Home Secretary had touched him to the quick—Home Secretaries, indeed! "Please understand that we don't bully any one, and certainly not Miss Longden. She saw fit to refuse to answer my questions—"

"I know," Anne interrupted again. "That's what I was saying. You've got the poor kid into such a state that she can't get a word out. She just sits there and uses up a week's supply of handkerchiefs every two minutes. I expect you think that a great triumph."

"We don't," roared the colonel.

"Well, then, why did you?" demanded Anne.

"We didn't," protested the colonel, though by no means sure what it was he hadn't.

Anne raised her eyebrows delicately.

"Indeed," she said, and oh, how insultingly she managed to utter that simple word. "Indeed. Well, both grandmother and I have seen her, you know. We are both inclined to believe our own eyes."

"I am only trying to explain—"

"Exactly, and I am trying to explain that I do not find your explanations convincing. If that is all you have to say to me, perhaps I may as well go and get on with things. There is a great deal to attend to."

So far Anne had conducted the conversation brilliantly. She had reduced the colonel to a state of incoherent rage, all the more incoherent for being also suppressed. But this last remark of Anne's was a mistake. As so many do in great things and in small, when they feel they are being successful, she overplayed her hand. True, the colonel was almost on the point of letting her go, but the attempt to evade further questioning was just a little too obvious, and now Bobby interposed.

"Possibly," he said, "as Miss Hoyle seems to wish to make such a point of believing that you, sir, are responsible for Miss Longden's tears, which I expect have a different cause, you would allow me to ask a few questions. Miss Hoyle will, I am sure, not think it necessary to warn me so continuously that I need not try to bully her."

Anne turned to look at Bobby, whom hitherto she had been inclined to regard as just another and quite uninteresting piece of furniture. Her expression became wary.

She did not quite know what to make of the stolid, matter-of-fact way in which he was regarding her. A very ordinary young man to all appearance, she thought, and yet somehow with an odd suggestion that there was something extraordinary in his very ordinariness. Was it that he possessed ordinary qualities to an extraordinary degree?

"Never been so bullied in all my life if it comes to that," Colonel Glynne was muttering under his breath, and then added aloud to Bobby: "All right. Carry on."

"Suppose," Bobby suggested to Anne, "that we forget about Miss Longden. Any complaint she may wish to make will of course receive careful attention. Any explanation she may require will be most readily furnished. But that is not the question for the moment."

"I was only warning you that you couldn't bully me," Anne repeated.

"I am sure of it," Bobby answered.

They looked at each other for a moment in silence, two adversaries measuring each the other's strength. Bobby noted the closely-set mouth, the firm chin, the hard and resolute eyes, the general expression of a determined will that seemed to show so clearly in feature and expression. On Anne's side she noticed how steadily and how searchingly those clear eyes of his rested on hers. Penetrating eyes, that looked as though they could smile very readily, but now had in them no hint of a smile, showing only indeed a stern and settled resolution nothing would ever shake or change. Bobby went on slowly:—

"So we will consider ourselves warned, shall we? Now, we have been looking again at the statement you made earlier to-day and you mention that you went to your room about eleven o'clock last night and that you did not leave it again till this morning."

"Well?"

"We have now received," Bobby explained, "another statement according to which the door of your room was open about half-past eleven and the room itself was seen to be unoccupied."

"Well, it wasn't."

"Apparently a witness is prepared to swear it was. You realize, of course, that such a conflict of evidence bothers us a lot, and we have to consider it. Especially as the murder almost certainly took place about then."

"I suppose it's Bertram told you that, isn't it?" Anne remarked.

"Why should you think so?"

"Because he was sneaking round. I saw him. I don't think any one else was."

"If you saw him and he says you weren't in your room...?"

"Where was I? Well, if you want to know—behind the window curtains."

"A little unusual," murmured Bobby, while the colonel was beginning to look very worried, for murders were within his experience, but young ladies hiding behind bedroom curtains were altogether outside it. A murder, he felt, might happen anywhere, but young ladies behind curtains, and open bedroom doors were not to be expected in houses of the standing of Castle Wych.

He definitely disapproved.

He also disapproved of the fact that Bobby seemed quite unperturbed and Anne quite undisturbed. Anne had not answered Bobby's comment and so Bobby murmured again:—

"I wonder if you would mind explaining a little further."

"I suppose you'll keep it to yourselves," Anne said. "Not that I mind. Only once gossip gets started! Well, Bertram's been trying rather hard to make love to me. I'm not particularly flattered. I should imagine he tries to make love to every one he comes near. He's that sort. He doesn't mean marriage, though. He's definitely not that sort. Thinks marriage would cramp his style, I suppose. It would," said Anne with a sudden involuntary tightening of her lips that somehow made her look twice as formidable. "The way he turned up so suddenly—the long lost heir and all that sort of thing—was rather intriguing. I expect I showed I was interested and he got wrong ideas. I found him hanging about near my room once or twice. Well, I didn't like it. That sort of thing soon sets the servants talking. I didn't say anything. He could always make some excuse. He had been using the backstairs as a short cut from the library or the billiard room or the garden. We all do sometimes. If you do, you come along the passage past my room. If I had said anything I should only have looked a fool. Last night he was quite pressing when we were in the small drawing-room after dinner. He had had a good deal to drink, had some more to soothe his feelings after the upset with Ralph you've heard about. So when I went up to bed, I left my door partly open and I hid behind the window curtains. I had a jug of cold water. I meant to throw it over him if he thought the open door was an invitation and came in. I thought a little cold water would cool his enthusiasm without making too much fuss. I don't think," said Anne reflectively "that any man would be able to make love effectively when he was sopping wet. Do you?"

"I should hardly think so," agreed Bobby gravely, and the colonel looked more disapproving than ever.

This sort of thing, he was telling himself, was definitely not the sort of thing one wished to associate with the stately homes of England.

"But the best laid plans of mice and men—you know," Anne continued with a slight air of disappointment. "He only just poked his head round the door, took a good look, and went off. I never expected he would be so backward. I thought he would come in and wait for me to return. That's all."

The colonel was only just able to stop himself from saying severely:— "Quite enough, too." Bobby seemed to be deep in thought. He said:—

"That seems to explain the discrepancy in the evidence. Thank you very much. You have no idea what he did after that?"

"Went to bed, I suppose," Anne answered promptly, and then paused and for once looked a little uneasy, even frightened. "You don't mean," she said, "you think he went down the backstairs to the library and killed grandfather?"

"It is a part of police routine to consider all possibilities, however unlikely," Bobby explained. "I take it it is a fact that from outside your door any one could run down those backstairs to the library and back very quickly and that, at that time of night, no one would be likely to see or hear?"

"Yes, I suppose so," Anne agreed, and there was still that frightened look in her eyes where fear so seldom showed. "I suppose you are thinking I could have, too?" Then when Bobby did not answer she said rather loudly:—- "Well, I didn't."

Bobby made no comment. The colonel was looking more and more uncomfortable. He felt it simply couldn't be, and yet—certainly the evidence proved a possibility. Fortunately a possibility was not even a probability, much less a certainty. Bobby did not much wish to pursue this question of the possibility of Anne's guilt, for which at present there was certainly no hint even of direct evidence, and bringing the questioning back to Bertram, he said:—

"It is clear Bertram could have done just that, but do you think he did?"

"No," she answered instantly, "he hasn't it in him."

"Difficult to say what is in any of us," Bobby remarked. "Can you suggest any reasonable motive for his doing such a thing?"

She did not answer for a little. She was looking at him steadily, more warily than ever, he thought. She said presently:—

"You could ask him. You know as much as I do."

"Unfortunately, we don't," Bobby told her. "We know very little indeed of what you might call the background. And background is very important. There may be all sorts of things, of motives, we have no idea of, but that if we did know, might put us on the right track. We are not even sure how seriously or with what chance of success, Mr. Ralph Hoyle means to dispute Mr. Bertram's claim."

"Grandfather accepted Bertram," Anne reminded them. "Isn't that conclusive? Why should grandfather—grandmother, too—if it isn't true? Ralph says he's an impostor. Ralph doesn't say why, he just says it. Ralph is like that. If he says a thing he thinks it's all settled. I suppose it's only natural he should be upset. He was the heir and now he's nobody—at least unless Bertram dies unmarried without children. He's still the heir—only heir presumptive, not heir apparent as he thought he was. Perhaps," she added angrily, "you had better tell Bertram to be careful now, had you?"

"Good God," said the colonel, really startled by this unexpected suggestion which almost seemed as if it were meant to hint at Ralph's guilt, but Bobby ignored it and went on:—

"There is another piece of information we have received. I expect you know all police work depends on what we call 'information received'. We understand you are in possession of an automatic pistol?"

"Did Bertram tell you that, too?" she asked.

"I think a remark was made last night at dinner before every one there at the time, wasn't it?"

"Well, if it was, that doesn't make it true, does it?"

"Is it true?"

"No, it isn't."

"Can you suggest any reason why he should say such a thing?"

"You do want to dig it all up, don't you?" she asked resentfully. "If you must know, he was being a bit of a nuisance. I told you I found him prowling about near my room once or twice. Another time I met him in the wood.

I was coming back from the village. I don't much think it was an accident. His meeting me, I mean. I can look after myself. But I didn't want a fuss. It would have been all over everywhere in no time. I mean, if we had started scuffling. So when he began to get a little too pressing, I opened my handbag and let him see a glint of metal. My cigarette case, really, but I told him it was grandfather's automatic I had borrowed. I don't know whether he believed it. I suppose now he did. Anyhow, he took the hint and began to talk about the weather or the scenery or something. Stopped being troublesome. That's all."

"I see," Bobby said. "That, of course, is a very satisfactory explanation," and when he said that she shot him a look from under lowered eyelids that was more wary, more doubtful than ever. "By the way, do you understand firearms? would you have any idea of how to use an automatic?"

"Yes," she answered after a pause, and very much as if she would have liked to say 'No' instead, had she dared, and had she not been aware her acquaintance with the use of such weapons was well known. "What about it?" she asked, defiantly this time.

"My dear young lady," Bobby protested in his mildest voice, "we are merely collecting and collating facts. I expect you know that the pistol you were speaking of, your grandfather's automatic, that is, seems to have disappeared. At any rate, it is not in the case in the drawer of this table where apparently it was kept, and up to the present we haven't been able to find it anywhere else."

"I don't know anything about it," she answered briefly.

"One last question," Bobby said, "and then we shan't need to worry you any more. You heard nothing during the night, after you went to your room, that is?"

"No."

"There is nothing you can suggest, nothing you can think of or have heard that could be of any assistance to us in bringing your grandfather's murderer to justice?"

"No. Of course, I've heard what every one is saying about Ralph."

"What is that?"

"You know perfectly well. If you don't, I shan't tell you."

"You mean that Ralph and his great-uncle quarrelled violently last night?"

"Yes."

"It seems clear that Ralph left here about half-past ten, when Earl Wych was certainly still alive."

"What's the good of pretending you don't know he could have come back? Every one knows it. Every one knows he was furious at grandfather's accepting Bertram. Ralph said it was a conspiracy. He said he wasn't going to be swindled out of his rights. He said grandfather must be senile, in his dotage. He said softening of the brain must have set in. That made grandfather pretty angry. He just hated being thought too old."

"Do you think he was? In his dotage, I mean?"

"I never saw any sign of it," Anne answered. "No one ever suggested such a thing before. Not that I ever heard of."

"I think we may take that as established," Bobby agreed. "I think we may agree it is plain that Earl Wych was in full possession of all his mental faculties. The doctors tell us, too, he was in unusually good physical condition. He would probably have lived another ten years or even longer. It's just possible that was the reason for the murder."

He waited to see if Anne would make any comment on this. When she remained silent, he said:—

"Do you think it likely that Ralph Hoyle is guilty?" She stared at him a long time in silence after he had said this, yet almost as though she were not even conscious of his presence but only of her own thoughts. After a long interval, and, again it was almost as if she were speaking to herself, having forgotten others were there, she said:— "I do not know. I am not sure. Perhaps he is."

Bobby made no comment, but the colonel interposed sharply.

"You and Ralph are engaged, aren't you?" he asked.

"Would that make any difference?" she countered. "Engaged or not, does it affect facts?" Then she said:— "Besides, we aren't."

"Not engaged?"

"No." She held out her left hand. There was no ring on it. She said: "He's been running after that little chit of a Sophy a little bit too much for my liking."

Both Bobby and the colonel received this statement in silence. They did not quite know what to make of it. But they found it interesting.

"It's not her," Anne went on presently. "She's a pretty little thing. I'm quite fond of her. There's not much in her, but she's rather sweet, and she does try to be nice. I daresay she doesn't realize about Ralph. He wouldn't admit it, either. But you soon know it when a man begins to get interested in someone else." She rose briskly to her feet. "You feel a bit snubbed," she said. "I suppose it's silly. Of course, our engagement was always just a family affair, taken for granted." She was silent for a moment and then said resentfully:—"You're clever. You've made me tell you things I never meant to tell any one. I think I'll go if I may."

Bobby got up to open the door for her. She went through without noticing him. Bobby came back to his place. He said:—

"I would give quite a lot to know if we are clever."

"Eh?" said the colonel.

"I mean," Bobby explained, "whether we did make her tell something she had meant to keep to herself, or whether it was something she had been planning to tell us all the time."

"Um!" said the colonel. Then he said:— "What do you think of her?"

"I don't know," answered Bobby.

"Do you think she's our man?"

Bobby was too engrossed with his own thoughts even to notice this fine confusion of sexes. He said absently:— "It might be."

"Do you think she means to marry this claimant chap?"

"I think that much is clear," Bobby answered, and with a faint grin added:—"Anyhow, I'm sure he thinks so. I wonder if it's true that Ralph is attracted by Miss Longden. Or if Miss Anne has invented that for an excuse to break off the engagement? If it is true, can Miss Anne have shot her grandfather so that Bertram could succeed at once and then she could marry him and so become Ralph's boss and make things hot for him?"

"Roundabout sort of idea," the colonel objected.

"It might attract," Bobby said. "I mean a jilted woman might recover her self-respect by getting to be the boss of the man who let her down. It's only an idea, of course."

They were still talking when there came a message from Mr. Clinton Wells to say that he had various appointments and other business to attend to; and if the chief constable wished to question him, could that be done at once, or, alternatively, could he be allowed to go?

CHAPTER XIII
CLINTON WELLS

Clinton Wells, who had been told that Colonel Glynne would be most happy to see him without further delay, came briskly into the room.

"I don't want to bustle you," he said, "and of course I'm entirely in your hands, but if you could see your way to let me get off, it would be a tremendous convenience."

The colonel, favourably impressed, relieved to think that this time he was safe from any sharp, feminine tongue, waved him amiably to a chair.

"I don't suppose there's really very much you can tell us," he explained expansively, so happy was he to think that this time he would be talking as man to man, and not as mere man to an indignant old lady or to a young one with an exceedingly sharp tongue. "You were at the A.R.P. meeting last night, I think, but you didn't stay to dinner here, did you?"

"No," admitted Clinton Wells, grinning a little, "I invented a business appointment. Damaging admission, I'm afraid, when I've just told you the same story. But this time it's true. I have appointments with two clients. One of them doesn't matter much, but the other's important—or thinks he is. Last night I wanted to dodge the dinner."

"Had you any special reason?"

Clinton rubbed his nose and looked doubtful.

"Well, I don't know," he said finally; "possibly it's violating professional confidence as between client and solicitor, but the fact is Ralph and I had a bit of a row, and I felt we were better out of each other's way for the time. You know I have resigned from my firm in order to act for him in this succession business?"

The colonel nodded.

"So I understand," he said. "It is—er—a big thing for you to do, a big risk. I daresay most people would think it showed a good deal of courage, chivalry, too, to take up such a forlorn hope."

Clinton Wells made a deprecating gesture.

"Oh, I don't want to appear too much of a knight errant," he protested. "Of course, no one wants to see a gross injustice done merely to satisfy an old man's senile vanity. All the same, I admit I'm quite aware that if I can establish Ralph's claim, I expect I shall be sure of the Wych estate business for the duration—and my partnership back again in a hurry and on my own terms, too. The Blacklocks would be on their knees to get me to join them again."

"But if the case goes against your client?"

"Well, I daresay I shall have to whistle for my costs," Clinton admitted. "And my partnership would be up the spout for good. They wouldn't touch me with a barge pole. No one in Midwych would. I should have to make a fresh start somewhere else. Still, I'm facing that. You've got to risk something, and I hope I should have got my name known as a good fighter, so I might still expect a few clients. After all, one doesn't like to see a good, decent sort of chap like Ralph done out of his rights."

"Does you much credit, I'm sure, if you don't mind my saying so," said the colonel in a slightly embarrassed voice, and Clinton made a slightly embarrassed bow in acknowledgment. The colonel went on:— "I suppose the— er—row you spoke of with Ralph wasn't very serious?"

"Oh, no. He has the devil of a temper, you know. Awfully good chap, but he'll flare up in a minute. You think he is going to throw you out of the window or something, and then it's all over. I just thought I would keep out of his way for the time. Besides, I was feeling a bit worked up myself. I still feel he ought to have paid more attention to my advice. Why have a solicitor if you won't listen to him? My view was that it was both useless and unwise for Ralph to insist on having a 'show down', as he called it, with his great-uncle."

"That was what your—er—difference of opinion was about?"

"Yes. Ralph insisted on having his 'show down' with the old man. Trying to get the truth out of him, he said. I knew very well what the result of that would be. Both of them with tempers like barrels of gunpowder. I didn't want the breach between them to be final—or made worse by a lot of heated language. I like to be on the best of terms with the other side as long as possible. One of the first things I was taught. Good advice, too, I've found. I expect you've heard the result of Ralph's having his 'show down' was a blazing row, just as I expected. You know about that?"

"A good deal of shouting seems to have been heard," the colonel admitted. "We've been told about it by one or two different people."

"I expect they went for each other hammer and tongs," said Clinton with a half smile. "Said a lot of things neither of them meant most likely. But as I told Ralph by way of rubbing it in, it's just as well Martin saw him off the premises an hour or two before the murder."

"Quite so," murmured the colonel, "quite so. Yes. I am right in supposing that you consider this man, Bertram, to be an impostor?"

"Oh, yes. I thought so from the first."

"Do you mind telling us why? Telling us all you know about it, in fact. It may be a very considerable help. In theory, of course, it's no business of ours. Matter for the civil courts. But murder is very much our business, and anything that would enable us to understand the situation here better might be a very great help."

"I see that," agreed Clinton thoughtfully. "Of course, you have a right to every help any one can give you— especially a solicitor. A solicitor is an officer of justice, too. I don't know if you've heard that the original Bertram got himself into serious trouble at Oxford. I don't know the details, I never bothered to try to find out. But I know he had to leave the country in a hurry, and that it was bad enough for there to be some danger of a criminal prosecution. Most likely, if he had been a poor boy, he would have gone to Borstal. But grandsons of peers don't go to Borstal, and young Bertram went to America instead. It's a good distance, and not the first time a British aristocratic family has been grateful that when Columbus discovered America he discovered it such a long way away. You understand Bertram wasn't the heir then. In the line of succession, of course, but not the direct heir. There were two or three lives between him and the title. But they all fell in, accident and illness and so on. This claimant fellow turned up at my office about three weeks ago. He didn't know that owing to various deaths he had become next heir. At least he said he didn't. What he wanted to know, he told me, was whether it would be safe for him to appear again, and also what sort of reception he was likely to get from his grandparents. At first, you understand, I accepted him at face value. Took him for granted. It was unexpected, of course, and rather startling, and even then I felt it was hard luck on Ralph. When I told the chap that owing to various deaths he was the heir he was either very surprised indeed, or else he is a jolly good actor. But I began to have my doubts. I can't say exactly why. Somehow, it didn't seem right. Or that's what I thought. But then I thought that might be because he had been knocking about America so long. Of course, I had no right to ask him questions. Not my business. I rang up and told the late earl. He wasn't impressed. He didn't say anything when I dropped a sort of careful hint that personally I wasn't quite happy about it. But he said he would see the chap. So I brought him along. I admit he puzzled me. He seemed to know a lot. He recognized places and he knew names. But there were holes. There were things I felt he ought to know he didn't seem even to have heard of. I was inclined to think he knew the district, knew a good deal about the Hoyle family, probably had met the genuine Bertram in America—did I tell you he showed me letters and papers the genuine Bertram would certainly have had?—and had somehow got hold of, stolen, perhaps, the proofs of identity he showed me. Bertram's death had been reported, you know, and it's not difficult, if you are on the spot, to get hold of a dead man's papers and so on. That's what I thought. That's what, I'm dead certain, the old earl thought at first. The fact that I can show letters written to John Smith doesn't necessarily prove that I am that particular John Smith. The old earl asked him one or two testing questions our man couldn't answer. I was fully prepared to see him kicked out—and to help for that matter—when he asked for a private interview. Said he could convince the old earl in two minutes. Well, it didn't take two minutes. It took half an hour or so. Martin came to ask me to go back to the library to join them. I was completely and utterly bowled over, flabbergasted, when the old earl said quite calmly that he had now recognized his grandson. So, he said, had the countess. I could hardly believe my own ears. But they both stuck to it, and the chap was publicly accepted as their grandson and heir. That was conclusive to most people. Every one knew how intensely proud of the family name and tradition were both the old people. It simply wasn't thinkable that they would accept a wrong 'un, and put an impostor, a stranger in blood, in possession of title and estates. Inconceivable. If they were satisfied, then it must be so. You can't wonder most people took it all for granted."

"You didn't yourself?"

"Well, at first I simply didn't know what to think. I supposed the grandparents must know best. I felt I had been a fool to let my doubts be so plain. Not the best way of standing in with the new heir to let it be known you thought he was a fraud. I began to think I had done for myself and the firm, too. My partners rubbed that in rather vigorously when they heard about it all. I was told I had probably lost the firm the Wych estate business as soon as the new heir succeeded. Or sooner. He wasn't likely to forget in a hurry that I had as good as called him an impostor. There was a fine old dust-up in the office. I believe my partners would have thrown me out of the firm then and there if they had known how. Or sued me for damages. Well, there it was. I might have let them buy me out only for Ralph making it quite clear he didn't accept the new Bertram, and that he meant to fight. So I thought, all right, I'll go in with him. Right's right, all the world over. It meant I had to resign my partnership instead of being bought out. Couldn't be helped, and they were so glad to get rid of me, there was no trouble arranging things. I knew if Ralph said he meant fighting, fight he would. He's that sort. What he said confirmed my own ideas. I swung back to my first belief that this chap was another Arthur Orton and the whole affair another Tichborne case. You remember Lady Tichborne recognized Orton as her son, and if a mother could be mistaken in her own son and stick to it through thick and thin, then why couldn't grandparents be mistaken, too, no matter how they stuck to it? So I told Ralph I would sink or swim with him."

The colonel nodded approvingly.

"One can't help liking a good fighter," he remarked, and the remark was evidently intended to include both the absent Ralph and the present Clinton.

"Oh, Ralph's a good fighter all right," declared Clinton with a laugh. "I mean to do my best, too," he added modestly. "But then I'm just a lawyer. I've got to make my way in the profession. I don't deny a good fight is good fun, and I'm looking forward to it. And you don't much care for seeing a decent sort of chap like Ralph being done down by a dirty fraud. But I don't want you to think that I'm taking a sentimental view of the job. I'm not. I'm not taking it on out of friendship or sympathy or sense of justice or that sort of thing. Merely a plain business proposition."

"Business that a good many people would go a long way to avoid, I think," observed the colonel, and Clinton made a little deprecatory movement with his hands as if to wave the implied compliment aside.

"I suppose," observed Bobby unexpectedly, his eyes still fixed on the ceiling, "I suppose that only the late earl's death makes it possible to test the succession in court?"

"Well, I was considering that," admitted Clinton.

"Libel, scandal, an injunction to prevent Bertram from putting himself forward as heir, something on those lines, perhaps."

"I don't quite see—" began Bobby, and Clinton interrupted him.

"Oh, I agree it's much easier to put a case now," he said. "Of course, I've not had time even to begin getting evidence. There'll have to be inquiries in America. We must try to establish the real facts about Bertram's reported death. Then there's the question of this chap's actual identity. If he is—and I think he is—a native of this part, we shall have to try to trace every one who lived here about that time and has left since. A big job, but it can be done, and with luck we might get on the chap's trail very quickly. If we can prove who he really is, we've won at once. There's a lot to be done, and a plan of campaign will have to be thought out. It'll be a long time before we shall be ready to go into court."

"I suppose so," agreed the colonel. "The thing might take years. The Tichborne case did, didn't it?"

"Years," agreed Clinton. "The two trials alone took nearly a year, taken together. I don't know," he added, hesitatingly, "if I ought to ask you, but I suppose it is quite clearly established that Ralph left here an hour before the murder occurred? I'm inclined to suspect there's a certain amount of gossip going on, and I think it ought to be checked at once."

"Martin is quite clear on that point," the colonel admitted; surprised that so acute and zealous a lawyer as Clinton Wells seemed to be, did not see at once that such an early departure did not in any way prevent a later return. "It's most unfortunate there was this violent quarrel between Ralph and the late earl just before the murder. You can't wonder at there being gossip. Ralph says he went straight back home and to bed, and only heard of what had happened this morning. By the way, when you left here last night, you went home for your dinner?"

Clinton shook his head.

"Oh, no," he said. "My poor housekeeper would have had a fit. I told her I would be out for dinner, and there wouldn't have been a thing ready. Ought I to account for my movements?" he added smilingly. "I had dinner at the Midland Hotel." He began to search in his pockets. "There's the bill," he said, "if you like to see it— nineteen and six, it comes to. I don't always do myself as well as that, but they've a rather good Romanee Conti I treated myself to. To put myself in a good temper after my little upset with Ralph, I suppose. Then I went home, rang up one or two chaps I know to see if I could make up a four for bridge, found I couldn't, and spent the rest of the evening more usefully, I suppose, in looking up succession law and so on. I meant to make Ralph's case a big thing, win or lose. Put in the shade now, I suppose."

"Why?" asked Bobby.

"Well, isn't it?" Clinton retorted. "Murders are much more exciting, much more sensational than missing heirs."

"There seems a connection," Bobby remarked. "There's a reference in your statement you made earlier to an automatic pistol you all, yourself, Mr. Longden, Ralph, seem to have handled in the Wych estate office last night?"

"Oh, yes," Clinton answered. "But we all saw it securely locked up in the big safe in Ralph's office, and I understand Mr. Longden walked off with the keys by mistake. So Ralph couldn't have got it out, and Mr. Longden wasn't near the office till after the murder."

"There's evidence," Bobby agreed, "that Mr. Ralph Hoyle came straight here this morning when he heard what had happened, without going to his office. The housekeeper found the door bolted on the inside as usual when she came down about seven. She noticed, too, the keys on the floor where they had fallen when Mr. Longden pushed them through the letter-box."

"Well, that seems all right," observed Clinton. "The pistol must be still in the safe where we all saw it put away. Impossible for any one to have got hold of it. Longden had the key of the safe but not of the office. Ralph had the key of the office but not of the safe. Cancel each other out." Bobby made no comment on this, though he wondered, much as the colonel had wondered before, how it was that so acute a lawyer did not see at once how easy it would have been for Ralph, who had sole charge of the safe key, to provide himself with a duplicate. In a slightly embarrassed voice, Clinton said:—

"I suppose you know the old earl kept an automatic in a drawer of the writing-table here? Martin said anything about—well, about it and me?"

"I don't think so," Bobby answered. "No, he didn't. Why?"

"Well, it's like this," explained Clinton, still slightly embarrassed. "I was in here the other day talking to the old earl, and he happened to show me the thing, the automatic I mean, a point three-two Colt automatic, I remember. Well, I happened to have it in my hand looking at it when Martin came into the room. I thought I had better mention it. You know, I don't trust that fellow, Martin. He would make mischief fast enough if he got the chance. I wouldn't put blackmail past him. It did just strike me that if he said he had seen me with it, well, that would prove I knew about it, which I did, and I've had plenty of opportunity of getting hold of it since, if I wanted to. I thought I had better mention it. My legal mind did suggest that it might look a trifle fishy, if that was the weapon used. Not that I had any reason for trying to get rid of the poor old boy, only in a case like this, it's better to mention everything, isn't it?"

"Very much better," agreed the colonel warmly. "I wish every one would be as frank. We haven't identified the weapon yet, and as a matter of fact, the automatic you mention can't be found now."

"The devil it can't," exclaimed Clinton, looking worried. "I didn't know that. Suggestive, eh? Looks as if it were the one used."

"We can't be sure," the colonel answered cautiously. "All we can be sure of is that the bullets were fired from a point thirty-two, and that that is the calibre both of Earl Wych's pistol and of the one which presumably is still in the Wych estate office safe."

"If the earl's pistol were used," Clinton said slowly, "that does seem to suggest possibilities."

He seemed to become lost in thought. Bobby said:— "Yes. What possibilities?"

"Hanged if I know," Clinton answered with a half smile. "Can't say. Lawyers must be cautious, you know," he added, his smile more marked now.

He wouldn't say any more, and presently was allowed to go. When the door had closed behind him, the colonel said:—

"I must say I rather like the way he sticks up for Ralph and all the time pretends he is just thinking of his own interests. A fine fellow."

"Yes, sir," said Bobby, who had resumed his inspection of the ceiling above their heads.

The colonel stared out of the window, fidgeted, hesitated. Unconsciously he imitated a favourite gesture and rubbed the tip of his nose. Then he said:—

"Or is he?"

"I don't know," said Bobby.

"A bit odd," the colonel said, "the way he dragged it in about Martin having seen him handling the automatic here. Why was he so keen on our knowing that?"

"There were one or two other things he said rather worried me," Bobby said. "It all came in quite naturally about Ralph's temper and opportunities but it all did come in. Why shouldn't it for that matter?"

"You don't think," said the colonel hesitatingly, "you don't think he can be our man?"

"It might be," agreed Bobby cautiously.

"What possible motive could he have?" asked the colonel. "None," he answered himself firmly. "So that lets him out. Hang it all, we mustn't get into the way of suspecting every one. Or must we?"

"Well, sir," answered Bobby, "at present I think we must."

CHAPTER XIV
RALPH

The next and last on the list to be interviewed was Ralph, though first there was an interlude when an offer of refreshments brought by Martin was gratefully accepted. Not much time was spent in this way, though; not half enough indeed in the considered opinion of the stenographer, and then Ralph appeared, looking very grim and defiant. But his voice was quiet and steady as, without waiting to be questioned, he began abruptly:—

"I suppose you know what's being said about me?"

"We pay no attention to what people say," the colonel told him at once.

"Don't you?" Ralph asked. "Well, I do. I don't like being called a murderer. If any one says it to my face, I'll—"

He stopped there, with an effort that was evident, with eyes so fiercely alight, a mouth so ominously set, that the colonel was quite startled—and not too favourably impressed.

"No violence, please," he said sharply.

"May I suggest to Mr. Hoyle," interposed Bobby, "that if any one is suspected of an act of violence, the best way to strengthen that suspicion is to commit a further act of violence."

Ralph, who hitherto had hardly noticed Bobby, swung round in the chair he had just taken and stared at him. Their eyes met in a long and steady gaze, as those of Anne and Bobby had done a little before. But this time the long, searching stare they exchanged was not so much as if exchanged between two open adversaries, but, searching and questioning, an effort to divine each what was in the other's mind. 'Are you guilty?' Bobby seemed to be asking and Ralph to be retorting: 'What do you think?' Both of them seemed for the moment to have forgotten the colonel, who himself seemed loath to interrupt that silent, not so much duel as intensity of search into another's secret and most hidden thoughts. But then he coughed, almost apologetically, and said:—

"Ralph, I've known all of you a good many years. That makes no difference now. But I warn you again that any show of violence will only make things worse."

Ralph swung round on him.

"Well, what would you do," he demanded, "if people were going about behind your back saying you were a murderer?"

This was a difficult question, and the colonel made no attempt to answer it. Ralph did not seem to expect any reply, for he went on immediately:—

"I was fond of him—of uncle, I mean, great-uncle really—I always called them uncle and aunt. You know we had a blazing row last night?"

"Ralph," the colonel said, speaking slowly and with some care, "it is not our duty—or our practice—to warn people unless we think there is likely to be sufficient evidence to justify a charge. I don't think that about you and so I didn't mean to give you any warning. But now I will. I remind you formally that anything you say may be used in evidence, that you are not obliged to answer questions, and that if you wish you can have your solicitor present."

"Thank you for making it so plain," Ralph answered with some bitterness. "What you mean is the handcuffs are all ready but you are keeping them out of sight for the present. Well, anything I say you may use any damn way you like. I'm quite willing to answer any sensible"—he laid a slightly offensive emphasis on this last word—"any sensible question you want to ask me. As for a solicitor, I wouldn't mind old Clinton being here. He's been such a decent scout all along." Ralph's bitter, angry expression softened momentarily as he mentioned his friend's name. "He's stood by me from the first," and now Ralph's expression hardened again as if he were thinking of others who had emphatically not 'stood by' him. "He's the one person I feel I can trust. But I don't think we need bother him just at present. He's got his own work to attend to, he's gone haring off to his office where his clients have been lining up all day, waiting for him. But I'll tell you one thing. No one's going to call me a murderer to my face and get away with it."

The colonel took no notice of this renewed threat. He was turning over the papers before him. Bobby was idly jotting down his impressions on a scrap of paper. Why he did so he hardly knew, and when he had finished he tore the paper into small scraps and threw it into the waste-paper basket. What he had written ran much like this: "Strong emotions. Confiding. People with strong emotions generally are. If he trusted any one, would do so to the limit. Generous, hot-headed, truculent, sensitive. Interesting sort of chap. Eat out of your hand or fly at your throat, and a toss up which."

It may be added that if Ralph had ever had an opportunity to read this summing up of his character, he would have read it with bewilderment and declared that almost the exact reverse was true in every single detail. He did become aware that Bobby was once again regarding him with a deep and searching intentness. He returned the scrutiny with an angry glare.

"Well?" he said with a truculence that fully justified one item at least of Bobby's jottings. "Well?" he repeated, this time still more truculently.

"Yes?" said Bobby amiably.

This interchange of interjections was hardly a promising conversational opening, and in fact conversation ceased therewith. The colonel was still busy with his papers. Ralph turned his defiant stare to the window as though wishing his challenge now to embrace the whole outside world as well. Bobby continued to tear into very small pieces the jottings he had been putting down. The colonel gave a preliminary cough as a warning that he was now ready to begin again.

"The dispute with your uncle," he said, "I suppose was about the return of the man claiming to be Bertram Hoyle and now therefore succeeding to the title and estates."

"You may as well understand at once," Ralph interrupted, "that I don't admit for a moment that the fellow is anything but a bare-faced fraud."

"His grandparents accepted him?"

"Yes, I know," Ralph admitted, frowning heavily. "I can't make it out. I'll swear uncle knew well enough the fellow's an impostor. He must have known it. He as good as admitted as much when we were rowing at each other last night. He started talking about the honour of the family. I asked him what the devil the honour of the family had to do with accepting as a Hoyle, as the next Earl Wych, a fellow who hadn't a drop of Hoyle blood in his veins. He doesn't even look a Hoyle. He's no more a Hoyle than the first tramp you meet on the road or the first Irish labourer who comes over here to make a bit digging potatoes and goes home to pay his subscription to the I.R.A. to buy bombs for murder. And uncle had the cheek to tell me he was doing nothing in any way to affect my rights. It was none of my business, nothing to do with me, he said. Kicking me out to put a fraud in my place wasn't supposed to be any business of mine. That made me madder than ever."

Bobby said thoughtfully:—

"It seems a curious remark. I mean, saying it was no business of yours. Can you suggest what it meant?"

Ralph only answered by a gesture of helpless and angry bewilderment.

"Did you ask your uncle for an explanation?"

"Well, what do you think?" retorted Ralph. "I did nothing else."

"I'm asking," Bobby explained, "because our information—it's in one of these statements—is that your first reaction was to call your uncle a liar."

"Well, so he was, lying like blazes," answered Ralph, though now a little on the defensive.

"Not exactly asking for an explanation, though," murmured Bobby. "You see, from what I gather about Earl Wych he was very conscious of his—well, his rank and position. Proud of being Earl Wych. I suppose any one would be. So I was rather wondering if calling him a liar was quite the best way of getting him to explain.

Especially when the word was used from a young man to a much older man, from a nephew to his great-uncle, indeed from any one at all to the Earl Wych."

"Rubbing it in a bit, aren't you?" grunted Ralph sulkily. "All the same, if you don't want to be called a liar, you shouldn't tell lies."

"You see," explained Bobby as gently as before, "what I'm really trying to get at, is:— Did your talk with your uncle last night run on the same lines? I mean, did you start off by calling Earl Wych a liar?"

"I suppose I made it pretty clear what I thought of the whole business," Ralph admitted. "I don't think I called uncle a liar again. Not that I remember. I may have said it was all a blasted lie or something of that sort." He paused for a moment and seemed to be reflecting. "Oh, well," he said, "I suppose really I didn't give uncle much chance to explain. I felt too sore. I suppose I might have gone a bit slower. I think he must have gone the way old people do sometimes—second childhood, that sort of thing."

"Did he give that impression to you or to any one else apart from his recognition of his grandson?"

"No, he didn't," admitted Ralph. "Not in the least. Vigorous as any one half his age—especially when he was telling me things. None of my business, he told me. That's what made me so mad. But I didn't call him a liar again. At least I don't think I did. Anyhow, he called me much worse things."

"In fact," suggested Bobby, "a somewhat undignified slanging match on both sides?"

"Well, if you like to put it that way," Ralph admitted again. "What you are getting at is that I was a blasted fool to lose my temper; and if I had had the sense of a year-old baby, I might have got a reasonable explanation?"

"The words are your own," said Bobby gravely, "but the meaning is more or less mine."

"All very well for you to talk," grumbled Ralph. "If someone came along and kicked you out from where you belonged you mightn't be quite so calm and cool and reasonable and all that. Besides, old Clinton did try to get an explanation. If any one could have talked uncle over, he could. He didn't, any more than I did, though of course they didn't row at each other. Clinton just got shown the door. That was all. Clinton didn't quite like it when I said I would have a try. He said it would only make things worse. He was right enough all right. He generally is. Got quite huffy with me about it, and said he hoped I would take his advice another time or he would chuck the whole show. So I suppose next time I shall have to. I suppose you are thinking it's a pity I didn't this time."

Both Bobby and the colonel assured him with some emphasis that that was exactly what they did think. If Clinton's advice had been followed, this unfortunate and violent quarrel, just before the occurrence of the murder, would never have taken place.

"There's one other question I want to ask," the colonel went on. "I understand an automatic, point three-two, was kept in a drawer of this writing table. Can you say when you saw it last?"

"I haven't the least idea. I expect I knew it was there —or was there at one time—but I haven't seen it or thought of it for years. Not that I remember. It didn't figure in the row last night, if that's what you're getting at. We didn't get as fair as threatening each other with automatics." He was silent for a moment and then said, shuddering slightly, as though the question brought home to him more vividly what it was that had happened:— "Do you mean it was the one used to kill uncle?"

"We can't tell that yet," the colonel answered. "No one seems to know what has become of it."

"Does any one know if it was there recently?" Ralph asked. "Uncle may have got rid of it or put it away somewhere."

"There seems proof it was in its case in the top drawer of this table a day or two ago," the colonel answered. "The empty case is there still."

"I see," said Ralph gloomily. "You know I left about half-past ten? I suppose you think I could easily have come back. I could. I didn't."

"Will you tell us what you did after leaving here?"

"I went straight back home."

"Did you meet any one on the way?"

Ralph shook his head.

"No," he said. "I've no proof—no—what do you call it?—alibi. I walked back as fast as I could, thinking of all the things I wished I had said to uncle—and all the things I wished I hadn't. I walked pretty fast, trying to walk off my temper. You know where I live? It's the house built for old Anderson. He was estate agent till he died and I took it on. It's much too big a place for me, but there isn't anywhere else. When I got back I didn't feel like turning in at once. It was a fine night and I sat down in the garden and smoked a pipe and thought of some more things I wished I had told uncle—and some more things I wished I hadn't. And I thought how old Clinton would rub it in next time and remind me he had warned me what would happen and tried his best to stop me. Only all he said only made me more determined."

"In what way?" Bobby asked. "Why was that?"

"Oh, I suppose I am an obstinate beggar. Clinton's a real lawyer. He trotted out all the 'pros' as he called them, and then all the 'cons', and all he said only made me more pig-headed. I wasn't scared of what uncle said or of his giving me the sack right away and making this sham Bertram agent in my place. When I let myself into the house I stayed up for a time and made some notes for a talk I ought to have had to-day with the Argentine bloke I was to have seen in Liverpool—a thousand-pound deal washed out, probably. He won't wait. Well, I suppose that doesn't matter much."

"There are servants in the house?"

"Housekeeper and maid. It's a big place. Old Anderson had a large family and got it built to suit himself."

"Did they hear you come in?"

"I don't suppose so. Why should they? Fast asleep probably, and I didn't make any awful amount of noise."

The colonel was looking at his papers again.

"You and Miss Anne Hoyle are understood to be engaged," he remarked.

Ralph stiffened perceptibly.

"I don't think there is any need to discuss our private affairs, is there?" he said.

"I mentioned it," explained the colonel, "because it may help us to know how all you people stand to each other, and because Miss Hoyle told us the engagement has been broken off."

"It is for her to decide," Ralph answered as stiffly as before. "I think you must ask her if you want to know anything more."

"I am sorry," the colonel continued, "if you think I'm intruding on private matters, but there may be some kind of bearing on your uncle's murder. I'm afraid I must ask if the engagement was broken by Miss Anne's wish? If so, is there any reason you know of or is it a result of Bertram's return? If so again, does that mean that she believes he is the genuine Bertram, and therefore now the rightful Earl Wych?"

"You must ask her yourself what she thinks," Ralph retorted. He went on angrily:— "I daresay she is like every one else and thinks the old people ought to know. Every one seems to think that settles it. Every one," he added with a sudden softening of his expression, "except Miss Longden."

"Miss Longden," repeated the colonel, surprised, "why, what does she know about it?"

"As much as any one else, I suppose," retorted Ralph. "Got a right to her opinion, hasn't she? She seems to be about the only one who thinks I've any business to stand up for myself. She told me she would fight it out till she dropped." He smiled again, and his smile had the effect of altering his whole expression in the oddest way—of changing him from a scowling, angry combatant likely to be at your throat at any moment, into a grinning, friendly school-boy likely at any moment to confide to you the last piece of fun he had enjoyed. 'Two men in him,' Bobby said to himself, 'only which is fundamental?' and Ralph went on:—"She's a quiet little thing, and you would think she was scared of her own shadow, but she's got guts all the same. Once she has made up her mind to a thing, I don't believe she would ever budge."

The colonel didn't say anything. But privately be agreed. He knew because he had tried. She had made up her mind—not to answer his questions—and nothing had made her budge. Suspicious, the colonel thought darkly. Unless she knew more than she ought to know, why had she taken up that attitude, that defiant attitude? He went on:—

"We know the murderer used a point three-two automatic pistol. We have heard of two. The one that ought to be in this drawer, and isn't, and no one seems to know what has become of it. Then there's the one generally kept in the Wych estate office, the one you were cleaning yesterday. Mr. Longden and Mr. Clinton Wells were present, and both say they saw you lock it up in the estate office safe." Fumbling amidst the mass of papers before him, he found the account of the incident and read it aloud. "That is correct, is it?" he asked. "In every detail?"

"Very correct and very detailed," Ralph agreed. "You don't suppose that it was used last night, do you? I don't think that's possible. I don't suppose you suspect Mr. Longden, do you? He had the key of the safe in his possession till next morning apparently. But not the office door key. My typist was there till after five, and after she had gone the housekeeper cleaned up, bolting the door on the inside when she had finished. After that, no one could have got in except through her kitchen, and she was sitting there till she went to bed at eleven. I've taken the trouble to make sure of all that because I remembered about the pistol. And you've had a man there watching the safe nearly all day, haven't you?"

"Yes, that's so," agreed the colonel. "Mr. Longden seems an absent-minded gentleman. Could any one have got the key from him and then returned it somehow?"

"Difficult, I should think," commented Ralph. "Anyhow, you must ask him that. If any one did, how did he get into the office?"

"Perhaps it would be as well," suggested Bobby, "if we made sure first if the pistol is still in the safe. If it is, we can soon be certain whether it was used last night or not."

"Is that correct?" Ralph asked a little doubtfully. "I've been told that's possible, but can you be certain?"

"Quite certain," Bobby assured him. "It really seems that the universe is of an infinite variety—no two things are ever identical. Everything can always be distinguished from everything else, and the bullets fired from one pistol from those fired by any other pistol in existence."

"Well, we'll go and have a look," said the colonel briskly. "Will you come, too, Ralph?"

"I will," Ralph answered with considerable emphasis, "though I'm certain the thing is still there because it can't possibly be anywhere else, and so it can't have been the one used last night. That's rather a cracked idea."

"Oh, well," Bobby explained, "most detective work is trying out cracked ideas. By the way," he added after they had started, "can you tell me why it always seems to be Earl Wych and not Earl of Wych, like Earl of Derby and so on. I know there's no place actually Wych by itself. Is that the reason? There's Midwych, of course, Brimsbury Wych, Wychwood, half a dozen other Wychs, but no single Wych, is there?"

"Not that I know of," Ralph answered briefly and without replying to the first question.

"Is that why the title is Earl Wych and not Earl of Wych?"

"Might be," grunted Ralph, and added somewhat irritably:— "What do you want to know for? some more subtle detective work?"

"Might be," Bobby answered good-humouredly. "I was just wondering. British titles are a bit complicated, you know. I've heard of a British baronet and when he went to the States, because of the 'Bart' after his name, he got called either 'Bart' under the impression that that was his surname, or else 'my bart', on the analogy of 'my lord'."

Ralph stood still and stared at Bobby suspiciously.

"What's the idea?" he demanded. "What are you getting at? Trying to be funny? I don't think this is the time, if that's it. Not now. Or trying to pull my leg? I don't like that idea either. Not just now."

"I assure you," Bobby said earnestly, "it's not that. I'm asking a serious question and I have a serious purpose. Will you answer it?"

"Can't," Ralph replied, "because no one knows. I can tell you the family legend, but there's nothing to support it. The story is that when the Baron Hoyle of that time was created an earl he meant to be Earl Wych of Wychwood. He owned part of the forest and meant the title to sort of make a claim to the rest of it. But he was so pleased about getting his earldom that he wanted every one to celebrate and sent round a cask of wine to the chaps who were making out the patent. The result was that they all imbibed a bit freely, and the 'of Wychwood' got left out. So the title went through as 'Earl Wych' and Earl Wych it has been ever since. That's the yarn. But there's no real authority for it. Interested?"

"I find it very interesting," Bobby answered; and then they arrived at the estate office where, when the so carefully guarded safe was opened with the key that had been so long in Mr. Longden's possession, they found indeed the case for the automatic. But it was empty.

Of the automatic itself, there was no sign.

CHAPTER XV
SUMMING UP

The closest investigation, the most prolonged inquiry, threw no further light on the disappearance of the estate automatic. Three witnesses, the vicar, Clinton Wells, Ralph himself, were all prepared to swear they had seen the weapon locked up in the office safe. Yet now it wasn't there, but only—as in the library at the castle—an empty case that once, no doubt, had held a pistol and that, again, as at the castle, bore no finger marks upon a polished surface eminently suitable for taking such impressions. Miss Higson, the estate office typist, who liked to call herself secretary, had been at work in the outer office till half-past five and no one could possibly have entered the inner office without her knowledge. No one had even, as it happened, with the exception of herself, been in the outer office between Ralph's departure and her own. At half-past five she had locked up and gone home, taking the office key with her as usual, so as to be able to let herself in in the morning. During the evening Mrs. Gregson, the housekeeper, who occupied rooms above the offices, had cleaned and swept and tidied as usual. There were only three ways of reaching the inner office where was the safe. Through the outer office, its door locked by Miss Higson on her departure; through Mrs. Gregson's kitchen, where she was sitting all evening; by the front door admitting to stairs that led to the upper floor occupied by her. But that way led also through the kitchen. She had locked up carefully at night as usual and there were no signs of any forcible entry.

"Duplicate keys," said the colonel gloomily. "Any one may have had them. Mr. Longden had the safe key in his possession till early morning. He may have had a duplicate key to the office door as well. It's a perfectly simple lock. Plenty of keys would open it. Most unsatisfactory. I could open it myself with a hairpin."

That was about as far as their inquiries took them that night, though it was late before they agreed that nothing more could be done till morning. And then Bobby sat up till the small hours, putting on paper, as he always liked to do, the chief impressions he had derived from the events, the talks, the interviews of the day. One by one he passed in review the various actors in recent events, and if he began to see, or, rather, to think he saw, the faint outline of a pattern beginning to appear, it was an outline so faint, so strange, indeed so fantastic, involving so many suppositions, that until he could secure some solid evidence to support it, he felt his wisest course would be to keep it to himself.

"It might be," he said half aloud. "Cold-blooded devilry," he mused. "Quick thinking and quick action, too. Only—too much guess-work. Won't do to say anything yet. Won't do to let my bird suspect there's any suspicion yet. And then," he added, this time quite aloud and with sudden depression, "I may be entirely wrong. Probably 9am.

Next morning, at the Midwych county police headquarters, which incidentally he entered by the back way so as to avoid the many newspaper men who were clamouring for information, and so thronging round and about the front entrance as to make access thereby a complicated process—but how magnificently had the colonel strode through their serried ranks, just like the hosts of the Israelites passing through the held-up waters of the sea —Bobby showed his chief the long memorandum he had drawn up.

"I thought," he remarked, "those talks and interviews we had were all extraordinarily interesting. So many different motives turned up we had had no idea of before, there seemed such a complicated interplay of character and interests, the people concerned were themselves all so striking and unusual in their different ways."

"All very well," grunted the colonel, "but what solid conclusions do we get out of it all?"

"I don't think any as yet," admitted Bobby. "I think that's what makes it so fascinating. It's like watching through a smoke screen. You get a glimpse and then it's gone again. You see what looks like something solid and next moment you see it's only a smoke wreath. You see a figure clearly and even while you are watching you see it turn into another and then vanish entirely, so that there's nothing there at all. I jotted down a few notes last night," he added.

As he spoke he handed to the colonel the memorandum he had written during the night. The colonel began to read, impressed already by the heading.

'TEN POSSIBLES'

"Ten possibles," he read out. "Ten? how do you make that out?"

"Well, sir," Bobby explained, "we examined nine people who all seem in it more or less deeply—all their interests touched in one way or another. And then I thought it better to include an unknown. It may be there's someone we have had no hint of as yet. It's even possible the murderer might be a burglar Lord Wych interrupted. Or someone we don't know about but deeply concerned in getting the claimant safely in possession at once. Or something like that. I don't think we must forget the possibility. I don't think it is more than a bare possibility, but I think we must keep it in mind."

"I only wish it would turn out like that,' the colonel said slowly. "I don't like to think of any of these people having been guilty of such a brutal murder of such an old man—people like Ralph." He paused, a little disconcerted that the name had got itself uttered like that, for indeed it was the one uppermost in his mind. "Incredible," he said loudly. "Or Lady Wych. More than incredible. A disgraceful idea." He glared so fiercely he might almost have been hoping to annihilate utterly such a thought. But it remained. He said:— "There's the vicar or Clinton Wells for that matter. It might be either of them, I suppose." He said this almost longingly, so pleasant would it be to think that none of the Hoyles were concerned in this murder of the head of their family. "Only why should they?" he added in a more depressed tone. "Or Martin," he added, this time still more longingly, for the butler would have been an even more acceptable culprit. "I don't trust the fellow, but then again: Why should he? And there's that little chit of a Longden girl," he concluded darkly. "Enough impudence for a dozen." Bobby did not entirely agree with this last judgment, but he said nothing, and the colonel picked up the memorandum again, and began to read it.

It started with a list of the ten suspects—or 'possibles' to adopt Bobby's more prudent phraseology he had recently a opted on a suggestion made by his wife, who thought it a shame that people should be called 'suspect' when all that was really meant was that it was possible—and often not more than possible—that they were guilty.

"Suspect's a propaganda word," Olive had said severely. "It's what the lawyers call 'imparting prejudice'. And it's not fair."

So Bobby had written 'possibles' and not 'suspects', and the colonel, not very much liking this innovation, read on:—

'A

THE POSSIBLES

Three women.
A1. Lady Wych (wife)
A2. Anne Hoyle (grand-daughter)
A3. Sophy Longden (companion-secretary)

Three men (relatives)
A4. Ralph Hoyle (great-nephew)
A5. Arthur Hoyle (cousin)

A6. Bertram Hoyle (soi-disant)

Three men (outsiders)

A7. Mr. Longden (vicar)

A8. Mr. Clinton Wells (lawyer)

A9. Martin (butler)

and

A10. X, a possible unknown, and, at present, wholly hypothetical stranger.'

"Seems a fairly complete list," observed the colonel. "Who is your favourite? Might as well shut your eyes and stick in a pin, as far as I can see."

"Yes, sir," agreed Bobby. "I don't think any one of them can be ruled out at present."

The colonel went on reading:—

'B

Focal Points.

B1. Is the claimant, Bertram, genuine or a fake?'

"I should have thought," commented the colonel, "that the first focal point was the murder."

"Well, sir, in my view of the case," Bobby answered, "I should say the murder was more the symptom, the symptom of a deep-seated wrong. My own suggestion would be that the cause lies in these rival claims to the title and estates. If we knew more about that, we might find we knew more about the murder."

The colonel looked a little doubtful, but he said nothing. He went on:—

"'Focal points'—where is it? Oh, yes."

He read:—

'B2. The weapon. The Wych estate office pistol and the Castle Wych pistol are both missing. Presumption is that one or other was the weapon used. But which? And why has the other vanished?'

"Now there," said the colonel, "I'm with you. Find the weapon, find the murderer. Difficult, though, to understand why both have gone."

He continued to read:—

'B3. What is the meaning of the statement made by Lord Wych to Ralph that it was no business of his, and no injury had been done him?

The colonel passed this without comment, evidently thinking it a minor point, and proceeded to the next section.

'C

IDENTITY OF PLACE AND TIME

I

Regarding the three women

They were all on or near the scene of the murder at the relevant time.

C1. *Lady Wych*

Mr. Longden states that he saw the figure of a woman he believed at the time to be that of Lady Wych, near the open french windows of the library about the time of the murder. Questioned on this, Lady Wych had a heart attack, which may have been genuine or a convenience. It is not improbable that she will always have heart attacks when questioned, and, as these may be genuine, it will not be possible to press her too closely. As the vicar is also to some degree under suspicion, his statements cannot be accepted at their face value, unless confirmed, as this is not.

C2. *Anne Hoyle*

Her bedroom is near the service stairs, giving quick and easy access to the library. At night, the servants having gone to bed, this could be used with little risk of observation or interruption. Bertram states that Miss Anne was not in her room at the relevant time, and that he saw a pistol in her possession shortly before the murder. She denies both statements and offers plausible explanations. If his story is true and she was not in her room, where was she? It must again be remembered that all statements made by Bertram, himself one of the possibles, must be received with caution, unless confirmed.

C3. *Sophy Longden*

Finger-prints prove she was in the library at a late hour, probably about the time of the murder. But that does not prove there was not someone there later, without leaving finger-prints or other traces. She refuses to answer questions, and it may therefore be assumed that she saw something about which she intends to remain silent. It seems probable, therefore, unless she is guilty herself, that she is shielding someone. This may be Ralph, with whom she evidently sympathises, her father, Lady Wych, or, of course, someone else. No way to decide this at present.

II

The three male relatives

C4. *Ralph Hoyle*

Admits violent quarrel with the late earl. Left the castle about half-past ten. States that he went straight home, sat outdoors in the garden for a time, made some notes for a business interview, and then went to bed. No corroboration, and he could easily have returned to the castle had he wished to do so.

C5. *Arthur Hoyle*

Strong likelihood, but no actual proof, that he was hiding in the castle grounds during the evening. His motive might have been curiosity concerning the result of the interview between Ralph and the late earl, Ralph having openly stated his intention of having a 'showdown'. He denies presence in castle grounds, states that he spent the evening taking a drive in his car for pleasure. Can produce no supporting evidence.

C6. *Bertram Hoyle*

Admits being out of his room and near head of service stairs at the relevant time. States that he was on his way to the bathroom, but there are two other bathrooms nearer. A suggestion coming from Anne Hoyle is that he was trying to enter her room. Does this suggest complicity between the two?

III

The three outsiders

C7. *Mr. Longden*

Admits presence in castle grounds at the time of the murder and that he was in possession of the key of the safe in which the Wych estate office pistol was kept.

C8. *Martin*

Denies that he was near the library after eleven, but is certainly lying, since he betrayed knowledge of the late earl's having been smoking, which seems to have been unusual with him so late at night. Naturally Martin is accustomed to using the service stairs, which lead almost directly from the door of his room to that of the library. Query: Did the late earl catch Martin listening at the door, threaten to kick him out then and there, and was the result a struggle and the murder?

C9. *Clinton Wells*

Is able to give very full account of his movements and reasonable explanation for his absence from the dinner. But no corroboration for the relevant time. The castle is within reach by car or cycle from his house. He knew there was likely to be a serious quarrel between Ralph and his great-uncle. No motive known, but, as with Martin, possibility that he was eavesdropping, was detected by the late earl, and that a struggle and the murder resulted.

IV

Finally *X, the unknown quantity*

A possible and hypothetical burglar of whose existence there is no evidence and of whom nothing can be said since of him nothing is known.'

"I only wish there were," sighed the colonel as he laid down the memorandum and looked sadly at Bobby. "Or that there was something to show it was one of the three outsiders—clergyman, lawyer, butler. But I'm afraid—" He shook his head and left the sentence unfinished. Then he said:— "What your memo comes to is that the whole lot of them had the opportunity?"

"Yes, sir," agreed Bobby.

"Doesn't take us much farther forward," pronounced the colonel glumly and resumed his reading.

'D

WEAPON

D1. A point three-two self-loading pistol (commonly called an automatic) was employed by the murderer. Two such weapons are known to have been accessible. Both have disappeared. One, belonging to the late earl, was kept in a drawer of the library table. The case is still there. All concerned had access at one time or another to the library, and could easily have secured the pistol by simply opening the drawer at any convenient moment. Anne Hoyle is said (by Bertram, all of whose statements must at present be accepted with reserve) to have been in possession of a pistol that was presumably on a balance of probabilities, and if Bertram's story is true, the one taken from the library. It is a strong point in favour of the truth of his statement that it was made before the murder occurred. Anne Hoyle's explanation is that she gave him a glimpse of a metal cigarette case and told him it was a pistol and that he believed her.

D2. The second pistol of the required calibre known to have been available is that kept in the Wych estate office safe and seen there on the morning of the murder by Mr. Longden and Clinton Wells, both of whom support Ralph Hoyle's statement that he locked it up in the safe. Mr. Longden admits he picked up Ralph Hoyle's keys by mistake and had them, including the key of the safe, in his possession till the following morning. The key of the office was, however, in the possession of the typist, Miss Higson, and her evidence and that of the caretaker and office-cleaner, Mrs. Gregson, is that no one entered, or could have entered, the office after Miss Higson left. Obviously Ralph Hoyle had every opportunity to provide himself with duplicate keys, both of office and safe. The evidence of the typist and office-cleaner is only negative and can only be accepted with reserve as indicating that in their opinion the office was not again entered after the typist left.

D3. It is even possible that Ralph Hoyle deliberately offered Mr. Longden, a notorious wool gatherer, the chance to go off with his keys—in the way which conjurers call "forcing" the card or other object they want selected by the person supposed to be making a free choice. Clinton Wells, since Ralph is his client and apparently inclined to be careless about the custody of his keys, had probably equal opportunities of providing himself with duplicates.'

The colonel laid down the memorandum again and looked more worried than ever.

"What it comes to," he said, "is that almost every one had a chance to get hold of the keys at one time or another. And every chance to get hold of one or other of the automatics. But then why are both missing?"

"Yes, sir, that's a very puzzling feature," Bobby agreed, looking almost as worried himself. "I can't think of any reasonable explanation."

"There must be some connection," the colonel remarked hesitatingly. "Can't be merely a coincidence—or has it just happened that one pistol got mislaid?"

"Well, it doesn't seem very probable," Bobby said. "I can't say I much care for coincidence as the explanation of a puzzling detail. Too simple."

"The doctrine of economy," suggested Colonel Glynne, "that the simplest explanation is probably the true one?"

"I shouldn't say that applies in a case like this," Bobby answered. "If two automatics are missing, there's a reason, and one of them was probably the one the murderer used."

"Yes, but which?" asked the colonel. "Until you know that, we don't know—" He was about to say 'which', but just in time changed the word to 'much'. "We don't know much until we know that," he repeated firmly, "and we can't know until we find them and where the devil are they? tell me that."

As Bobby made no effort to supply the desired information the colonel scowled heavily, picked up the memorandum and began to read it again:—

'E

MOTIVE

E1. *Countess Wych*

Family honour? It has been much talked about and may be the motive, but the reason is obscure. Could she and her late husband have had different ideas of what "family honour" means? Is there any significance in her reference on the night of the murder to an ancestress who shot her son to save disgrace to the family name? Could she have intended to shoot the earl for some such reason?'

The colonel paused in his reading and put the paper down.

"I can't think it," he said angrily. "I won't think it. Good God, we don't live five hundred years ago, do we? when that sort of thing was possible."

"Throwbacks to ancient ways of thinking are possible," Bobby answered. "Traditions do survive in some old families. Queer things have been done in the name of honour, strange sacrifices offered up on that altar."

He spoke heavily and with reluctance, but he felt the possibility was one that had to be kept in mind.

"Lady Wych is an old lady with plenty of courage and determination. Capable of anything she put her mind to," the colonel agreed.

Then he went on reading:—

'A further possible motive in Lady Wych's case is jealousy.'

At that he banged the memorandum down and fairly shouted:—

"At her age? at her age? at his age? Nonsense, Owen, nonsense."

"Yes, sir," said Bobby meekly, "but a woman is always a woman, and a wife is always a wife, no matter at what age. You remember, sir, the suggestion has been made that Earl Wych might have been carrying on an intrigue with Miss Longden. Probably only spiteful gossip, but all the same a possibility to be kept in mind, I think."

"Oh, all right, all right," snapped the colonel irritably. "Absurd, but there it is." He relaxed into a grim smile. "Plenty of stories about the old man in his younger days. If they were all true, he would have as many bastards scattered about the country as Henri Quatre himself. Luckily all stories never are true. I suppose," he added hesitatingly, "this Bertram claimant fellow can't be an illegitimate son the old man wanted to succeed him? He may have had the idea that he would like his own son, even a bastard, to follow him. Would Lady Wych have stood for that? Is that another possible motive in her case?" The colonel looked very unhappy. "Getting worse and worse, more and more muddled," he muttered. "She may have been insisting on his giving it up, refusing to consent to it, threatening to tell the truth, the earl may have been giving way, and the Bertram fellow known it and thought murder the only way to make himself safe. Anything in that?"

"Well, sir," Bobby admitted, "there are stories going about like that. About Bertram being an illegitimate son, I mean, and that explains the late earl's acceptance of him. But it's pure guess-work, merely a theory to explain what seems inexplicable. No evidence whatever."

"Sometimes guesses hit the truth," muttered the colonel uncomfortably. "It would fit in with Lady Wych's character and her talk about saving the family honour. I don't like the idea, but then the more you think of it, the more inconceivable the whole thing seems."

Once more he picked up the memorandum, now beginning to show some signs of wear, and went on reading aloud:—

'E2. *Sophy Longden.*'

"Obstinate little baggage," snorted the colonel in parenthesis. "I could believe anything of her."

He continued:—

'She may be in love with Ralph Hoyle'—(Here the colonel snorted again)—'and may have committed the murder to help him and assure his position. If so, it may have been in a sense a disinterested crime, committed without Ralph's knowledge and out of sympathy with him.'

"Bah!" said the colonel indignantly. "Girls are queer, God knows, damn queer, but not so queer as that. Or are they?"

Bobby did not answer because he did not know, and again the colonel continued:—

'E3. *Anne Hoyle*
The earl's death would assure the succession of the claimant, Bertram, whom she intends to marry—or why has she broken off her engagement to Ralph? Was there any reason to fear Earl Wych would withdraw his recognition of Bertram?'

Once more the colonel hurled the unlucky memorandum down on the table before him.

"Why on earth," he shouted, "should Anne want to marry Bertram? He's not so attractive as all that, is he? Why, she's been engaged to Ralph since—since she was born pretty well."

"Possibly she thinks that's an engagement a little too long," suggested Bobby, "and if she believes Bertram to be the true heir—well, he becomes eligible and Ralph merely a poor relation. And then there's their chins."

"Chins?" repeated the colonel, puzzled.

"Three interesting chins, sir," Bobby asserted. "Miss Hoyle's sticks out like a dictator's. So does Ralph's, only more so. Not only their chins, I mean, but everything about the two of them suggests a lot of what is called character, meaning pig-headedness as often as not, or at any rate a tendency to believe your own way is the best way and you are jolly well going to have it. Bertram hasn't any chin at all, and gives me the idea he has neither a will nor a way of his own, beyond wondering where the next drink is coming from. Married to Ralph, Miss Hoyle would be Countess Wych. Married to Bertram, she would be countess and earl as well, both together. I think that's a prospect that might tempt her."

"Even to murder?" asked the colonel doubtfully.

"To a dominating and ambitious woman, I think there might be a temptation," Bobby answered gravely. "I don't say that it's more than another possibility to be kept in mind."

"Well, that's enough for the three women," the colonel said. "What about the three men relatives?"

Once more he began to read:—

'E4. *Ralph Hoyle*

Bitterly resented the recognition of Bertram and the putting of Bertram in the place Ralph believed to be rightfully his own. Only an hour before the murder he is known to have quarrelled violently with his great-uncle. Said to be subject to violent fits of temper.'

"I know, I know," commented the colonel. "I hate to say it, but on the face of it, he's our man. Every motive, every opportunity, every characteristic. Obvious."

"The obvious isn't always the truth," Bobby remarked.

"No, but it is as a rule," said the colonel and went on to the next name.

'E5. *Arthur Hoyle*

If Bertram Hoyle were proved an impostor and Ralph Hoyle were hanged for murder, Arthur would succeed to title and estates.'

"Good God," gasped the colonel, "so he would. I never thought of that. It's subtle, it's round-about, it's possible. If he had an idea that something like that might happen, that would be why he was snooping that night. Wanting to see what happened, wanting to get evidence. I never did like that man," the colonel concluded thoughtfully; "an efficient, go-getting business man of the worst type."

Again he continued reading:—

'E6. *Bertram Hoyle*

The present (if his claim is genuine) Earl Wych, Baron Hoyle, baronet and various other things, including the ownership of Castle Wych and the Wych estates. Very nice things to possess, too. But if his claim is genuine, why commit the murder merely to come into actual ownership a little earlier? If an impostor, the motive would be evident and pressing, if he had any reason to suppose that the late earl might be going to repudiate him. Only why should a claim be admitted by both earl and countess only to be repudiated in a few weeks?"

"Doesn't seem to make sense," commented the colonel this time. "Besides, I don't believe that that fellow would have the guts to do anything of the sort. He got cold feet at the mere idea of joining up and if he doesn't, well—"

The colonel shrugged his shoulders, unable to conceive what would happen to an Earl Wych who showed reluctance to join the regiment an Earl Wych had founded and that subsequent earls had always commanded—with the help of competent non-commissioned officers, of course, to tell them what to do.

"Perhaps he'll turn into a conscientious objector," said the colonel suddenly, naming the most degrading supposition he could imagine. "Well, what have you got down about the three outsiders—vicar? lawyer? butler? What a combination!" and he went on:—

'E7. *Mr. Longden, vicar*

Hints have been dropped that there was gossip about the late earl's relations with Miss Longden, the vicar's daughter. Could this have led to murder? Mr. Longden is a clergyman. Could he have come to regard himself as the avenging instrument of Providence?'

"No," said the colonel loudly, and then "Yes," equally loudly, after which he glared at Bobby as if he had detected him in a flagrant confusion of thought. "All the same," he added, "I don't much care for this father-avenging-his-daughter's-honour idea. Too theatrical."

"Yes, sir, I know," agreed Bobby, "only sometimes the theatre does resemble life—and even more often life resembles the theatre. I don't think we can rule out the possibility at present, though there's not a shred of evidence to support it, except gossip probably started by a malicious and nasty-minded butler."

"Well, your next is this butler fellow himself," the colonel said, and read out:—

'E8. *Martin.*'

("Marmaduke seems to be his first name, I didn't know that till this morning," interposed Bobby, and the colonel snorted indignantly, for Marmaduke seemed to him a most inappropriate name for a butler, and to go a long way to confirming the worst suspicions.)

'Martin,' the colonel re-read. 'In his case no known motive.

E9. *Clinton Wells*

Only motive apparent would be a desire to bring to a head a lawsuit certain to attract universal attention and that, if Wells conducted it successfully, or even in a way to win general approval, would probably make his name. He is certainly very ambitious. He might regard the case as his road to fame and yet feel the difficulty of bringing it to a head while the earl was alive and no question of succession had arisen. Again, success might seem impossible while the old earl was still alive, and presumably ready to go into the witness-box on Bertram's behalf. Dead, he couldn't testify to his belief.

Finally. E10. *X. The unknown quantity.*

F

EVIDENCE.'

"Ah!" interpolated the colonel. "I wondered when you were coming to that—scanty and contradictory about sums it up. Well, let's see what you think we've got."

He went on reading:—

'Against

F1. *Sophy Longden*

Finger-prints.

F2. *Lady Wych*

Mr. Longden's statement that he saw her outside the library window about the time of the murder.

F3. *Anne Hoyle*

Bertram's evidence that she was not in her room at the relevant time. Bertram's second statement that she was in possession of a pistol—presumably the missing automatic from the library drawer.

F4. *Ralph Hoyle*

His known violence of temper, his possession of a pistol of the requisite calibre and type, his quarrel with his great-uncle shortly before the murder.

F5. *Arthur Hoyle*

Hiding in the vicinity at the relevant time.

F6. *Bertram Hoyle (soi-disant)*

Presence near head of service stairs giving access to the library. He had no legitimate business there at that time—the bathroom story being evidently an invented excuse.

F7. *Mr. Longden*

Presence near at time of murder. Knowledge of the estate office pistol and possession of key of safe.

F8. *Clinton Wells*

Knowledge of the same pistol.

F9. *Martin*

None except presence near the scene of the murder and his denial thereof.

F10. *X, the unknown quantity*

No evidence even of the existence of any X.

G

GENERAL REMARKS

All the three women concerned seem to have strong and unusual characters. Not many young girls could hold out in refusing to answer questions as did Miss Longden.'

The colonel paused in his reading.

"I've a good mind—" he began, glaring at the door, as if intending to send again for Sophy then and there. He did not do so, and he did not explain what he had "a good mind to". (It was in fact a "good mind" to make Sophy speak and a total inability to see how.) "Oh, well," he said crossly and went on with his reading:—

'As for Anne Hoyle, she seems of an extraordinarily ambitious and domineering type. She resents bitterly the old world conventions that on account of her sex deprive her of what she considers to be her rights. One feels she would be likely to go a long way if she saw any chance of asserting them. That is not possible under the present law. But as the wife of a man of weaker type than her own, she would probably be able to get her own way in everything. As Ralph's wife, she would certainly find he had his own ideas about things. Then there's Lady Wych, a remarkable old lady, certainly a good deal taken up with what they call the family honour. Family honour undoubtedly comes into the picture somehow. Ambition, love, family honour, three strong motives for which strange things have been done in the past and will be again in the future.

'The three men of the family are also interesting and contrasting types. There's Ralph, desperate, it may be, at the thought of losing all he believes rightfully his; Bertram, possibly afraid the old earl may be going to change his mind, balanced between getting kicked out or established as heir, and resorting perhaps to murder to make one scale tip the balance; Arthur, known to be a bit of a gambler, perhaps seeing a chance, if he plays his cards well, of securing so great an inheritance. Finally, the three outsiders, vicar, lawyer, butler, hovering at present, so to say, on the outer verge of suspicion, but each one of the three liable to become the central figure at any moment.'

That ended Bobby's memorandum, and the colonel laid it down on the table and shook his head doubtfully.

"All very interesting," he said, "and they all seem to have a motive of sorts. It's all tied up with this question of whether Bertram is a fraud or the genuine article. And yet that's a point we are not supposed to be concerned with, and can't investigate directly. Making things difficult," grunted the colonel indignantly. "Reminds you of little Jack Horner. Put in your thumb and you pull out a— murderer. Only which?"

The telephone bell rang. Bobby went to answer it. Presumably it was of importance or the outer office would not have put the call through. Bobby took the message and then turned to the colonel.

"Mr. Clinton Wells," he said. "He wants to know if we have arrested Ralph. He says if we have, we should have warned him so that he could take immediate steps. He seems very indignant, and wants to lodge a protest."

"About something we haven't done?" growled the colonel. "Tell him not to be an ass. Why should he think we have arrested Ralph—or any one else for that matter? I only wish we knew enough."

Bobby was at the telephone again. He turned round presently, looking puzzled.

"He says that's the story going about. He says no one has seen Ralph this morning. He says Ralph slept at home, but got up early, went out without stopping for his breakfast and no one has seen him since."

"Bolted?" said the colonel slowly. "Bolted? I suppose that's conclusive."

CHAPTER XVI
THE CHARLES THE SECOND OAK

None the less, though Colonel Glynne spoke with such emphasis, though Bobby expressed no disagreement, neither of them was quite convinced that this flight— if flight it were, this disappearance—to use a word that went at least no farther than the actual fact proved—carried with it the obvious significance of confession of guilt.

"Panic? Ralph's not the sort to panic, and where there's been one murder there may be another," Bobby heard the colonel mutter, half to himself, and later on was called upon to confirm this utterance that, later on still, the colonel, who had been intensely interested by some of Mr. J.B. Priestley's 'time' plays, was inclined to regard as a proof of how events to come impinge upon the conscious present.

Then as they were preparing to leave to investigate upon the spot the circumstances of this new and startling development, there came in a report of another disappearance.

"Man of the name of Brown, Bertram Brown," explained the inspector on duty, to whom the report had come in the first place. "Booked a room at the Chambers Temperance Hotel, in Carlyle Street, two days ago. Went out and hasn't been seen since. His luggage is still in his room. Not a great deal apparently, one bag with contents the hotel people don't seem to think much of or likely to cover their bill if it runs on any longer. They say he had had a bit too much to drink—the Chambers is one of those temperance hotels which are run rather on bottle-party lines, you can have as much as you like if you send out for it—and they were afraid he might have met with an accident. It seems he landed in Glasgow from America, spent the night there at the Northern Lights Hotel—that's the label on his bag at least—and then came on to Midwych."

Colonel Glynne gave the necessary routine instructions for looking into the matter, and Bobby noted, without thinking much of it, the trifling coincidence that here was another Bertram, though Bertram is not one of the more common Christian names.

Then they started off and were soon at Ralph's home, the house he occupied, or had occupied, as Wych Estate Agent.

All their questioning produced no further information. Ralph seemed perfectly normal on retiring to bed the previous night. He had risen early this morning, gone out without waiting for his breakfast, and had not been seen or heard of since. The house was on a road that lay between the village and the castle. If he had turned east he must have passed through the village, where, even at that early hour, many would be astir and he would almost certainly have been seen. So presumably he had gone west, past the castle, where they were not such early risers, and so he might have escaped notice, and on possibly towards Midwych itself. Or he might have turned off across the fields and so made his way towards the thickets and groves and wide open spaces of Wychwood Forest. Traversing these he could emerge anywhere west or north of Midwych; or indeed in the safe concealment of that great expanse of solitary and deserted country, it would be possible for a young and healthy man, used to country life, to maintain a kind of Robinson Crusoe existence almost indefinitely.

There seemed to be a general impression that that was what he might intend doing, and that, if so, then those deep forest recesses afforded safe concealment. The colonel said gloomily:—

"Take an army to search Wychwood—and then they mightn't find."

A fox-hunter's expression Bobby did not much like, for he did not care to think of Ralph as the hunted creature pursued thus with horn and dog through the indifferent forest trees. An ugly picture, he thought, and an offence to human dignity, and yet, if Ralph were indeed the murderer of the old earl, what better fate did he deserve?

Having learned nothing by their inquiries in the village and neighbourhood the colonel and Bobby went on to the castle in the hope of getting some information there. No one seemed to know anything though all were closely questioned. Countess Wych was in bed and Sophy thought her unfit to see any one. However, when asked she declared herself both fit and willing to receive the colonel.

"But not that young man of his," she sent the message down. "I don't like him. He gets on my nerves."

The colonel thought this a little hard on Bobby, but thought it would be better to see the countess on her own terms, rather than not at all. So, leaving Bobby downstairs, he went off; and to Sophy, who also had stayed downstairs, since Lady Wych had stipulated that she and the colonel were to talk alone, Bobby said:—

"You know, I'm awfully sorry to think I got on Lady Wych's nerves. Especially as she doesn't strike me as a nervy person. In fact, I shouldn't have said she went in for being nervy."

Sophy made no answer to this, though it was plain that she was of much the same opinion. Abruptly she said:— "Mr. Ralph didn't do it."

"If he is innocent he should have stayed here," Bobby said. "Innocent people don't run away."

He used the expression deliberately, in the hope that it might sting Sophy into a defence of the absent man. If once she could be induced to talk, any information she had and was keeping to herself might presently get itself uttered. He thought the attempt had failed, for she remained silent, though it was easy to see that there was deep fear and unease in the bright clear eyes fixed steadily on his. Since she did not speak, he said presently:—

"Is not running away as good as a confession?"

"Mr. Ralph didn't do it," she repeated.

" If you have any reason to think so," Bobby said gravely, "or if there is anything you know, or think you know, or suspect, won't you tell us? If Ralph Hoyle is innocent, it can only help him."

"I don't know anything," she answered, and added unexpectedly:— "I suspect everything. It's all so vague, like a nightmare, when you feel you must and yet you can't. There's something... you don't know what... all around you... something horrible... it's like that... only you can't do anything."

She had begun by speaking calmly enough, but at the end her words came in gasps, in broken sentences. Bobby, watching her closely and not without sympathy, felt that he understood well what she meant. He had often felt like that. Groping in the dark for he knew not what and knew not even if it were there, whatever it might be.

"If you think of anything, no matter how trivial, won't you let us know?" he asked, almost pleadingly, for he could not get away from the feeling that those small hands, however unwittingly, might hold the vital clue still needed. "No harm would be done by telling us, even if it turned out to be quite unimportant."

She made no reply to that, and presently he went on:— "I expect you feel very sorry for Ralph, don't you?"

"I do think it's such a shame," she burst out as though this question released depths of feeling hitherto held up. "I just know he would never do anything like that, and now Anne says she won't be engaged to him any more, and I think it's wicked, I do, and I don't know how any one can think of marrying Mr. Bertram, not if he's Lord Wych ten times over, and he isn't, I know he isn't."

"Then why did the old earl recognize him?"

For once her eyes dropped before his. He wondered if she knew or suspected the true reason. But he knew also that she would say nothing unless and until she thought the time had come.

"Lady Wych is still willing to accept him, isn't she? to let him inherit the title?" Bobby asked after a time.

Perhaps... I don't know..." Sophy answered slowly. "It's all so difficult... I don't think she has made up her mind... knows what to do... everything is such a dreadful muddle... I think she's all confused and upset."

"Miss Longden," Bobby said slowly, "don't you think you ought to be willing now to answer us, to tell us everything. Police have no power or authority to insist on your speaking, but if you are called as a witness, the courts have authority. They can make it very unpleasant for any one, who won't answer reasonable questions."

"Yes, I know," she answered, as one who long ago had seen what was inevitable, and, since it was inevitable, knew there was nothing to be gained by trying to avoid it. "I looked in a book and it had all about what they can do to you. I think being shut up in prison must be worse than almost anything, don't you?"

"Miss Longden," Bobby repeated, "if you refuse to answer questions, you must not wonder at what we think. There are two possibilities. Either you shot Lord Wych yourself..."

"Me?" said Sophy and looked very surprised. "Oh, I wouldn't ever do a thing like that," she assured him. She shook her head gravely. "I don't think I could, not really. Do you?" Bobby expressed no opinion, and she continued: "Of course, I'm an awfully good shot."

"Eh?" said Bobby, a good deal startled.

"Didn't you know?" she asked. "I thought detectives always found out everything. It was Uncle Jim. He's an officer in the Territorials. He showed me their shooting range, and it was awfully interesting, and I said could I try, and he looked ever so superior, and said all right, and promised me a pair of silk stockings if I hit the target once in five shots, and I hit it every time, right on that round black spot in the middle, only he wouldn't give me five pairs of stockings, and I think it was rather cheating not to, don't you? and then he got his revolver and told me to try with that, and I did, but he wouldn't promise me anything for hitting, though I wanted him to."

"Were you as good with the revolver?" Bobby asked.

"Oh, yes, nearly, not quite. I hit the black round thing three times and uncle said two hits were inners and one missed altogether—I can't think why. It's quite simple really. All you've got to do is to point the thing straight. Uncle said lots of people couldn't. I think that's rather funny, don't you? because it's only pointing straight."

"I suppose that is all," agreed Bobby, feeling a little worried by this unexpected light thus thrown on Sophy's powers and capacities.

He remembered having once heard a firearms expert remark that sometimes people—almost invariably women —were extraordinarily successful the first time they shot. But almost equally invariably they failed just as badly at a second attempt. A kind of beginner's luck, probably. Bobby did not know in the least what to make of Sophy's apparently spontaneous and naive tale. Or had she known he was sure to hear sooner or later the story of her skill, and had she thought it wiser to tell it herself in this apparently simple and innocent way? Was, in short, the girl as simple as she seemed? He reflected grimly that all women are the most inexplicable mixture of child-like simplicity and Machiavellian subtlety. The devil of it was that you never knew which they were turning on—the child-like simplicity or the Machiavellian, more than Machiavellian, subtlety.

Sophy was saying thoughtfully:—

"I don't think I could ever possibly shoot any one. At least not an old man like Lord Wych. I was awfully frightened of him," she added, "he always seemed so grand and imposing, and rather nice with it, only his being nice made you all the more frightened because somehow it made you feel how awful it would be if he stopped being nice. No," she decided firmly, "I'm sure I could never possibly have shot him."

Then we are forced to the second conclusion," Bobby said. "That you know something, and that you won't tell us because you are shielding someone."

She made no answer, but she looked full at him, and he perceived with exasperation that now she was a third woman, neither simple nor subtle, but the very incarnation of an oxlike and immovable obstinacy.

"Oh, hell," said Bobby, losing his temper.

"I don't think," Sophy told him, "that that is a very nice way to talk. My father says it's very sad that young people"—she said this as one of immeasurable age rebuking callow youth—"have got into such a way of using so lightly what are really very dreadful words—like hell and damn—as if they didn't mean anything. They do," Sophy told him sternly, "they have very dreadful meanings indeed."

"Sorry," muttered Bobby, and Sophy at once put on so smug an air of feeling that her rebuke had done him good that he longed passionately to box her little ears for her— the usual coarse masculine reaction when the feminine shaft has struck fairly home.

Another bull's-eye she probably thought, he told himself resentfully.

Partly to change the subject, he asked:—

"Does Lady Wych know Miss Anne has broken off her engagement with Ralph?"

"Oh, yes. Anne didn't want her to know, but I told her at once," Sophy answered primly, and Bobby wanted to shout 'sneak' at the top of his voice, only he didn't dare.

All at once he perceived that now she was neither simple nor subtle, nor prim, nor smug, but entirely different—a larky schoolgirl enjoying a rag on an unpopular mistress.

"Bertram's ever so frightened," she said. "I mean about Anne marrying him. He doesn't want to one bit. You can't imagine how scared he is."

"Well, he hasn't got to if he doesn't want," Bobby remarked, and Sophy surveyed him with quiet contempt. "You don't know Anne," she said simply.

"Oh, well," Bobby muttered.

"I heard Lord Wych say once that Anne was like Parliament," Sophy went on, "and I asked Lady Wych why, and she said it was because Parliament can do anything except turn a woman into a man, and Anne can do anything except turn herself into a man. If she's made up her mind, Bertram just simply hasn't got a chance, and he knows it, and it makes him most awfully sick. Because he is slack all through, and Anne won't have that. He's tremendously upset now he knows what she means. He was upset before, I mean about being the new Earl Wych. He didn't know there was such a lot to it. Being Earl Wych, I mean. He thought it was just being rich and having a good time. And it isn't. Not a bit."

"Being an Earl Wych is a whole-time job," Bobby agreed. "You've got to live up to it—in person, too."

"I showed him Earl Wych's appointment book," Sophy said. "All dinners and speeches and meetings and one thing and another. And Anne to see he didn't shirk. He said it would be like gaol, only in gaol you did get some time to yourself. I don't know if earls are necessary," Sophy added musingly. "Our socialist club in Poplar used to call them an excrescence, only a lot of adjectives as well, but they are kept on the go. And with Anne—"

"Rubbed that in, did you?" Bobby asked when she paused.

"I don't know what you mean," she answered with dignity. "I was only telling him. And he doesn't like the idea of going to the war, either. There's a picture in one of the rooms of an Earl Wych leading a charge or something, and looking awfully fierce, and waving his sword about, and telling the rest to come on. I used to think it was the charge of the Light Brigade at Waterloo or somewhere, but it was only practising in the park really."

"Show it to Bertram?" Bobby asked.

"Well, I did happen to be looking at it while he was there," Sophy admitted, "and I asked him if he thought they were all killed, and then he went away. That's all."

"Rubbing it in?" asked Bobby again.

"I don't know why you keep saying that," Sophy answered with still greater dignity. "He's got to know, hasn't he? It's the Wychwood Dragoon Regiment, only they use motor cars now instead of horses, but it's really all the same, and they say they are going to be the very first to be sent to France."

"Did you tell him that, too?" Bobby asked.

"I think it was mentioned," Sophy admitted again. "He's got to know, hasn't he? What with going to the war, and Anne going to marry him, and having to live up to being Earl Wych, I don't think he is feeling awfully happy."

"Well, thanks for telling me," Bobby said. "Most interesting. Especially why."

"Why what?"

"Why you told me," he explained, and she looked at him doubtfully, as if she understood but was not quite certain that he did. He added:— "I see you are a psychologist."

"What's that?" Sophy asked suspiciously.

"You," said Bobby.

"Oh," said Sophy. "Well, I hope a what's-its-name is nice."

"Generally bald and stuffy and awfully old clothes and big spectacles and a nose in a book," Bobby told her.

"Oh!" said Sophy again, and contemplated this picture without pleasure. "Sike—what is it yourself," she said, and then asked abruptly:— "Why does Mr. Clinton Wells want to know where the

Charles the Second oak is?" Bobby blinked, bewildered by this sudden change of subject. Then he asked:—

"What is the Charles the Second oak?"

"It's where he hid once when there had been a battle and he was running away or something," Sophy explained. "There's all about it in the Midwych County History— it's an awfully dry book and I read it all, at least nearly all except what I skipped—when we came here first—and it says doubts have been thrown on the story, but it doesn't say why. I think it's an awfully nice story, and besides it's still there—the oak, I mean—only Mr. Clinton Wells didn't know and Mr. Bertram didn't either, though nearly every one does, so they asked me, and I told them. But why did Mr. Clinton Wells want to know?"

"There's quite a lot of things I don't know," Bobby answered, "and that's one of them."

He noticed that Sophy was looking hard out of the window. Bertram was strolling along one of the garden paths with his hands in his pockets, and certainly he looked very depressed. Sophy looked away from him at Bobby and then back at Bertram, and Bobby received the conviction that he had been given a hint. He said:—

"Well, if you don't mind, I'll go and have a talk with him."

"I think that would be a very good idea," Sophy approved gravely.

CHAPTER XVII
TEN STAR CLUES

On his way, however, to obey the unspoken hint he felt he had received, Bobby, in crossing the hall, met Martin, busy about some of a butler's duties. Moved by a sudden impulse, Bobby stopped.

"Martin," he said, "can you tell me—you know I'm a newcomer about here—where there's an oak they call the Charles the Second oak, after some old story or another?"

Martin did not answer for a moment, and the look he gave Bobby was sly, calculating, puzzled. That he saw some significance in the question was plain, equally plain that he did not know what that significance could be.

"The Charles the Second oak, sir?" he repeated, obviously trying to gain time.

"Well," said Bobby sharply. "Where is it?"

"Very well-known spot, sir," Martin answered then. "In the forest, sir. Fine view from the top of the nearby hill. Favourite place for picnics."

He proceeded to give directions for finding it. It was about seven miles by road, but by paths through fields and the outskirts of the forest not more than four miles, if as much. Bobby listened attentively, and when Martin had finished, thanked him and remarked casually:—

"I shall be able to tell Mr. Clinton Wells now where it is, if he asks me."

"Oh, Mr. Wells would be sure to know," Martin answered. "Born and bred about here, sir. He's sure to have been there for a picnic or something."

"Apparently he doesn't know, for he was asking about it," Bobby said.

"Well, sir, that's funny, very funny indeed," said Martin, and once more the look he gave Bobby was sly and wondering and suspicious.

"Very funny," Bobby agreed and walked on, aware that he had nearly said:—"Very fishy."

Clear, he thought, that Martin did not believe in Clinton Wells's ignorance of the position of so well known a local landmark, and equally clear that in this pretence of ignorance Martin felt there was some significance about which he was anything but clear.

Nor was that significance clear to Bobby, who was still turning the problem over and over in his mind when he joined the new earl, who, hands in pockets, looking very glum and depressed, had slumped down on one of the seats with which the castle grounds were well provided. He looked up as he heard Bobby approaching and favoured him with an ugly scowl.

"Oh, it's you, is it?" he snarled. "Well, better a cop than any more of that blasted lawyer."

"Has your lordship—?" began Bobby, and Bertram interrupted him angrily.

"Oh, can the lordship," he snapped. "I used to think I would be tickled to death getting called 'my lord', and now I only want to reach for a club. Strikes me being 'my lord' in this damn old country just means being odd-job man about the house. That old stick of a lawyer—"

He paused, apparently for lack of words to express himself, and Bobby said:—

"I suppose Mr. Blacklock has a lot of business to discuss with you?"

"Business?" almost wailed Bertram. "Business? You ought to hear the old geeser." He tried to mimic an old, dry, precise voice. "'It's due to your lordship's position.' 'Your lordship carries heavy responsibilities.' 'Your lordship will be expected—'" Bertram threw up both hands in an almost comical gesture of despair. "Seems to me the whole blessed country isn't doing a thing but expect my lordship. A chain gang isn't in it."

"The duties and responsibilities of an Earl Wych—" began Bobby formally, and then dropped into the vernacular. "There's a hell of a lot he's jolly well got to do."

"You've said it," grunted Bertram, and looked gloomier and more depressed than ever, as though he saw nothing before him but a life of toil, trouble, and hardship. "Speeches, too," he added, as mentioning the last straw.

"Speeches? oh, rather," agreed Bobby warmly. "Part of the job."

Bertram had taken out his handkerchief and was wiping his forehead on which had gathered small drops of perspiration, as at the very thought of speeches he might have to make.

"Couldn't get a word out," he muttered, "not me."

"Oh, Miss Anne will help," Bobby told him cheerfully, and Bertram put his elbows on his knees and buried his face in his hands in an attitude of the most complete dejection.

Bobby surveyed him, not without satisfaction, nor did he offer the reminder that these duties, responsibilities, public appearances, any Earl Wych would be expected to undertake, could only be enforced by public opinion; and could be, and indeed sometimes were, utterly neglected by those called upon to accept them. But then Bobby, thinking of those weak, scowling, uncertain features, did not much think they showed the degree of resolution that would, after all, be needed to resist such general pressure. Besides, those who set themselves against the current of public opinion and expectation, defying all tradition, must feel their own position secure.

But was this man's position sufficiently secure for a display of such defiance of public opinion, when already legal action to test his claim was threatened? A jury would not be favourably impressed by the claims of a man to a great position when he was refusing or neglecting to carry out the duties and responsibilities belonging to it.

These reflections Bobby kept carefully to himself and said instead in his most cheerful voice:—

"Oh, that'll be all right. Miss Hoyle will always be there to see you don't forget or overlook any of your duties."

Bertram fairly jerked himself upright in his seat.

"What do you mean by that?" he almost shouted.

"Well, I understood your engagement—"

"Engagement nothing," snarled the other. "See?"

Bobby tried to look very bewildered.

"But Miss Hoyle..." he began.

Bertram interrupted with a volley of picturesque and most unseemly comment on that young lady, her appearance, her manners, everything about her. Then suddenly he broke off and looked inclined to cry.

"Do you think she really means it?" he asked.

"I do," Bobby answered with all the emphasis he could command. "From what I've seen of her, when she means a thing, she means it, and she gets it."

Bertram looked round so wildly that for the moment Bobby almost thought he contemplated flight.

"I don't deny I made a pass or two at her," he said moodily. "She's a good looker all right, a high stepper from the word 'Go', but, lordy, if I had known her as well as I do now I'd as soon have made a pass at a rattlesnake."

"Oh, come," protested Bobby, "she's not as bad as all that surely."

"Worse," Bertram declared. "Well, not rattlesnake. Boa constrictor." He seemed rather pleased with this comparison. "Boa constrictor," he repeated, and looked up at Bobby as one seeking sympathy. In a voice trembling with resentment and sorrow he said:—

"She's cut down on the drinks already."

"You don't say," murmured Bobby.

"Take my solemn oath," said Bertram. "If I tell that sneaking butler fellow I want another, he says 'Yes, sir' and off he goes. But," said Bertram impressively, "it don't come."

"Too bad," said Bobby.

"I know it's her," declared Bertram moodily, and Bobby could not resist saying:—

"It's all for your own good, you know."

Bertram indulged in another outburst of picturesque and most improper comment, reflecting, by the way, in passing, on all Anne's ancestors, who were, if his story was true, his ancestors, too. Possibly, however, he hadn't thought of that. When he had exhausted his available stock of adjectives, he paused, sighed, and, in a meek little tone contrasting oddly with the violence of his outburst of the moment before, he said:—

"She's got me scared. That girl—slave-driving is as natural to her as swallowing a highball. There's a way she has of looking at you—"

He broke off, seeking a suitable comparison, and Bobby supplied it.

"Like a cat at the mouse she's cornered."

Bertram nodded in gloomy agreement.

"All the same," he muttered, as one whistling to keep up his courage, "she can't make a fellow."

"She doesn't have to," Bobby told him. "She just sees that things happen the way she wants them to happen and they do."

Bertram made no comment on this, but looked more depressed than ever. Bobby sat down beside him, lighted a cigarette, and smoked in silence, leaving Bertram to muse in equal silence on the fate before him. When Bobby thought these musings had lasted long enough, he remarked as by way of making conversation:—

"I was interested to read in one of the Midwych papers about you taking your place in the ranks of the Wychshire Dragoons, and hoping presently, like your heroic ancestors, to lead them into action."

Bertram turned and gave Bobby an even more malevolent glare.

"I'm joining no Wychshire Dragoons," he announced. "Not me. That was a lot of guff I pumped into the fellow because he seemed to expect it. This isn't my war. Nothing to do with me."

"I am afraid," Bobby said gently, "that the Conscription Act is even more compelling than Miss Anne Hoyle, and that is saying a good deal. It applies to all British subjects—dukes, earls and dustmen."

"Suppose I ain't one? British subject, I mean."

"You mean you got naturalised in America?"

"Would that stop me being earl?"

Bobby did not answer this question. He said instead:— "You came in on a British passport?"

"What's that got to do with it?"

"If you claim American citizenship, it was hardly consistent, was it? And you will have to show your naturalization papers, if you want to avoid being called up. Are they complete?"

Bertram made no reply; and with a quick inner excitement, Bobby thought:—

"He doesn't want to show them."

And this seemed to him to throw a clear and sudden light on the situation.

"You will have to show them," he repeated aloud.

"I don't have to," Bertram answered sullenly, and then: "I ain't going to no war."

Bobby looked at him thoughtfully. The fellow was quite simply and plainly a born coward. Not his fault perhaps. None the less, without courage there is nothing on which any foundation of character can be built. That no doubt explained the essential weakness which made him feel so helpless before Anne. Bobby told himself grimly that weaknesses are there to be played on when they are weaknesses in a crooked game. He said slowly:—

"It'll be an ugly war. Worse than the last. Bombs and sitting in trenches all day being shelled. That sort of thing. Only more of it and worse. Beastly. But it's there."

"Aren't there conscientious objectors?" Bertram asked suddenly.

The idea of an Earl Wych as a conscientious objector made Bobby gasp. Nor did he think Bertram likely to impress any tribunal before whom he might put forward such a claim, "You would need rather a long record of religious work," he said drily. "Perhaps you have it. No business of mine. Our job is to find a murderer."

"Better ask Martin," grunted Bertram. "He knows something. Snooping, sneaking guy. You ought to see the way he looks when he goes off to fetch another one he never brings."

"I have asked him, but I haven't got much of an answer," Bobby said. "Why not try yourself?"

"Blackmail," Bertram muttered. "That's his game."

"Shouldn't wonder," agreed Bobby. "Only—who?" Bertram shrugged his shoulders, and after a time Bobby said:—

"Oh, by the way, there's one thing I wanted to ask you. In the States, you knew Mr. Bertram Brown?"

It had been a long shot, a very long shot, born merely from Bobby's instinctive dislike of even so small a coincidence as that between two Christian names. But it hit the mark. Bertram turned pale, and once again his hands flew up, but this time that instinctive gesture was of fear.

"What... what... what's that?" he stammered. "What do you mean?"

"Just what I say."

"Well, why? what's it matter if I did? what about it?"

"He landed in Glasgow two or three days ago," Bobby explained: and to his surprise this information, instead of intensifying the other's fears, seemed to dispel them entirely.

"Gave me a bit of a jolt," he said, looking quite jaunty again. "Some other fellow. I did know a Bertram Brown on the other side. But he's dead—as good as dead," he added under his breath. "Upset me for a moment when you said he had landed. Thought for a moment there was a ghost come chasing me."

"The Bertram Brown you knew is dead?" Bobby asked, remembering the original report of the death of Bertram Hoyle and the suggestions made that this man was an impostor who had somehow got hold of the dead man's papers.

"Just about," Bertram answered grimly. "Not landing here anyway, not him."

Bobby looked thoughtfully at the new earl, new certainly and doubtful perhaps as well. For it began to seem to him that possibly those two words 'Just about' held yet another and important clue—a star clue, so to say. A strange clue, too, no doubt, and yet it might be as significant as the thread that leads to the heart of the labyrinth. He said:—

"Well, a Mr. Bertram Brown has landed. At Glasgow. He came on to Midwych and he has vanished from his hotel. A second disappearance. We don't have so many in Midwych as all that, and now two have happened together, I do rather wonder if there is any connection.

Bertram was beginning to look worried again.

"I don't know anything about it," he muttered. "Anyway, it can't be the fellow I knew. Not possible."

"I hope," said Bobby, again guilty of a long shot, "the disappearance doesn't turn out another murder."

And at that Bertram looked more worried than ever. For a moment indeed Bobby thought he was going to jump up and run away, and he thought that instinctive reaction interesting as throwing yet additional light on the other's character.

"I wish to God—" he muttered under his breath.

"Yes?" Bobby said when he paused.

"Nothing. It's a hell of a mix up. I never meant... I never thought," and now Bertram's voice had grown a little wild. "It can't be... just can't... how could it be?... the fellow I knew, I mean... if it is... well, what's it mean?" He got to his feet and looked round with a furtive and a frightened air. "Oh, hell," he repeated.

"Hadn't you better make a clean breast of the whole thing?" Bobby asked. "I don't think you'll find it's an awful lot of fun being Earl Wych, especially when you are no more Earl Wych than I am. I don't think you much want to marry Anne, but she goes with the title and you'll have to. She'll see to that. You don't want to go to the war, but Lord Wych will have to—at the head of his regiment."

Bertram winced. The picture of himself leading a regiment into battle was evidently one that he found singularly unattractive. Bobby saw Colonel Glynne come out on the castle terrace and stand there, evidently looking for him. Bobby said:—

"There's my boss. I'll have to go. Thanks for what you've told me."

"Told you? what have I told you?" Bertram asked, looking startled, and Bobby smiled on him amiably and said:—

"Why, everything, I think."

Then he walked away towards the waiting colonel, and as he went added to himself: 'Everything, that is, except the murderer's name—unless it's this vanished Bertram Brown.' He wondered uneasily if thus suddenly and unexpectedly had appeared upon the scene the unknown, the 'X' postulated as a mere possibility but now, as it were, emerging into the light.

As he came up Colonel Glynne said to him:—

"Was that Lord Wych you were talking to? I can't get anything out of the old lady. She talks round and round, and if you press her, she shuts her eyes and asks for one of those pills for her heart the doctor left her. Then you have to shut up. At the same time she doesn't want you to go, and I'm sure there's something she wants to say, only for some reason she can't bring herself to it. Get anything out of his new lordship?"

"He's in a very interesting state of mind," Bobby said. "He thinks it would be fine to be Lord Wych, but he's deadly scared of the things a Lord Wych is expected to do, and I think he feels he wouldn't be strong enough to defy public opinion, and that if he did it would attract too much attention. He is still more scared of going to the war, and yet he knows as Lord Wych he would have to. And most of all I think he is scared of Miss Anne. She's cut down his drinks already. I've tried to give him as much as possible to think over. Miss Longden has rather been rubbing things in, too. I'm quite hopeful that if he is left alone for a bit he may decide to throw in his hand."

"Suppose he doesn't?"

"Well, sir," Bobby said slowly, "I've made a list of ten points I think significant. Ten Star Clues, so to say."

He took out his notebook in which he had jotted them down, and while the colonel listened carefully, he read out:—

'TEN STAR CLUES

1. Bertram's hint that he is a naturalised American citizen.
2. Bertram's statement that the Bertram Brown he knew in U.S. is "as good as dead".
3. Earl Wych's statement that his action had done Ralph no harm.
4. Lady Wych's statement that "ill would come of it".
5. Lady Wych's reference to her homicidal ancestress.
6. Anne Hoyle's dogs.
7. Sophy Longden's silence.
8. The Charles the Second oak.
9. Messrs. Blacklock's office boy.
10. Clinton Wells's chivalry.'

When he had finished he handed the notebook to Colonel Glynne, who for some moments sat knitting his brows over it. Then he said:—

"I can see what you mean sometimes, but what is this about the office boy?"

"Only that I thought I should like to know what strangers called recently at their office."

The colonel said moodily:—

"It's still: 'Put in your thumb and pull out a murderer'." Then he said:—"Where's your proof?"

"Yes, sir, I know," Bobby admitted. "I do feel confident that the answers to my 'ten star clues', taken together, give the murderer's name. But we need to find the pistol used in the murder to have a case for a jury."

"And when and if we do find it," the colonel pointed out, "it may knock your 'ten star clues' higher than the skies where stars ought to be."

"Yes, sir, I know," admitted Bobby again, looking more worried than was often the case with him. "It's in my mind—"

He broke off. Anne Hoyle was coming towards them. She looked angry and disturbed. She said:

"Why is the ornamental pond being drained? Who said it could be? If it's you, what authority, what right, have you to interfere like that on our property?"

"Miss Hoyle," the colonel said, "a murder is being investigated. The police have a good deal of authority in such cases. In point of fact, Mr. Owen here spoke to both Lady Wych and to Mr. Blacklock, who is one of the executors. Neither of them raised any objection. Do I understand that you see any reason for objecting?"

She looked at him, sullenly and with fear, and did not answer. Bobby told himself that probably it was the first time in her life that she had ever shown fear. The colonel resumed:—

"It is of course quite usual, when a disappearance is reported, to drag all ponds and so on near by. By way of precaution."

"You don't think, you don't mean...?" she asked, surprised and scornful, and also, Bobby thought, a good deal relieved, "Ralph would never commit suicide," she said abruptly. "He hasn't drowned himself, if that's what you are thinking. I suppose it's the sort of idea police would get."

This last was said to Bobby, and accompanied by a look of great scorn. To her, Colonel Glynne was hardly 'police', she thought of him as a neighbour, one of her own class. It was Bobby whom she regarded as responsible for all that was being done, and it was Bobby who now answered her. He said:—

"When the pond is dry, we shall know for certain. Then, too, it is not only Ralph Hoyle who has disappeared."

"What do you mean by that?" she demanded.

"There are two pistols which have vanished," Bobby reminded her. "Ponds are natural places for hiding such things. Handy if there's one about and somebody has a pistol to get rid of—a colt automatic point three-two, perhaps."

Once again, as once before, their eyes met in a long and silent challenge. Anne was white to the lips when in a voice that was low and steadied only by an effort, she said:—

"What do you mean?"

"That I wondered a good deal why, with your grandfather murdered only a few hours before, you could still find time to play with your dogs, throwing sticks into the water for them to bring out. I wondered if it was only sticks for your dogs to fetch, that you threw into the water." Even then her pride did not desert her. She held herself erect, she brought her voice more under her control, she turned from Bobby as though he were beneath her attention. She spoke to the colonel as equal to equal:— "I suppose this man was watching. I suppose he saw me. Very well. I had my grandfather's pistol. I took it. To keep Bertram sensible. I fired one shot to make sure it would not go off accidentally. I didn't kill grandfather. I expect you think I did. I fired one shot in the air to prevent accidents. That's why you will find one cartridge has been fired."

"The precaution would make no difference with a self-loader," Bobby remarked. "It is true people often leave the first chamber of a revolver unloaded."

They all turned as they heard approaching steps. A man was coming towards them from the direction of the pond. He was carrying something. When he was nearer they could see it was a pistol.

Anne said:—

"Well, you've got it."

She began to walk away towards the castle.

CHAPTER XVIII
GLASGOW VISIT

Nothing else of importance happened or transpired that day, and Bobby was in a somewhat dispirited mood when at last he was able to return home, eat a belated supper, and recount to Olive the events of the day. This was a preliminary adopted since his marriage to his favourite device of putting everything down on paper in as clear a form as he could manage. Her expression grew very grave as she listened to the tale of the discovery of the automatic in the ornamental pond in the castle grounds, and Anne's confession that it was she who had thrown it there.

"Is that enough for an arrest?" Olive asked doubtfully. "The pistol has been sent for expert examination," Bobby explained. "I imagine if it turns out to be the one used, the colonel will feel an arrest necessary. But what's bothering me most is where this Bertram Brown comes in, and why he has vanished."

"He may have nothing to do with it," Olive suggested.

"I know," Bobby agreed. "But in a maze like this, one has to consider every possibility, however remote. Very likely it'll only lead to a dead end. You get used to that in our job. All the same, the whole thing begins with the arrival from America of a chap called Bertram. Another Bertram arrives, also from America, and Bertram No. 1 is very upset, but recovers when he decides it can't be the Bertram he knew, because that Bertram is 'as good as dead'. The next thing that happens is that Ralph Hoyle clears out. Then Bertram No. 2 vanishes. It all seems to me to form part of a pattern, a very carefully laid out pattern, too. But I don't quite see yet where or how to fit in the bits. Or even where to make a start."

"Well," Olive pointed out, "you know one starting point. The Northern Lights Hotel in Glasgow is where the second Bertram begins, isn't it?"

"Glasgow has had a look round there," Bobby objected, and then rubbed the end of his nose and thought hard, while Olive wondered why stimulation of the end of a nose should increase, as it so often seemed to do, masculine cerebral activity. "It's just possible," Bobby went on, having concluded his nose-tip rubbing, "that they may have overlooked something I could spot. They aren't familiar with all the ins and outs of the case, and there might be some trifle I could spot they couldn't tell mattered. Only there's one thing—you remember, I wanted to have a chat with Messrs. Blacklock's office boy, and I can't do that if I go to Glasgow. Besides it's Sunday to-morrow."

"I could find the office boy for you if you like," Olive volunteered. "I expect there will be a housekeeper or caretaker or someone at the office who would know where he lives."

"It might be an idea," Bobby agreed. "No one would suspect police activity if it was a woman asking, and you have to go a bit carefully with a firm of lawyers, especially when it is all so jolly vague."

That then was to be Olive's task for the Sunday; and late as it was Bobby risked official wrath by ringing up the colonel. Fortunately that gentleman had not gone to bed, but in his study was thinking as hard as Bobby himself had been doing, though perhaps with less effect. To him Bobby was put through at once, and from him duly received permission to make the Glasgow trip and, since on Sunday trains were inconvenient, to use a car.

"That's all right, then," Bobby said, returning from the 'phone. "It'll be a bit of a drive, too. And another wild goose chase most likely. It's long odds there's no connection. I'll swear Bertram No. 1 knew nothing about Bertram No. 2's arrival till I told him. He doesn't seem to have been near the castle, so that rules them out. But there's Arthur Hoyle in the background, and the Vicar and Clinton Wells and so on. Any one of them may be concerned. And of course Ralph Hoyle's disappearance is suggestive—though what of goodness knows."

"You don't think anything has happened to him?" Olive asked hesitatingly, for though the fear was in her mind she did not like to give it expression.

"When murder starts you never know where it'll end," Bobby said grimly. "Some seem to get the taste for it, like the Croydon unknown who was never caught. My own idea is that Bertram No. 1—Bertram, Lord Wych, that is —is only a puppet, and that there's someone in the background pulling the strings."

On that they went to bed, and first thing in the morning Bobby was on the road to Glasgow, making such good speed as law and occasion permitted. He arrived about noon, and after a brief interview with the Glasgow police who seemed a little amused at his having come so far on so futile an errand, was allotted a plain clothes sergeant to guide him to the Northern Lights Hotel.

It was a comfortable-looking though quite unpretentious establishment, and the Glasgow police had made their inquiries so thoroughly that plainly not the tiniest item of information had escaped them. With some complacence the plain clothes sergeant remarked on the care and thoroughness his colleagues had displayed, and Bobby agreed warmly, and said it was only what in Midwych they always expected from Glasgow. He explained, too, that he had brought with him a photograph of the missing Bertram Brown's signature in the Midwych hotel and would like to compare it with that in the Northern Lights guest register.

The sergeant suggested that that was in the nature of a work of supererogation, and, in saying this, stole a sideway glance at Bobby to see if the southerner was duly impressed by a word theology has made more familiar north rather than south of the Tweed. A little disappointed that Bobby took the word as it were in his stride, the sergeant added that he knew Mr. Owen was a careful man—and how like to distant thunder he rolled his 'r' in 'careful'—and certainly no precaution was ever unnecessary.

So the register was duly produced, but photograph and original were never compared, for at the first sight of the register Bobby gave a little jump and then pointed to one of the last entries, one that recorded that Ralph Hoyle, of Brimsbury Wych, near Midwych, had stayed the night there.

"That's your man, probably," said the Glasgow sergeant, taking the blow bravely, but rolling his 'r's' more than ever. "Well, now, ye'll note that entry was made after our visit, so it couldn't have been seen then. Travelling under his own name, too, as open as the day."

"I expect that's how he managed to escape notice," Bobby said. "Often enough the best concealment is no concealment. Only—why did he come here?

The sergeant thought that was clear. Making his escape. Lying low till he got a chance of a passage to the States. Wouldn't it be as well to ring up headquarters, report their discovery, and suggest a sharp look out being kept at the docks?

"Trying to get through by running a bluff in the open," said the sergeant over the 'phone, and at the other end it was grimly remarked that an open bluff was as good as a capture, once it was known. Bobby, closely questioning the Northern Lights management, learned from them nothing of significance. Mr. Hoyle had attracted no special attention, but then an hotel guest has to be very eccentric indeed to attract special attention. It was vaguely remembered that he had hung about a good deal, had seemed to be expecting a visitor, had asked if any one had inquired for him, and finally had received a long telephone message, after which he had paid his bill and departed.

Not much the wiser, but wondering who the telephone message had been from, since obviously whoever it was had known where to find Ralph, Bobby returned to the police headquarters, where he was assured that everything possible would be done to trace the missing man, or at least to discover by what route he had left the city.

"He may have skipped over to Ireland," suggested the superintendent. "Get down to the south of Ireland and you only have to say you are dodging the police to be welcomed by all. Or he may have skipped anywhere. But we'll do our best."

With that assurance Bobby departed home. It was late, and he was thoroughly tired out with the long drive when he reached Midwych. There he learned that Glasgow had been as good as its word and had already sent information that a man answering to Ralph Hoyle's description had been seen to take the southward bound train from Glasgow.

"Apparently," said Glasgow with a touch of malice, "he made use of a return ticket, since none was issued to him here."

It was a fair deduction then, Glasgow thought, that the ticket had been bought at Midwych and therefore was available only to Midwych for return. No doubt excess fare could be paid to another destination, but that would be noticed and reported. So a strong probability existed, in Glasgow's opinion, that to Midwych Ralph was returning.

Bobby agreed it seemed likely, and presently received a report that Ralph had actually been seen by an acquaintance leaving the Midwych station about the time of the arrival of a Glasgow train. Once again it seemed that Ralph had evaded pursuit by the simple method of making no effort to evade it.

"Impudence or innocence," observed Colonel Glynne ruefully, and, tired as Bobby was by his long trip, he went on to Brimsbury Wych, though this time with a plain clothes man to drive for him, and accompanied by another, a sergeant, in case he required help.

Ralph's innocence or impudence had not however extended to making a public appearance in the village or at the castle. At the castle Bobby made careful and detailed inquiries, and Sophy, when he questioned her, pointed out with some asperity that Ralph had quite evidently and simply gone to Glasgow to keep an appointment, and was there any harm in that? Then he had returned home again and wasn't that perfectly natural? So what was all the fuss about?

"He doesn't seem to have returned home yet," Bobby remarked.

"Well, perhaps he has another appointment to keep," suggested Sophy, "Why not?"

"That's an idea," Bobby said and looked thoughtful.

It struck him as a possibility that Ralph had been called to Glasgow on some pretext or another and then, on some fresh pretext some new meeting place had been arranged whereto Ralph was now on his way.

But by whom? With what purpose? Whereabouts?

Somewhere in the neighbourhood, no doubt, since it was to Midwych Ralph had returned. But 'this neighbourhood' was a vague term, and then there flashed into Bobby's mind a sudden memory of the inquiry Clinton Wells had made concerning the exact position of the Charles the Second oak. Could it be there, he wondered, this new trysting place, and even as he wondered he saw how Sophy was looking at him, and understood at once that the same idea had come to her.

"Oh," she said, and ran out of the room so swiftly, so lightly, so unexpectedly, that her disappearance quite startled Bobby, and more than startled Martin, with whom she collided violently just outside the door.

"He was listening," she called over her shoulder as she disentangled herself and ran on.

"Were you?" Bobby asked; and Martin, whom only contact with the wall had saved from going full length on the floor, answered angrily:—

"I shall inform her ladyship that unless I receive a full apology from the young lady, I shall prefer to hand in my notice."

"Yes, but that doesn't answer my question," Bobby said, and walked on to find his sergeant whom he instructed to return to Midwych to ask there for two men to be detailed for special duty to watch the Charles the Second oak.

"Tell Colonel Glynne," Bobby said, "that it's only an off-chance, but Ralph Hoyle almost certainly went to Glasgow to keep an appointment and it may be he has come back to keep another."

The sergeant said nothing, but told himself it was lucky he had his promotion and so was no longer a constable and liable to be picked on to keep such useless, tedious, senseless vigils.

Alas for the vanity of human expectations.

Colonel Glynne said:—

"All right. It may turn out important, so you had better go yourself, sergeant, and take a good man with you."

The sergeant, with thoughts too deep for words, retreated. To the superintendent who was also in the room, Colonel Glynne said meditatively:—

"You know, Inspector Owen is a perpetual puzzle to me. He looks and generally acts like the most stolid matter-of-fact, unimaginative Englishman you ever heard of, and then he comes out with some sort of guesswork, intuition, subconscious reasoning, whatever you like to call it, that's as likely as not to hit the mark. The Welsh in him most likely. I suppose a good many English are like that—Celtic strain in us all that bubbles up from time to time. It's what upsets foreigners—a divine unreason the poets call it. It'll upset Hitler and his pals before this job is through."

So the colonel pursued his analysis in philosophical reflection; and Bobby, back at the castle and asking for Miss Longden, to whom he had wished to put another question, was told that she had gone out, leaving a brief message that no one was to wait up for her and delegating her duties with Lady Wych to one of the maids who had sometimes, on other occasions, taken her place for brief periods.

"Martin's gone out, too, and says he won't be back to-night," added the maid to whom Bobby was speaking, one of the older members of the household staff. "Every one seems to think they can do just as they like with his lordship dead, and her ladyship in her room, and Miss Anne not seeming to care. Everything at sixes and sevens," she complained.

Bobby said vaguely that it was all very trying, and he asked himself with some misgiving whether there was or could be any connection between Sophy's sudden resolve to spend the night elsewhere and Martin's abrupt departure.

He decided to go on to the vicarage, though by now it was late and pitch dark, and see if Sophy was there. Or perhaps Ralph, though of that Bobby had small hope, for it was growing more and more fixed in his mind that Ralph at Glasgow had been given an appointment at the Charles the Second oak.

But why? and for what purpose? and why the earlier summons to Glasgow? Was that to confuse the trail, so that any search made would be there and not here?

Bobby's looks were grave and troubled as he thought of that dark, solitary meeting place in the heart of the forest, and of how few and rare would be its visitors now that the summer season was over, how little the chance of anything happening there coming to light for many months.

Unnecessary fears, he told himself, vexed that his imagination should be so out of control as to present to him forebodings and fears for which the actual facts offered such slight foundation. A sign, he supposed, of the strain recent events had imposed upon them all.

He reached the vicarage. At this time the blackout in country districts was only very laxly enforced, and Mr. Longden stood framed in the light streaming from the hall as he talked to Bobby at the open door.

The vicar was, it seemed, worried and uneasy. One of the villagers had been saying he had seen Sophy hurrying along a field path that led nowhere save to the forest; to the heart of the forest where the trees grew most thickly, where the stretches of gorse and bracken, and of the comparatively open glades that abounded elsewhere, hardly existed. It was a dark night, however; the villager might easily be mistaken; and Mr. Longden, though worried, felt there must surely be some misapprehension, for what errand could Sophy possibly have that would send her so late to the lonely, the deserted forest?

"I was on the point of walking over to the castle to inquire," he said, a little in the manner of a man confessing to a nervousness he knew to be slightly absurd.

Bobby made no comment, for he thought to himself that it might be easy to guess the nature of Sophy's errand—if indeed it was for the forest she was bound.

He wondered if he could overtake her. He felt the attempt would have to be made. He asked what path it was on which Sophy was said to have been seen. It led, he learned, almost directly to the Charles the Second oak, and was often used by hikers and picnickers bound in the summer for that well-known view-point. But the path was not very easy to find or keep to, since it was crossed by many side tracks.

As quickly as the darkness and his ignorance of the ground permitted, he hurried on; for he had a feeling that haste was needed, and when he reached the verge of the forest, where the tall trees made the black night blacker still, he saw, or not so much saw as was aware of, a dark and shadowy form flitting lightly before him, only a short distance ahead.

He called her by name. She did not answer. He heard instead, in the quiet of the forest and the night, how instantly she increased her speed.

CHAPTER XIX
WYCHWOOD

Bobby called but got no answer. He called again, his voice lost in the vast and sombre silence of the woods. He began to run, but already those light footsteps he had been aware of had faded, they, too, into the all-prevailing stillness. He had a powerful electric torch with him. He flung its beam ahead, around, as he ran. Here and there its strong ray startled into life some denizen of the forest that even those light passing footsteps Bobby had heard had frightened into immobility. But the faint scampering such small creatures made as they sought safety, or the flutter of wings as some bird or another made its indignant and disturbed way to a fresh roosting place, alone broke the brooding quietude all around. Bobby tried to run more quickly, but in the darkness speed was not easy. After he had collided with a tree or two, stumbled once or twice, felt a branch like the lash of a whip across his face, he slackened to a walk.

After all, he might have been mistaken. What he had thought were light and running steps might have been in reality only dead leaves rustling in the slow night breeze. He looked at his watch. It was past eleven now, and only the faint and intermittent light of the stars shining here and there from behind a panoply of cloud, relieved the darkness beneath the trees. He wished he had more experience of life in the open air, of country life. A man felt so small, so lost, so insignificant in the heart of this great forest where forest had been since the beginning, where his remote, skin-clad ancestors would have felt so much more at home than he could ever be, with his sophisticated training of town and pavement. He found himself wondering if it could really be Sophy he had heard, and deciding that it was impossible. How could she, so small, shy, shrinking, ever have found the courage to penetrate into this sombre solitude at this dead hour of the night?

Abruptly he discovered that he was on the wrong path, one that was running north instead of due west, since the Charles the Second oak lay, he knew, due west of the castle, and, small knowledge as he had of the stars, he could at least recognize the north star, now shining directly ahead of him instead of on his left. By good luck he stumbled on a path that seemed to lead in the right direction. He followed it till it joined another, one also running west, and apparently more frequently used.

Suddenly he stiffened to attention. Always, all the small innumerable noises of the night, all the whispering movements of the little busy creatures that go about their business in the greater safety of the covering darkness, all had hushed to a wary stillness as he passed by, recognizing that here was something coming that was strange, unknown and formidable. Only his own footsteps, that even to himself sounded so clumsily, so almost indecently loud, broke that primaeval forestal tranquillity. Yet already his ears had in some measure attuned themselves to the all-pervading quiet, as if now they were recovering ancestral qualities only forgotten, not lost, in disuse; able, therefore, to distinguish quickly alien sounds that had no commerce with the life. He stood quite still and listened again, at once aware that here were sounds of approaching steps that differed altogether from those earlier ones that he had heard before. Hurried they were indeed, as those others also had been, but loud, uneven, clumsy, utterly alien to the life of the woods into which the earlier footsteps had seemed to merge, having with it something in common, as though they belonged to some belated dryad hurrying back to her tree home.

The steps came nearer. A man's, undoubtedly. Ralph Hoyle, perhaps, Bobby thought, or else that unknown who might be the missing Bertram Two, as Bobby was beginning to call him in his thoughts, who again might turn out to be the sender of the mysterious 'phone message received by Ralph at the Glasgow hotel. Bobby found himself wondering with dark fear if that message had been to make an appointment in this forest loneliness that had perhaps already been kept.

A disturbing thought there in the black and silent night, for if that appointment had been made, then for what purpose in so lonely a spot and why from it was apparently only one returning?

Those hurrying, stumbling footsteps were nearer now. In the night the approaching form began to take shape, to be recognizable as a man. Bobby stepped out into the middle of the path where the darkness was at least less intense. He was preparing to utter a challenge. It never got spoken, for with a howl scarcely human in the intensity of its fear and its surprise, of what indeed seemed its despair, the unknown hurled himself at Bobby.

Taken by surprise, astonished, too, by the fury of the assault, Bobby reeled backwards. He caught his foot on the root of a tree and went headlong, his assailant with him. Over and over they rolled, locked in a close, embracing fury. Bobby tried to wrench himself free. He received a heavy blow on the side of the head from some heavy instrument, and for the moment was dazed. A second blow he managed to take on his elbow. He wrenched himself free by an effort that called for every ounce of his strength. A blow he aimed at the glimmering patch of whiteness in the dark that he took for a face, had full effect. His assailant went sprawling, his grip loosened. Bobby got to his feet. His electric torch was still in his hand. He switched it on, turned its ray on the huddled form at his feet, almost indistinguishable from the bush into which it had been hurled by Bobby's well-aimed blow. But if the sharp, searching ray of the torch showed that, it showed also the muzzle of a pistol pointing straight at Bobby.

For an interminable moment, from the heart of the bush, that muzzle pointed thus, its deadly threat hanging suspended in the clear light of the ray from the electric torch. There flashed into Bobby's mind the thought that he made an excellent target. Then he thought that now he would never know who it was, for while the prostrate man held the pistol steady in one hand, he kept the other before his face, his hand and the branches of the bush concealing it completely.

"Get out, clear out, keep out," a high-pitched, screaming voice cried at him, a voice in which there mingled menace and panic in a way that Bobby knew, for he had heard it before at other times, carried with it deadly warning, the menace and the panic each reinforcing and strengthening the other.

He gathered himself together for a spring, his only chance. He thought:— 'He can't miss,' and then again:— 'He is as scared as I am—more.' A stone came flying over his shoulder, thrown from behind. A yelp showed that it had hit its mark. The pistol muzzle wavered. Bobby sprang. In the bush, fortunately it was not a bramble bush, not thorny, they wrestled to and fro, threshing confusedly in the dark. Then Bobby found himself uppermost, found his fingers grasping a coat collar, hauled with vigour, discovered he was standing upright, a little breathless, a trifle dishevelled, at his feet a limp, unresisting form whining incoherent protests, from which Bobby could distinguish that there had never been even the most remote intention of firing, that sooner would the speaker have shot himself than Inspector Owen, whom he had failed to recognize, and had absurdly mistaken for a highway robber, that he had only found the pistol that night, that he had fully intended to take it straight to Inspector Owen, that for that service he had expected to be thanked or even to receive some small reward, not to be knocked about something terrible as he had been, and the sight of one eye probably lost for ever, owing to a blow received from a stone, which, in his considered opinion, was hardly to be expected from a gentleman like Inspector Owen.

"Get up," said Bobby with an unsympathetic though not very severe application of the toe of his boot to an appropriate part of the anatomy of one whom he had now recognized to be Martin, the castle butler. "So it's you, is it? Well, what have you been playing at?"

"Playing?" groaned Martin bitterly, "playing?" and indeed with his torn clothing, his bruised eye, his nose and mouth still oozing blood from the blow dealt by Bobby, he looked anything but playful. "Playing?" he repeated still more bitterly.

Bobby was thinking:—

'Who threw that stone? someone threw that stone. Who?'

Martin went on whining:—

"It hit me in the eye, right in the eye, I expect I shall be blind in one eye, who will want a one-eye'd butler?"

Bobby, swinging his torch to and fro, searching the ground, saw now what he had been seeking—a pistol lying near the bush where it had been jerked from Martin s grasp. He picked it up. It was a Colt automatic point thirty-two. He said:—

"How did you get this?" Then he said: "Is this what was used for the murder?"

"I don't know," whined Martin. "How should I know? It might be. I thought to myself, I thought: 'What's he talking so much about that old oak for?' and I thought if I went there and I found anything same as I did, it being there all right, the pistol I mean, and I said to myself, I said, that'll be a help, I said, and maybe a trifle of a reward, too, just by way of acknowledgement, instead of which there's all my teeth out and very likely an eye gone as well. Who'll want a one-eye'd butler?"

"Shut up," ordered Bobby roughly. "Quiet."

He listened. He could hear them distinctly now. Fresh footsteps approaching and the sound of voices raised in argument.

Martin, seeing how intently Bobby was listening, seemed to think it an opportunity. He was trying to slip away when Bobby shot out an arm and caught him by the collar and jerked him back.

"You'll have a lot to explain if that does turn out to be the murder weapon," he said grimly. "Won't look too good for you, you know."

Martin began to babble excuses, protests, explanations, but once again Bobby cut him short.

"Keep that till later on," he said, "and don't spend the time thinking up lies. It'll only make things worse for you if you do, and they look bad enough already."

By now the newcomers had drawn near. Bobby threw the light of his torch on them. They were three in number. Two of them were the plain clothes men Bobby had asked should be sent to watch the oak. Between them was the missing Ralph Hoyle, indignant and protesting. He recognized Bobby at the same time.

"What in blazes is all this?" he demanded. "What's the game?"

"Don't know," Bobby answered. "Can't give it a name yet. It might be saving your life—or even your honour. Do you mind falling down?"

"What?" said Ralph, thinking he had not heard correctly. "What's that?"

"Yours not to reason why," murmured Bobby; and, taking Ralph completely by surprise, very neatly tripped him up and deposited him full length on the ground. "Lie still, you fool," he added in a quick whisper to the considerably astonished and even annoyed Ralph, and then in a loud voice, indeed in a very loud voice:— "He's fainted. It's a deep wound, probably fatal."

"What the hell?" protested Ralph furiously.

But Bobby had leaped away. He had heard a quick, rustling movement behind one of the trees. A moment later he emerged, accompanied by Sophy.

"I thought that dodge would work," he said complacently. "Gave herself away at once."

"What the hell?" repeated Ralph, making up for want of originality in expression by even greater depth of feeling.

"Now, now," said Bobby, soothingly this time, "you said that before."

"Oh, he isn't hurt, he isn't hurt a scrap," declared Sophy.

"Well, aren't you glad?" asked Bobby, innocent now.

Enlightenment came to Sophy as she glanced from Bobby, looking now a trifle smug, to Ralph, looking much more than a trifle bewildered. To Bobby she said with tremendous emphasis:—

"You—you beast."

"What in thunder—" began Ralph, and then gave it up for sheer want of words to continue.

"I suppose what you mean," observed Bobby, "is: What is Miss Longden doing here at this time of night?"

"I was having a walk," said Sophy hurriedly.

"Well, now, think of that," murmured Bobby.

"I suppose," said Ralph, throwing in his hand, "this is some sort of new game—charades, probably."

"How did you know?" demanded Sophy, still indignant, of Bobby.

"Detectives always know," answered Bobby impressively, and Sophy wasn't at all impressed and said very loudly.

"Fiddlesticks."

"Well," explained Bobby, "when at what is called the psychological moment a detective sees a stone arrive out of the blue, a well-aimed stone, and it saves what is called, vulgarly, that detective's bacon, and when he remembers that a young lady who thinks that to hit the mark all you have to do is to aim straight, is somewhere about, then he adds two and two together and decides that the answer makes—Miss Longden.”

“I think it's very horrid of you,” said Sophy, unappeased.

“It hit me in the eye,” wailed Martin. “I expect I shall lose the sight. Who'll want a one-eye'd butler?”

“Martin, too,” groaned Ralph, who had not previously noticed him. Resignedly he asked Bobby:— “Who else have you got in your pocket?”

“It's like this,” began Martin, but Bobby stopped him.

“You keep quiet,” he said. “You've plenty to explain, but that can wait.” To the two plain clothes men, he said:— “Got a car anywhere around? Good. Take this man to headquarters. Detained for inquiries.”

They departed, Martin still bewailing his injuries, still protesting the excellence of his explanation if only it were listened to. But Bobby was in no hurry to hear it. His experience told him that Martin would be the readier to talk the more his panic increased with the reluctance shown to listen to him. He would be sure to think that that reluctance was due to the police believing that they had all necessary information already. Which would make him all the more anxious to give his own version. To the still very bewildered Ralph, Bobby said:—

“He had the pistol I think was used in the murder of Lord Wych.”

“Martin? Martin had it?” repeated Ralph. “You mean Martin is the murderer?”

Bobby did not answer. He was deep in his own thoughts. Ralph, looking at Sophy, suddenly forgot all about Martin.

The utter bewilderment her appearance had caused him changed abruptly to an almost equally bewildered admiration, for now it was as though he had never seen her before. Strangely lovely she looked in the dim light beneath the trees that the two beams, one from Bobby's strong electric torch, another from one of Ralph's that he had now produced, shone on the tree trunks and the foliage around, mingling with the faint starlight falling through the leaves and branches overhead. The hard daylight might have deprived her of some of that strange beauty which at the moment was hers, for beauty it was that hung about her now till it seemed as though she were some strange, ethereal spirit of the woods that hovered there, hesitant upon the point of going.

"It's Miss Longden," Ralph muttered. "Is it?" he said, still bewildered. It seemed he could hardly believe what he saw, almost as though he thought it must be some phantom of his own imagination that hovered there. He said again:— "Why, Miss Longden...?"

"Well, don't ask her, because she won't tell," Bobby interposed with a faint grin; and then froze to sudden attention as he realized that the magazine of the automatic he was holding had only one cartridge left.

Three had been fired at Lord Wych. One was left. What had become of the others? Why had they been fired? Why? and—at what mark?

He said abruptly to Ralph:—

"I must hurry off. You can see Miss Longden home."

With that he nodded to them and hurried away, and as he did so it came into his mind that Olive, a matchmaker like all women, would highly approve of what he had just done, and of the opportunity he had thus almost accidentally given Ralph.

"Oh, well," he thought, "if they send me a piece of the wedding cake I shall have earned it," and with that he dismissed all thought of them from his mind that he might busy it with grimmer things.

CHAPTER XX

ACCUSATION

When, after an almost all night long conference with Colonel Glynne and but an hour or two of hurriedly snatched sleep, Bobby arrived at the castle next morning it was to hear from an excited maid the information that the engagement of Miss Anne to the new Lord Wych was to be formally announced that day.

Bobby said that was grand. Notwithstanding murders and disappearances and so on, it was engagements and betrothals and marriages that really mattered. The maid agreed heartily—heartily is the appropriate word here. Bobby said he must find Lord Wych to congratulate him. But no one seemed to know where the happy man was to be found, so at a venture Bobby wandered off to that remote and hidden seat in a solitary portion of the grounds where once before he had found him.

He greeted Bobby with a scowl and a general air of 'Hast thou found me, oh, mine enemy?' and Bobby beamed on him in response.

"I heard the happy news up at the castle," he explained. "I just couldn't help coming along to congratulate you." He sat down by the other's side, produced a cigarette, offered his case to his companion, and beamed afresh at a sulky refusal. For a moment or two he smoked in silence. Then he said gently:—

"Well, she's brought it off all right."

His lordship squirmed.

"I knew she would," said Bobby meditatively. "Not much Miss Anne wants she doesn't get." He added:— "Just as she's got you."

Once more his lordship squirmed.

"I have more good news for you," Bobby went on.

His lordship looked at him suspiciously.

"The Wychshire Dragoons are ordered on active service. As a mechanized unit they expect to lead the attack." (This, by the way, was an addition of Bobby's own, but then there is much virtue in an 'expect'.) "I expect" (again, how useful a word is 'expect') "you'll be given a commission direct without having to bother to apply. That'll be so you can lead them into action, like that chap in the picture in the castle. You know. The one showing an earlier Lord Wych waving his sword in the air to lead the way to the enemy."

"They don't catch me," said his lordship sourly.

"Shot at dawn," murmured Bobby. "That's what happens in war to chaps who try to shirk."

His lordship didn't so much squirm this time as turn pea green. He suffered from a vivid imagination, and he actually saw a picture of himself standing against a wall with half a dozen grim looking men, all extremely like Bobby, standing opposite, rifles in their hands.

"Look here," Bobby said. "You are in a spot. A bad spot. If you're a British lord, you've got to live up to it— and Miss Anne's there to see you jolly well do. There's a war on, and the Earl Wych will have to be in the thick of it. Or people will talk. Talk a lot. You know best what that may lead to. Well, there it is. Hadn't you better make a clean breast of it?"

"I don't know what you're getting at," the other mumbled.

"Oh, yes, you do," Bobby answered. "You are no more Earl Wych than I am. You've given that away half a dozen times. For one thing, you didn't even know why it is Earl Wych and not Earl of Wych."

"Can't expect a chap to remember everything," retorted Bertram, trying to pluck up spirit. "Not after all the time I've been in the States."

"Rubbish. People don't forget things like that they hear when they are children. Another point. More important. You let slip you had taken out your papers over there. That can be traced. May take some time because I believe you can do it anywhere in any part of any State."

"How do you know I gave my right name?" Bertram demanded, evidently thinking that there he had scored a point.

"That's a matter for the American authorities to consider," Bobby answered amiably. "What matters is that it gives us a starting point. Something to work from—to trace your identity."

Bertram mumbled something indistinct. Easy to see that he was growing more and more disturbed. Relentlessly Bobby continued:—

"I told you about the disappearance of a Mr. Bertram Brown from his hotel in Midwych."

"Nothing to do with me," Bertram answered with more confidence. "Nobody I ever knew."

"I wouldn't be too sure of that," Bobby said. "You admitted you knew someone of that name in the States, but you say it can't be the same man because he is 'as good as dead'. I wonder if that means he had been given a long term of imprisonment?"

"Good at guessing, aren't you?" Bertram snarled, now all his former unease returning and in even greater measure.

"Detectives never guess," Bobby protested, a little hurt. "They draw exact deductions from given premises."

Bertram looked impressed but said nothing.

"Parole system in the States, isn't there?" Bobby asked. "Do you think it might be applied to a Britisher so as to get rid of him, get him out of the country and save his keep and so on?"

Bertram's jaw dropped.

"I... I never thought of that," he stammered. "Well, think of it now," Bobby said grimly. He added:— "If that Bertram Brown you knew, is this Bertram Brown—well, who is he and where is he?"

By this time his soi-disant lordship was beginning to perspire gently.

"Now you know," Bobby went on, "why I told you you were in a spot. Why I told you you had better make a clean breast of it."

He paused, watching with scientific detachment his victim's ever-increasing doubts and fears. He thought to himself with a touch of surprise:— 'Why, this is the third degree I'm giving him. What would the papers say?' He continued aloud:—

"There's been one murder. You're under suspicion still. Every one is. Not much evidence yet, but we may get some soon. Was it to your interest old Lord Wych should die before he could change his mind about acknowledging you? Perhaps it was only a temporary arrangement he had been talked into. Perhaps he never meant it to stand. Mr. Bertram Brown has disappeared. Was that to your interest also? and has he been murdered, too?"

Bertram was on his feet now, very pale, gesticulating wildly.

"I wish I had never started the damn thing," he shouted. "Hell, it's no catch being a lord in this damn old country. Hell, I don't want to marry that slave-driving vixen, me that's been married twice already and both of 'em still alive most like, trust 'em for that. Hell, you don't find me getting blown to bits sitting in trenches all day, not me, and me a full American citizen five years and more."

"Clinton Wells put you up to it in the first place, didn't he?" Bobby asked.

Bertram nodded gloomily.

"Know it all, don't you?" he mumbled.

Bobby never denied knowledge. He said:—

"Do you care to make a statement? For you to decide, of course. But it may make a difference. It's generally taken into consideration."

Bertram hesitated.

"Just as you like," Bobby repeated. "Your affair. I think we know enough. I'll have to take you along to headquarters. Not an arrest, you understand. Detained for inquiries, that's all."

Bertram looked as if he thought that 'all' was enough and more than enough.

"Will you promise?" he began.

"No," interrupted Bobby sharply. "You get no promises, my lad. All I say is, if you make a voluntary statement, that fact— provided you don't tell a pack of lies—may be taken into consideration. You'll need it, too," he added grimly.

"Oh, all right," Bertram said, his last shred of resistance broken down. "It was him started it, Clinton Wells, I mean. I'd never have thought of it, never had the gall to try it on. He said it was on Easy Street. If you ask me, he was in a spot himself. At his office. That's my idea. It was Bert told me to go to the lawyers first, to find out how the old man was likely to take it, the old lord I mean. That was after they had handed Bert a ninety-nine-year sentence. Hadn't had as much to do with it as the rest of the boys, but it was him had to stand the racket."

"What was it?" Bobby asked.

"Bank," explained Bertram. "A guy got himself shot. Bert wasn't in it. But the cops picked him up where they found some of the dollars. So they soaked it to him. He got word to me to come see him. Asked me to go back home and tell his people so they could do something about it. Ninety-nine years, that's a packet. Gave me all his papers and such like. Told me where to get 'em, so the cops wouldn't know who he was. Talked a lot about the honour of the family, and him with a ninety-nine-year stretch to do. I was to go to the lawyers first so they could break it to the old lord and see how things lay with him. Bert hadn't a notion then it was him was to be the next lord. He reckoned there was several in the family came first. When I got back home—I was born round these parts, that's how Bert and me first got pally—it was Clinton Wells I saw at the lawyers' office. He's a smart guy all right. Worked it all out while I was sitting there. Smart as the devil. I said: Nix. I said: The old lord, he'll know I'm not the goods. But Clinton Wells, he showed me how we could fix him."

"How?" Bobby asked.

"Mixing it. Half truth, half lies. A story always goes best if part of it's true. Noticed that?"

"I have," agreed Bobby. "So have the poets. A lie that is half a truth is always the stuff to give 'em."

"That in poetry?" asked Bertram, impressed. "He knew his stuff, that poet."

"Sometimes poets do, though it is not generally known," Bobby remarked. "Well?"

"He fixed it so I was to tell the old lord how Bert hadn't got ninety-nine years but only nine months in the cooler, and how the cops and the newshawks, too, had their noses to the trail who he really was. So how about me being him for nine months, because if the old lord handed out a certificate I was him, I mean, that I was his genuine grandson, then when they heard that on the other side, then cops and newshawks, too, would lay off, thinking the lad in the cooler wasn't any more a British lord's grandson than they were themselves."

"What was to happen when the nine months were up and no grandson appeared?" Bobby asked.

"I was to have the job of finding him," Bertram answered. "The idea we put up to start with was that I was to have a fat wad for being him while I was here, and then another wad to go back to the States and hunt him up and bring him home."

"You mean the real Bertram? But he was serving a ninety-nine-year sentence?"

"That's so, but the old man thought it was nine months. When the time came, we reckoned to let on what it really was. Clinton Wells said maybe rather than have such a scandal break, the old lord would go on letting me be—it the grandson, I mean. Because of the family honour. Dead nuts they all were on the family honour. Used to make me laugh, with that ninety-nine-year packet in the background. But they were all so keen on it, Clinton Wells said maybe they wouldn't see any other way to have it saved."

"Nonsense, and Clinton Wells knew it," Bobby told him. "Once Lord Wych knew the truth, he would have faced it. He would never have dreamed of accepting a stranger as heir to the family title and estates. Also he would have known the truth would be sure to come out in the long run. Ralph Hoyle was already threatening legal action. For nine months perhaps, until the real heir got back. Not a day longer. But that explains why he insisted that he was doing Ralph no injustice. He wasn't in a sense, since there actually was then an heir who came before Ralph."

"Clinton Wells said it might be that way," Bertram answered. "If when the old lord knew it all, he wouldn't stand for me being the next lord after him—and mind you, I was tickled to death at first at the notion of being a British lord, me being had for a sucker, and never suspicioning what it meant, or knowing anything about Miss Anne what ought to be running a farm down Tennessee way, nor how there was going to be a war and every one taking it I wanted to be the world's little hero. I thought it was a cinch being a British lord, but now I'm just as glad as not to be out of it."

"I suppose," Bobby remarked, "you hadn't sense enough to see how entirely, if the scheme had gone through, you would have been under Clinton Wells's thumb. He would have had the last penny out of you. If you had tried to kick, he could have posed as having been deceived by you, but having gradually discovered the truth. And so established a claim on Ralph, made sure for ever of the Wych estate business, and made sure, too, of a first-class reputation as the man who unveiled the great Wych peerage conspiracy. A foot in both camps and all ready for it if you tried to kick. But you would never have dared."

"I figured it might be that way," the other answered composedly. "I remember first day I thought that was going to be his game when he staged that bit about being Ralph's attorney and acting for him against me. I didn't like it much, but he talked me down. Said having it that way, he would know every move on Ralph's side and have all the answers pat. I never trusted him, but me being had for a sucker, same as I said before, I reckoned the chance of being a British lord was worth it. Now I know a whole heap more about the job, and I'm not so keen."

"We had better go back to the castle," Bobby said "I must ring up Colonel Glynne and see what he thinks."

"Mind you," added the sham Bertram as they walked along, "I haven't an idea who corpsed the old lord—Ralph, I thought, along of being peeved about me. Only afterwards I wasn't so sure. I did think at times it might be Miss Anne in a hurry to put her hands on me and the rest of it all at once."

Bobby made no reply, and when they reached the castle he got the use of one of the 'phones. He had his story to tell, but there was news for him also. Presently he rang off.

"Clinton Wells is on his way here," he said to his companion. "At least I think he is coming here. He seems to have guessed there are developments, and probably he is coming along to tell you what to say. Or perhaps," Bobby added thoughtfully, "he means to double-cross you now things are getting warm. Pretend he has just found you out. It's pretty certain that's a card he was keeping up his sleeve. I've my instructions, though."

They had not long to wait, for soon Clinton Wells arrived, driving up the long avenue that led to the castle. Bobby had asked that he should be brought straight to this room without being told who was there. Yet he showed little surprise when he saw who were the occupants. One quick glance from Bertram to Bobby and back, and he seemed to divine instinctively what had happened.

"Inspector," he began, "I'm glad you're here. It's a bit of luck. I may as well tell you at once I have found reason to believe that this man is an impostor."

"You dirty, double-crossing—" began Bertram in a fury, but Bobby checked him with a lifted hand.

"Mr. Clinton Wells," he said, "last night we detained Martin, the butler here, for inquiries. This morning he has made a statement. I have just been informed by 'phone. It seems he is prepared to give evidence that on the night of the murder he heard shots fired and he saw you running away. That, of course, makes him an accessory after the fact, but he will probably be accepted as king's witness." Clinton Wells listened quietly and with a faintly contemptuous smile.

"Do you really think any jury is going to believe that yarn?" he asked. "As a matter of fact, Martin meant blackmail, he tried it on a few days ago, he hinted at some such yarn. I only laughed. I thought it too ridiculous. I kicked him out. This is his revenge."

"I agree Martin is not a very reliable witness," Bobby answered. "I am inclined to believe, when we go into it, we shall find he is on record for something like blackmail before. All the same, as I am to take you to headquarters where you will be charged with murder, I must warn you before you say anything more."

"You seriously intend to charge me with the murder of old Lord Wych on the word of a scamp like Martin?" Clinton Wells asked incredulously. "You'll be the world's laughing stock."

"For a long time," Bobby answered slowly, "I have thought you were probably the murderer. It was almost certain the pistol used was either the Wych estate office pistol or the one kept in the castle library. But there was evidence Miss Anne Hoyle had the one from the castle library, and though she very foolishly attempted to hide it, it has been found now, and we know from expert examination that it is not the murder weapon. Nor did it ever seem likely that she was guilty. But your own story of what happened in the estate office the day of the murder, the last time the pistol there was seen, showed that you had the opportunity to secure it. You were the only person left alone in the office with the key, the pistol, and the safe. Mr. Longden never had the key of the office door. Ralph hadn't the key of the safe. He might have provided himself with duplicate keys, but there was no evidence that he had done so, and if he had contemplated committing murder with the pistol it seemed unlikely that he would have gone to such pains to advertise his possession of the thing. So you see, you seemed indicated, but I had to wait till we could get hold of the pistol before we had the proof we wanted. Expert examination of the weapon and the bullets taken from Earl Wych's body give it now. What bothered me was that at first I couldn't imagine any possible motive. But now I know about your elaborate scheme to put up an impostor as the next Earl Wych and then be able to blackmail him to your heart's content. You would have been almost earl yourself, wouldn't you? When Ralph Hoyle threatened legal action, and when Earl Wych showed he was beginning to be suspicious, you got frightened and tried to make yourself safe by egging Ralph on to quarrel with the old earl and then murdering the old man before he could repudiate the impostor, at the same time fastening suspicion on Ralph. I don't suppose you cared very much whether Ralph were actually hanged or not, the mere suspicion would have ruined his chance of being successful in a lawsuit."

Clinton Wells had listened quietly, smiling all the time with what seemed a confident and slightly contemptuous amusement. Whatever Bobby had hoped for by way of reaction or self-betrayal failed to materialize.

"Of all the ingenious fantasies spun out of nothing at all," he said coolly when Bobby paused. "Good gracious, if you were mad enough to attempt to take such a case into court, you would very soon be laughed out again. No jury would listen for a moment."

"Well, perhaps not," Bobby agreed unexpectedly. "So we are not charging you with the murder of old Lord Wych. It might be difficult to secure a conviction."

"Glad you think so," Clinton Wells sneered. "Good morning." He turned towards the door, and then stopped and frowned when he saw a plain clothes constable lounging there. "Of course, you understand," he said, "the matter will not end here. You will hear more of it."

"But we are charging you," Bobby continued, once more unexpectedly, "with the murder of Bertram Hoyle, passing as Bertram Brown, but actually having succeeded to the Wych peerage, though he himself never knew it. He was recently released under the parole system from an American prison, he called to see you at your office in Midwych, he left there in your company, his body has now been discovered, in Wychwood Forest, near the Charles the Second oak—"

Abruptly Clinton Wells's composure deserted him, he made a step forward, staggered, collapsed on the nearest chair.

CHAPTER XXI
CONCLUSION

On the sea front at Torquay, for this was still the period of the
'phoney' war, with the Maginot Line complex in full force and the
British government still murmuring complacently that ' time was
on our side', Bobby and Olive were seated together. The strenuous
days Bobby had endured during the inquiry into the Castle Wych
case had earned him a brief special leave. On his knees lay the
morning paper in which he had noted three items of very different
import. For one recorded the dismissal by the Court of Appeal,
without any reply thought necessary, of the appeal Clinton Wells
had made against the death sentence passed at his recent trial; the
second mentioned the departure for the United States, 'on a long
visit', of Miss Anne Hoyle, grand-daughter of the late Earl Wych,
and cousin to the present earl; and, thirdly, an announcement of
the engagement of Ralph, Earl Wych, to Sophia, daughter of the
Rev. Louis Longden, of Brimpton Wych, Midwych, Wychshire.

"And not a word or a hint in the papers anywhere," Olive said
admiringly, "about the real Bertram having been in an American
gaol and only released on parole."

"Decent of the papers," Bobby admitted. "There have been one
or two hints, though, in some of the less responsible gossip
columns, but luckily they weren't sure enough of their facts to say
much, and the tale was too extraordinary for much to be said
without the full information they hadn't got."

"I never believed it would be possible to keep so much back,"
Olive said. "I thought everything would have to be told at the
trial."

"Well, most of it wasn't relevant to the simple question of
whether Clinton Wells did or did not commit the second murder,"
Bobby answered. "Nothing either need or should be said at a trial
that isn't strictly confined to the question of guilt or innocence in
the one particular instance. The fact that Clinton had also shot the
old earl was implicit in the evidence, but, strictly speaking, was
irrelevant to the charge on which he was being tried. A man can
only be hanged once, and once that one charge was proved there

was no need to open another. The evidence was as strong as evidence could well be. There was Messrs. Blacklock's office boy to identify the dead man as haying called at the office and as having left with Clinton Wells. There was evidence that he had accompanied him home. They were seen entering the forest together. Clinton Wells was seen leaving it alone. There was Martin's evidence that he heard shots and the evidence of the farmer he was talking to at the time. Martin's story that he found the automatic under the Charles the Second oak is confirmed by the traces of soil on it. There are the footprints to show Clinton Wells was actually on the spot earlier, there are half a dozen other points adding up to complete certainty. Clinton Wells had grown careless. I think he had no idea how closely he was being watched or that our suspicions were already pointing very strongly to him."

"I suppose it was through him that Ralph went off on that Glasgow visit that looked so suspicious?"

"Oh, yes. Ralph refused, or rather he thought he had refused, to take Clinton's advice about not having his 'show down' with his great-uncle. Actually, of course, Clinton, while pretending to dissuade him, had been cunningly egging him on, just as he took every opportunity to talk to us about Ralph's hot temper, so as to give an edge to our suspicions. But Ralph trusted him, felt he mustn't neglect his advice a second time, and so when Clinton came along with his tale of someone staying at the Northern Lights Hotel, who could give proof of the claimant's real identity, he went off obediently to see about it. So that no one should know, Clinton persuaded Ralph that secrecy was necessary, and that he must get off quietly without letting any one know why or where he had gone."

"And then I suppose rang him up again to send him off to another promised meeting near the Charles the Second oak?"

"That's why," Bobby explained, "he dropped those hints he knew would reach us, about the oak. Then he got the genuine Bertram there by telling him some yarn or another, shot him, hid the body, and took care to leave the Wych estate office automatic he had used once before where he knew it must be seen. That was to make sure we would search further and find the body we were expected to think had been hidden by Ralph. The calculation was that we should with luck discover Ralph on the spot, or if not, at least we couldn't help knowing he had been there. Clinton Wells thought that would make Ralph's arrest certain. So it would. And Ralph's arrest he thought would make his own position secure and put Bertram No. 1, the sham Bertram, in full possession of title and estates—and at the same time entirely in his power. Probably as soon as he knew that the genuine Bertram had been released and had reached England, he decided that only fresh murder could save him. A pretty desperate gamble, though it might have come off. But he didn't expect little Sophy Longden to guess, in some way she knows best, that mischief was being planned against Ralph, that somehow it centred round the old oak, and then to make up her mind that she was just jolly well going to see he was warned in time. Not every girl would have faced that long trip into the forest at that time of night. Not every one would much care for being alone in Wychwood at midnight. Lucky for me she took it on, though, or that fool of a Martin might have potted me. And Clinton Wells had not reckoned either on Martin's spotting there was something on and trotting off to see what it was. It was he who found the automatic left there for our benefit, and he got a nasty jolt, too, when he and I ran into each other, and he realised he was caught with the murder weapon in his possession. Lost his head completely. Well, the king's evidence he gave was very useful. Blackmail was his game from the first and it was the hope of blackmail, of course, that made him hold his tongue so long about what he saw on the night of the old earl's murder."

"Do you think Lady Wych suspected Ralph?"

"Very likely. She won't say. She knew, they all did, that there was sure to be a violent quarrel between the old earl and Ralph that night. Apparently her husband had promised to come in to say good-night and tell her all about it. When he didn't, she went to find him. She found his dead body on the terrace, but she didn't give the alarm. I imagine her first idea was that Ralph had done it and that she couldn't bear to help in his capture. When she had had time to think a bit, she began to wonder whether it might be someone else and not Ralph at all, and so she made up her mind to say nothing. Sophy knew nothing of the murder till morning. She had been to see how Lady Wych was and found her room empty. So she followed her downstairs and saw her leaving the library. Sophy went into the room, but it was empty, Lady Wych had drawn the curtain, and all Sophy did was to turn off the wireless and go back to bed, having first made sure Lady Wych was safe in her room again. When she heard about the murder in the morning she supposed Lady Wych must know something. Possibly she wondered if Lady Wych herself were guilty. She could say nothing without seeming to implicate the old lady, and so she made up her mind to say nothing. I expect she would have gone to the stake rather than speak. Obstinacy is her middle name. You should hear the colonel talk about her."

"You might call it loyalty," Olive said, "loyalty to an old woman who had been kind to her."

"Well, you might call it that," Bobby conceded. "The colonel doesn't. He says 'pig-headed'. To the ninth degree. Of course," added Bobby slyly, "what he means is:— 'She's just a woman.'"

Olive let this pass. She had another question to ask. She said:— "What's become of the sham Bertram?"

"Oh, he's off back to the States—scot free, money in his pocket, better luck than he deserved. Though he was never more than a pawn in Clinton Wells's game. Lucky to be out of it. Even if their plot had come off, Clinton Wells would have squeezed him dry. Anyhow, he's fully convinced that being a British peer is no soft job, and that marrying Anne Hoyle would be a fate worse than death."

"He was just a silly," declared Olive, dismissing him with a flick of her fingers, "but I do feel a little sorry for Anne. Still, even if she had married Ralph, it would have been a disaster. She would have wanted her way, he would have gone his, and the result would have been catastrophe."

"You needn't worry about Miss Anne Hoyle," Bobby told her. "She will soon land an American millionaire; a millionaire, too, who, bossing others, will then himself be bossed. But I do wonder a little what old Lady Wych will think of Sophy as the new Lady Wych."

"She ought to think what I think," Olive answered with decision, "that Ralph's in luck at last. How many girls would have had the courage to make that trip through Wychwood at midnight just on the chance of being able to find him and warn him?"

"Yes, I know, I've said that, too," Bobby remarked. "All the same, it's odd to think of that quiet, shy little thing as Countess Wych; even if no longer of Wych Castle, now the county council has taken it over." After a pause, he added:— "She does make you feel though that whoever she married, duke, dustman, costermonger, earl, burglar for that matter, she would understand her husband so well, she would understand his job, too, and play Aaron to his Moses's arm, so that her man would make a better job of his duking or dusting or costering or burgling, as the case might be."

"What you mean," said Olive, "only you go such a long way round, is that Sophy is just a woman."

THE END

9 781910 570968